THE
WATER TOWER

THE
WATER TOWER

A LAKEVIEW MYSTERY

AMY YOUNG

LEVEL
BEST BOOKS

First published by Level Best Books 2023

This novel is entirely a work of fiction. The names, characters and incidents portrayed in it are the work of the author's imagination. Any resemblance to actual persons, living or dead, events or localities is entirely coincidental.

Amy Young asserts the moral right to be identified as the author of this work.

First edition

ISBN: 978-1-68512-277-5

Cover art by Level Best Designs

This book was professionally typeset on Reedsy.
Find out more at reedsy.com

For Oreo, the best writing partner ever, and Kevin

Praise for The Water Tower

"Start with a suspicious death of a beloved student, add a devoted former starlet turned drama teacher, and a dash of the police closing the case far too quickly, and you have the makings of a twisting and propulsive mystery. Amy Young's *The Water Tower* will keep you flipping the pages to find out who killed the politician's young daughter, and then have you checking if your teenager is where they should be tonight."—Mary Keliikoa, multi-award nominated author of *Hidden Pieces* and the PI Kelly Pruett mystery series

"*The Water Tower* is an electrifying work of suspense that depicts a wonderful home town setting. This slow-burn mystery with sparkling prose has a well-crafted plot that is at once engrossing and fully realized beginning to end. I highly recommend this engaging mystery."—David Putnam, bestselling author of the Bruno Johnson series, and Dave Beckett series

Chapter One

She stood on the water tower, looking at the skyline she had only observed from the ground. You really could see the whole town from up here. Funny how your whole life can fit into one 360-degree glance. Peering down at the ground, she was no longer able to see individual blades of grass, all of them blurring into a sea of perfect emerald green. To her right was the roof of Lakeview High School, looking small from this vantage point. She felt as though if she leaned over far enough, she could almost touch it. But that was ridiculous; the school had to be several hundred feet away. Her vision came in and out of focus as she swayed, thinking about her life, her past, her future.

In her three years at the school, she had never been up on the tower. No one she knew had been up here, either. Most students wouldn't dare to scale it. Too scared of getting caught, too scared of breaking the rules, too scared of living. When she looked down at the ground, she thought she could see movement, like little grass men dancing and hopping around through a crowd of their peers. Kind of like high school. More like, *exactly* like high school. Everyone looks the same; maybe some are a bit taller, a bit shorter, a bit wider, but everyone dressed in essentially the same uniform, hopping over one another, trying to make their mark.

How many feet above the ground was she—fifty, sixty feet? Was that high enough to kill you, or maybe just break a few bones? It would probably depend on how you hit the ground. Here she was, high above the town, pondering the angle at which you might hit the ground and live through the fall, the velocity at which an object might fall from here.

Her body felt warm all over, despite the crisp air of late fall, and she took off her jacket and threw it aside. She leaned against the rail and spread her arms, allowing the breeze to blow through her, inhabiting every cell for just a moment, before moving off in another direction to go dance with someone else. Her seventeen years had all been spent here, in this one place, in this small, boring town where, it seemed, nothing was all that was destined to happen.

The clock tower chimed; it was eleven o'clock. She felt she had eternity in front of her, the rest of this night, the rest of her life, stuck here in this town. Would she ever get out? Did it even matter if she did? She thought about the college catalogs arriving at home, the hundreds of pages of sales pitches clamoring for her family's money. The sprawling campuses, the smiling students, the serious, but friendly, professors—what was the point? She would just end up back here, raising the same family as her friends, living the same life that her kids would eventually live.

Reaching out her slender arm, she twirled her wrist. She could hardly wait for graduation when, everyone said, "real life" would begin. "I can't wait to get out of here," her friends exclaimed, dreaming of big cities and even bigger lives in far-off places: Chicago, Los Angeles, New York, anywhere but here. But she knew they would return, just like their parents, raising 2.5 kids with a Labradoodle and a balding husband in one of the best-little-suburbs in the country. Was it really so bad? She watched all these super-educated women who had given up their careers to stay home and clean up after the kids and drive to soccer practice, instead of changing the world as they'd so hopefully planned when plotting their escape years earlier. Was that her fate? Was that what awaited her now? Dozens of similar thoughts swirled and crashed like waves in front of her, mixing in a fantastic spray of colors, lights, and sounds.

She was dead before she hit the ground.

Chapter Two

Josephine Ashbury woke with a start, sweating, and looked at the clock beside her bed. 10:47, the bright blue digital clock announced. She sighed, rolling back over, trying to will herself back to sleep. Most of her nights were like this, sleeping in fits and starts, awakening every few hours in a sweaty haze. "Maybe it's pre-menopause," she laughed to herself, thinking about her mother's teasing earlier in the week. At thirty-one, she thought she was a bit young for the big M, but perhaps not. Maybe this was how things would be from now on; long, restless nights punctuated by moments of lucidity and only fleeting glimpses of dreams. She never felt rested after one of these nights. Insomnia had always plagued her, but it usually came in waves that lasted for anywhere from a week to six months. But this time was different—she hadn't slept a full night for as long as she could remember.

Maybe a cup of tea would do her some good. Weren't people always talking about the amazing benefits of tea? Drawn in by the name, she had bought a package of a blend called "Sleep Well"; after trying it a few times, she was unimpressed. She swung her legs over the edge of her king-sized bed, and her feet searched the floor for her slippers. The air outside of her pillowy down comforter felt like ice as it hit her skin. Pulling on the long fleece robe she kept at the end of her bed, she stood up and stretched, yawning and rubbing her eyes. Presley, her male tuxedo cat, rolled onto his back lazily and looked at her with one eye, exposing his white belly. Her female cat, Monroe, a light gray and peach striped shorthair, was curled up on the other end of the bed, oblivious to her movement.

"Go back to sleep," she whispered to Presley, then padded down the hallway to her kitchen, turning on the light above the stove and grabbing the stainless-steel kettle that lived on top of it. As she ran water into the kettle, she gazed out her back window.

Her backyard seemed to stretch out for a mile, the lawn rolling in peaks and valleys before coming up against the ironwood fence at the back of the property. Lots of room for a dog, which had been a major selling point when she bought the house earlier this year. Beyond the yard was the parking lot of Lakeview High School, perfectly convenient, considering that was where she worked now. She had never planned on becoming a teacher, but she found herself more and more at home there as the days went by. It was a big change from her life in Hollywood, where she had spent the last decade of her life.

She looked up at the water tower beyond her fence and squinted her sleep-deprived eyes. The metal reservoir shone in the night sky, the waxing moon casting a haunting light over the imposing structure. Up, up, up it went, with splintering wood legs and steps zig-zagging up to the top. The small space between the ground and the steps was designed to keep everyone but designated personnel off the tower, but Josie knew that from time to time, a few daredevils found their way up onto the top where they sat, legs dangling off the edge, arms intertwined around the slim railing, drinking, smoking, or just relishing in the thrill of being so far above the ground.

At least, that's what kids had done when she was in school at Lakeview High. But every generation was different. Some years, the water tower seemed to go untouched; others, the police pulled kids off of it constantly. Since she had been back in town, she hadn't heard of anyone scaling the tower. Of course, that didn't mean it wasn't happening; that just meant the kids weren't getting caught.

Was someone up there now? She put down the kettle and rubbed her eyes, blinking off the sleep and focusing more intently on the spot where she had fixed her gaze.

Nothing. "Just hallucinating," she mumbled to herself, turning around to put the kettle on the stove and igniting the flame. The gas burner click, click, clicked to life, and she sat down in a kitchen chair, waiting for the kettle to boil. She had a funny feeling in her stomach, almost as though someone was watching her, and the hairs on her arms stood up.

"Meow," Monroe announced loudly from behind her, rubbing up against the doorway. Josie jumped and then laughed at herself. "Silly kitty," she said, bending over to scratch Monroe behind the ears, "sneaking up on me." Monroe purred happily and ran over to her food bowl.

She heard her phone ding from the bedroom, and when she went to grab it, she saw a text from her mother. "I hope you get some sleep. Sweet dreams," it read, followed by a smiley face and a heart emoji. Josie's mother, Sophia, had been a pediatric surgeon for decades at Lakeview Hospital, so her hours were long and erratic at times.

"You too! Don't stay up too late," Josie chided back with a silly face emoji.

When the kettle whistled, Josie returned to the kitchen, shut off the stove, and retrieved a mug from the cabinet. As she poured steaming water over the teabag and turned to look out her window one more time, that strange feeling of unease crept back over her. She studied the water tower again and, satisfied that there was nothing up there, returned to her bedroom. Getting subpar sleep was making her feel bizarre. Shaking it off, she put the mug of tea down on her nightstand, took off her robe, and settled back into her pillows. She glanced over at the clock again. 11:11, it winked. Time to make a wish.

Sighing, she sipped her tea and sat back against the fluffy pillows. Only five more hours until she would get up for her morning run. She hoped she would get at least a few solid hours of shut-eye in before morning.

Chapter Three

The alarm was screaming before she knew it. Josie opened one eye and checked the clock. 5:00, it waved. She exhaled slowly and set to dragging herself out of bed. How was it that she could spring up in the middle of the night, no hope of sleeping, but when she needed to get up, it felt impossible? Presley made a grunting noise and shifted but did not open his eyes. Fortunately, the house was warmer now than when she had awakened in the middle of the night; she had set the thermostat to warm up the house before she got up in the morning. Otherwise, she knew the temptation to bury herself under the covers would surely win out.

As she slipped one slender leg into her running tights, it occurred to her, as it often did, how different her life was now compared to even two years ago. Josie had struck out for Los Angeles with big dreams right after college, settling quickly into a series of office temp jobs with bad pay and zero perks. Despite her precarious financial situation, she managed to keep herself in a small studio apartment in Los Feliz, a trendy neighborhood at the foot of the Hollywood Hills. A combination of striking beauty and raw talent had landed her an agent relatively quickly, but months turned into years with only bit roles here and there. That is, until her big break.

A short film in which she had the lead caught the eye of a studio executive at MGM after winning acclaim at Sundance Film Festival. Before Josie knew it, she had a small role in the upcoming James Bond movie and was catapulted into the category of "Bond girl." Almost overnight, her agent was flooded with calls for auditions and meetings. Then her career truly took off. After many rounds of auditions with directors, producers, seemingly everyone under the sun, she landed the lead in a police procedural show starring James Bleecker, Hollywood's hottest leading man. James had a lethal combination of good looks and self-effacing charm, which he had leveraged into an extremely successful career. Women all over the globe swooned over his striking blue eyes, wavy blonde hair, and signature five-o'clock shadow.

Once the show began airing, Josie went from somewhat unknown to a face everyone recognized. The show was a major hit, and she and James just happened to fall in love during filming, as co-stars so often do. They embarked on a tumultuous six-year romance, all the while filming the show, which grew in popularity every year. She and James both became executive producers during the show's third season, and Josie found herself with the kind of money she had only ever dreamed of and a career that thousands of young actresses would kill for. Her face graced the cover of dozens of magazines, and she couldn't go anywhere without being stalked by paparazzi.

Then it all came crashing down. After a widely publicized on-set breakdown, Josie found herself in the midst of a media circus. She decided it was time to take a break from Hollywood and regroup, so she returned to Lakeview and bought a house she'd always loved. During a visit to see a former teacher at Lakeview High soon after she returned to town, Josie had encountered the superintendent. On a whim, she pitched the idea of teaching an acting class at the high school for a year, and the super latched onto the idea immediately. Josie's agent still called and sent scripts her way, but she wasn't ready to return to Hollywood. She didn't know if she would ever be ready.

When she was working in LA, she had gotten into the habit of exercising early in the morning since she was usually due on set by six o'clock. But no matter how hard she tried to retrain her body to favor the mornings, she would always be a natural night owl. She finished dressing quickly and pushed herself out the door, lest her desire to crawl back into bed overtake her and make her miss one of the few days she had left before it got too cold to run outside. Her years in LA had "heated her blood," as her dad joked; she did not run outside when the temperature dropped below freezing. Usually, she rotated running with kickboxing, which she loved but had to take a hiatus from when she dislocated her thumb a few months earlier. Now her runs either had to be out in the cold or on the treadmill, which she found intensely dull.

Giving Presley a final rub on the head, she stuffed her phone into her right jacket pocket and was out the front door. The air was brisk, and the mornings got colder as each day in October passed. Though winter would not officially begin until December, it was not unusual to see snow in Northeast Ohio by Halloween, and sometimes even earlier. Josie took a deep breath, the smell of frost melting into early morning dew filling her nostrils. She began walking, graduating to a slow jog as her muscles warmed. Finally, she hit her usual pace and settled into the routine thumping of her feet, her breath rhythmically carrying her into a pleasant trance.

She passed a tall, slender man running towards her with a loping gait. With his sinewy muscles and gaunt face, he had the look of a regular marathoner. She smiled and waved as they passed each other, and he returned the gesture. In a small town like Lakeview, greeting every person you passed on the street wasn't just polite, it was expected. When she first arrived in Hollywood, she would greet everyone she encountered on the street the same way she would in small town Ohio. Most of them looked at her like she was an alien.

But for all the differences, there were similarities between the two cities. As with LA, the residents of Lakeview strove to keep themselves fit, and running was a popular exercise choice. There was never any shortage of company on the roads, no matter how early Josie ventured out. She always passed at least five other runners on her morning trek, sometimes more. Yes, as the air cooled and winter began to take its hold, fewer people pounded the pavement. But still, long after she abandoned her early morning jogs for indoor activities, she saw plenty of people slogging through the snow and ice to get their daily fix.

Most mornings, Josie ran the same route—going east on Forest Road, the main vein running through the center of Lakeview that was lined with lovely, mainly colonial-style houses. The houses gave way to the main park in the center of town, run by the Cleveland Metroparks, which housed a nature center, planetarium, and soccer fields for the kids. Just after the park was the fire station, a modern building with a large driveway that branched from Forest Road and cut through to McBride Street. Occasionally, if Josie was doing a shorter run, she would cut down the driveway and wave to the firefighters milling about, if there were any out that early in the morning.

As she turned right on the next street, Huron Drive, she admired city hall, which had been remodeled a couple of years earlier into a more modern-looking structure of glass and metal, but still housed the old clock tower whose chimes she remembered so fondly from growing up. She completed her loop by going west on Lake Street. Lake Street was where many of the older, grander estates in Lakeview had a clear view of Lake Erie, including Senator Clinton Oldham's home. Senator Oldham was one of the more famous residents of the town, aside from Josie herself. Many wealthy professionals, athletes, and local newscasters in the Cleveland area also chose to call Lakeview home. With its long coastline, gorgeous views of the lake, and small-town charm, Josie could hardly blame them.

Once she passed the beach access area, she turned the corner onto a smaller side street to begin the trek back to her house. The Lakeview water tower loomed over her, no longer functional but preserved by the Lakeview Historical Society. The cool air felt good now that Josie was warmed up, and she smiled to herself. The sun was peeking over the horizon, bathing everything in a warm, gentle glow. Sunrise and sunset are, without a doubt, the best times in a lakeshore town. Picking up the pace as she grew nearer to home, Josie pushed her lungs until they felt as though they might burst. When she couldn't take any more, she slowed gradually to a walk, panting as she cut down a street that backed up to the high school baseball and football fields. Some mornings, if she was feeling ambitious, she would run sprints around the track. As she looked out over the damp grass and stretched her legs, she decided to skip it this morning.

Walking the gravel path towards the fields, a swatch of color on the ground near the water tower caught her attention. Was that a backpack? She started to trot over, then realized what she had stumbled upon. For a moment, she felt as if she had turned to stone, unable to do anything except stare at the horror before her. When she finally shook herself out of the shock, she reached with trembling fingers into her pocket for her phone.

"9-1-1, what's your emergency?" the operator said politely.

"Yes, this is Josephine Ashbury. Please send police to the water tower behind the high school. I—I just found a body."

Chapter Four

Flashing blue and red lights flooded the high school parking lot as faculty members arrived to start the school day. Each person got out of their car with the same incredulous look on their face, surveyed the scene, then hurried to the perimeter of caution tape surrounding the water tower. Josie sat on the edge of the ambulance bay with the doors open, a blanket wrapped around her shoulders. The EMT said she was in shock, which made sense—she could not believe what had transpired since she awoke this morning.

After she had called the police, she slowly approached the figure lying in the grass, recognizing the girl immediately. Amber Oldham, a Lakeview High senior, lay with her limbs splayed out in an unnatural manner. Her azure eyes were open wide, as though something had surprised her, her flaxen hair spilling around her face like a pool of white gold. The arm of her red designer blouse was torn, as though it had snagged on something, and the bottom of the shirt crept up to show just a sliver of her milky white abdomen.

Josie shifted her glance between the girl in the grass and the top of the water tower, trying to wrap her brain around what she saw. Had she jumped? At first, when she had seen Amber lying there, Josie thought her mind was playing tricks on her, that maybe Amber had simply fainted in the grass. But once she moved closer, there was no mistaking it: the girl was dead. Her hollow eyes gazed up at the sky, and her neck was twisted too far to the left. Was it possible that she had fallen? Amber was wearing little black boots with spiky four-inch heels, not made for climbing anything, much less the rickety wooden stairs of a six-story water tower. Those boots would have been hard enough to balance in on solid ground.

What had Amber been doing on the water tower in the middle of the night, alone? Josie twirled a strand of hair around her fingers. She knew that occasionally kids got caught sneaking up there to party, but *this* girl, alone, on a weeknight? It didn't make any sense. Unless…well, unless she had gone up there to jump. That seemed to be the consensus amongst the teachers that kept stumbling over, peering over at the water tower and talking about how "awful, just plain awful" it was.

But something nagged at Josie. Amber was in her acting class, and they had become close over the couple months since school began. The girl was sweet, smart, and well-liked, her friend circle wide and welcoming. Her easy charm, no doubt inherited from her politician father, allowed her to mesh well with every social group. As far as Josie knew, she would be off to college next fall, possibly an Ivy. She had the grades and extracurriculars for it and would have no trouble securing recommendations from any one of the many teachers who adored her. So why would a girl like that throw herself to her death? Why end everything when your life is just beginning?

Josie blinked herself back to the scene. She knew all too well that a person could seem perfect on the outside, while on the inside, they were falling apart. The incidence of teen suicide was skyrocketing with the rising prevalence of social media. Once news or a rumor got out, it was *out.* She'd heard rumblings in the hallway of a few scandals this year, but she hadn't heard a word about Amber. Sure, Amber had problems, but as far as Josie knew, it was normal high school drama, nothing that would have led to this. But she knew better than to jump to conclusions. Just because Amber didn't show her hand didn't mean she wasn't keeping secrets. Often, trouble was brewing right under the surface of an unblemished façade.

"Jose," she heard a voice call.

Sean Sullivan, Josie's high school sweetheart, and a Lakeview police officer, was striding toward her. A tall man of about six-four with a full head of dark hair, beautiful brown eyes, and a fit physique, Sean was the source of many a town crush. When she and Sean split up midway through her senior year, Josie had been heartbroken; but she'd managed to nurse her wounds, and the two became good friends. Since moving back to Lakeview, though, she found herself reminiscing more about their time together. Maybe she'd even developed a little crush of her own. But they were just friends now. Sean was dating someone, and she would never interfere with his happiness.

Sean's father was the police chief, and Sean had always planned to follow in his footsteps. The uniform, and the profession, suited him. He was one of the most honest and fair people Josie had ever met. There was something about hearing her first love's voice that made her stomach jump a little.

"Hey, Sean," she said, stifling a yawn.

"Hey. How are you doing?" he asked, his brow creased with concern.

"Other than finding the body of one of my students on my morning run? I'm great," she said, then bit her lip. That had come off much harsher than she intended. "Sorry, Sean, I'm just super freaked out."

"Understandable," he said, giving her a tight smile. "This wasn't how I planned on spending my morning, either."

"I'll bet," she nodded. She knew from Sean's accounts that mornings at the Lakeview police station were spent slowly waking up with bad coffee (better now with the advent of single-serve coffee pods) and chatting about the previous night's TV shows. There were at least a few officers who were big fans of her show, although some of them had made a point to tell her that they found it "unrealistic." Later in the morning, someone would make a run to the local coffee shop to get pastries. The death of a seventeen-year-old girl? Josie couldn't think of a time when anything even close had happened.

"Would you come down to the station and answer some questions?" Sean asked. "Just routine stuff. Maybe tomorrow morning? That'll give you a chance to, you know, recover a bit."

"Sure. How's ten o'clock?"

"Sounds good," he said, turning to walk away.

"Sean?" She called out. He returned to her side. "Did you get her jacket? It looked like it was draped over the railing at the top of the tower."

"Where?" Sean asked, turning to squint up at the water tower.

"You didn't see it?" Josie said, stepping over to Sean's side and following his gaze. "Look, it was right up—" she pointed, but when she looked to where she was pointing, she realized nothing was up there. She could have sworn that when she found the body, she'd seen the leather jacket that Amber wore every day flapping in the breeze on the railing of the tower. Looking around, she shrugged, "I don't know, maybe one of your guys got it."

"I'll make sure to check," Sean replied, turning to walk away again.

"Hey," Josie called after him, beckoning him back to her once more. "Do you think she jumped? It's just so. . ."

Sean looked to where Amber's form still lay in the soft grass, the baseball field acting as its own caution tape around her poor, tangled body. "That's the working assumption," he said gently. "We haven't ruled anything out. But that's certainly what it looks like."

Josie nodded, trying to swallow the lump in her throat. She shook her head and looked up at him. "I guess I'll go home and shower."

Sean nodded. "And Josie? I'm sorry you had to be the one to find her. I mean, no one should have had to find her this way, but I'm really sorry it was you."

Josie smiled faintly, then turned to walk home. As she made her way across the concrete path into the parking lot, she nodded at other teachers still arriving, but barely noticed who she was passing. She felt like she was trapped in a bad dream.

Chapter Five

Sean watched Josie enter her yard, her slim figure disappearing behind the fence. The old water tower loomed over him like a giant, ominous cloud. Standing about fifty feet tall, the wooden structure had been a subject of debate for years. Though it was blocked off with a chain link fence and had the bottom ladder rungs removed, the tower was still easily accessible, if someone really wanted to get up there. The wooden planks crisscrossed back and forth to the first level, about ten feet up, then there were three sets of stairs winding up to the top where the large metal drum sat, empty for as long as Sean could remember.

Many in the community wanted the tower torn down because, despite the city's best efforts, teenagers got up there and did, well, teenage things. A few kids had fallen, attempting to climb the tower over the years, but no one had ever fallen off the top. And there had never been a death. Since the tower had been decommissioned and designated as a historical landmark years earlier, and since it was the only water tower left intact of the many that were once used in the area, the historical society won every time a debate on the issue arose. The city had tried putting up all kinds of fencing around it over the last thirty years, but when kids wanted to get through, they found a way regardless of the roadblocks. Sean was in the camp that wanted to see the tower demolished or turned into lofts or shops like the others in the area had been. He supported preserving history, but that tower was definitely more trouble than it was worth.

He surveyed the scene around the baseball field carefully. During his decade on the police force, he had never had to handle the death of a kid.

Noise complaints, rowdy teenagers, and the occasional petty theft were the most frequent offenses in Lakeview; an event like this would shake the town to its core. As he tried to corral the arriving teachers into the building, they all craned their necks to see what the commotion was about, shaking their heads in horror when they realized why the field was crawling with police and emergency personnel. Kids would soon arrive, and then the police would have a full-blown panic on their hands. The school had canceled classes today, but it was too late to catch every kid before they left the house, especially those with before-school activities.

Before Sean knew it, a throng of media trucks had pulled into the parking lot and were unloading their gear. He had to get this situation under control, fast. Looking back towards Josie's house, he visually confirmed that the gate was shut, and she was safely behind it. Media outlets had been hounding her since she returned to Lakeview last year, and news of her finding the body would cause a frenzy. The last thing the Lakeview police needed was a video of this poor girl's body splashed all over the news and Internet, sensationalized further by the involvement of a famous actress. Amber's family was suffering enough. He glanced over at Congressman Clinton Oldham and his wife, Annelise, sitting together on a bench while several officers attended to them. Mrs. Oldham was weeping softly, Mr. Oldham's arm around her as he talked to the police. Andrew Oldham, Amber's older brother, stood behind his parents, pale and clearly in shock. Ordinarily a good-looking, energetic man, Clinton Oldham looked almost sickly as he hunched over his wife.

"Chief," Sean called out to a tall, thick man who looked more like an ex-MMA fighter than the captain of a small-town police force. Mike Sullivan, Sean's father, was standing with the Oldhams, attempting to console the family. With salt and pepper hair and a fit build, he looked like an older version of his son. He had been chief of police in this town for nearly thirty years. Mike quietly said something to the officer next to him, then made his way over to Sean.

"This is a disaster," he said gruffly as he reached his son.

"The press is here," Sean said, gesturing to the growing fleet of vans with their station's respective logos emblazoned on the sides.

"We need to get the body out of here. I'll go talk to Alistair," Mike barked, then stalked off toward the body. Alistair Smith, the Cleveland Medical Examiner, hovered over Amber, talking to the coroner as technicians loaded her lifeless figure into a black body bag.

One reporter made a beeline for the field, and Sean braced for an unpleasant confrontation. He hadn't had much interaction with the press in his time on the force, but he had not enjoyed the little he'd experienced. Sean placed himself squarely in the man's path, holding out his arms and blocking the way before the reporter could set foot on the field. "Sorry, sir, no press on the field."

The man sized up Sean quickly, flashing a way-too-white smile, the wind ruffling his perfectly coiffed blond hair. "Darren Jenkins, Channel 5 News," he said, putting out his hand.

Sean ignored the reporter's hand and looked at him pointedly.

Undeterred, the reporter's million-dollar smile didn't waver. "So, what happened here? We got a tip that someone found a body. Can you tell me anything about that, officer...?"

Sean didn't offer up his name. Frowning, he snapped, "The police chief will release a statement later today. Until then, I'm afraid there's nothing I can tell you." Why were reporters so slimy? Was it the way they were able to report a story about a murdered child, then switch happily to the weather? They all seemed like sociopaths.

"Come on," Jenkins said, leaning in, "There's got to be something you can tell me," giving Sean a wink as though they were old buddies catching up over a scotch. "Is it true that the victim is Senator Oldham's daughter? Well, I guess it must be, since the senator and his wife are sitting right over there. And is it also true that Josie Ashbury found the body?"

"Sorry, *sir,* but I'm going to have to ask you to go back to your van," Sean said, pointing towards the parking lot.

Jenkins snorted indignantly, turned on his heel, and stormed off, his cameraman in tow. Sean watched him go, shaking his head incredulously. When he turned back, he could see that Amber's body, now fully zipped into the body bag, was now on a stretcher. He peered up at the tower, searching for the jacket Josie mentioned, but saw nothing except the railing winding around the reservoir. For good measure, he walked the perimeter of the tower, craning his neck upwards the whole time to look at the railing, but he saw nothing. Finally, he beckoned one of the younger patrol officers over and asked him to go up and have a look. The officer looked pleased to have the task and scurried up the steps like a squirrel scaling a giant oak. After walking around the tank, he waved down to Sean and shook his head, indicating that there was nothing up there.

Sean frowned. Josie had seemed so certain that she saw Amber's jacket. Was she mistaken? He was about to take a trip up to the top of the water tower himself when he heard a commotion behind him and turned to see a group of reporters approaching him like a pack of rabid dogs.

"Hey, guys?" he yelled over to the group of officers milling around the field. They saw the reporters and strode towards them quickly, the two groups looking as though they were about to engage in a medieval battle. It was going to be a long day.

Chapter Six

Josie let the hot water from the shower run over her, still trying to come to terms with the scene she had stumbled upon earlier. Poor Amber, she thought. And Amber's poor parents. Losing a family member was tragic enough, but losing a child was unnatural. As she closed her eyes and shampooed her hair, a flash of last night rushed forward behind her eyes. She remembered thinking she saw a person on the water tower. Had she seen Amber up there? Frantically rubbing the soap from her eyes, she tried to remember. She had gotten up to make tea, looked out the window, and saw what she thought was a flash of red. Was her brain just filling in what she now knew had been there?

She got out of the shower, toweled off, and looked in the mirror. She looked like an entirely different person from the characters she played onscreen. Even with her hair up in a turban and no makeup, Josie was beautiful by anyone's standards, with long, wavy chestnut hair, porcelain skin, and wide-set light green eyes. At five foot eight, she was "all legs," as her mom said. One of the most endearing qualities that Josie had—and what had kept her grounded in Hollywood—was that she didn't see what the fuss was all about. Even when she was splashed across magazines from *Glamour* to *People* to *Maxim*, she didn't feel like she belonged there more than anyone else. She loved acting, and was so thankful for her success, but the fanfare that came with it felt excessive. Deep down, she was the same small-town girl she had always been.

Ordinarily, she felt pretty good about herself when she looked in the mirror, but today it was like she was looking into a stranger's eyes. She felt like she was looking at a stranger. As she stared into her own eyes in the mirror, she tried to force herself to remember last night clearly. Insomnia had followed her like a shadow since she was a child, and her memories of being up and down during the night were hazy at best. But she could swear she had seen something last night, what she had shrugged off as being a flash across her vision. The question was, what exactly had she seen? Closing her eyes again, she tried to pull up the memory, but all she could see was a blurred image of the water tower.

She would have to try again later. Pulling a wide-toothed comb through her hair, she reached under the sink for her hairdryer when she heard her phone buzzing. "Foxy" flashed across the screen.

"Hey, Nik," Josie answered, smiling and putting the call on speaker.

One of her best friends since childhood, Nicole Fox, was always the first to call whenever there was a breaking story. Nikki had always had a nose for news, ever since she was a reporter for the "Lakeview Ledger," Lakeview High's newspaper, and editor-in-chief of her college paper at Loyola University. With huge aqua eyes framed by curly black lashes and a smattering of freckles, Nikki had a face that people inherently trusted—which gave her an edge as a reporter. She stood about five-foot-five, so she was short enough to not be intimidating, and had dark blonde hair which, while beautiful, allowed her to blend in when she didn't want to be noticed. Blending in was useful when she was sniffing around crime scenes, something Nikki often did on assignment as a reporter for the city newspaper, The Cleveland Press.

"Have you heard?" Nikki said breathlessly.

Ah, so Nikki was behind. The occasion was rare when Josie knew more about a developing news story than Nikki, especially something this big.

"I showed up at the high school, but the cops have it on lockdown," Nikki continued. "I couldn't even get Sean to talk to me."

"Yeah, I know. They've got everything sealed pretty tight over there."

"Can you see anything from your place? Is it true that Senator Oldham's daughter fell off the water tower?" Nikki asked.

"Yeah…actually, I was the one who found her," Josie said, feeling sick to her stomach as she said the words.

"Oh, Jose," Nikki replied, "Are you okay? I'm coming over."

"No, no, I'm okay, I just want to lie down," said Josie. "The school was a madhouse this morning, with all the press showing up, and then teachers and students. Sean isn't even going to take my statement until tomorrow morning. The police were too busy fighting off the media and sending everyone home."

"Okay. Tell you what, why don't we have lunch tomorrow after you give your statement? I'll call the other girls, and we'll meet at SSP."

The "girls" Nikki referred to were Josie's other two girlfriends, Heather Spooner and Alexandra Ziebranowicz. The four women had been close since grade school, navigating growing up in a small town. As kids, they saw each other through good times and bad, and now in adulthood, they walked together through marriages, children, divorces, deaths. When they all went off to college, they'd managed to stay close, and while living in LA, Josie talked to them at least once a week, even when she was in the throes of filming fourteen hours a day. Nikki was the glue that held them all together. Whenever life started to get in the way of their friendship, Nikki scheduled a conference or video call, and the foursome picked up right where they'd left off, as though they'd spent no time apart. SSP, or Second Street Pub, was their usual meeting spot, a casual bar and grille where the staff knew them, and they could chat for hours without being rushed out.

"Yes," replied Josie. "Are you sure the other girls are available?"

"We'll see. I think they'll make time for this."

"All right, I'll see you tomorrow."

"'Kay."

Josie hung up and set about drying her hair. She looked at the clock on her phone. "8:04," it yelled. It would be a miracle if she managed to get anything done today.

Chapter Seven

On Tuesday morning, Josie pulled her Tesla into the parking lot of the Lakeview Police Station and glanced around. The lot wasn't even half full and everything was quiet, despite it being ten o'clock on a Tuesday morning. Even though she had grown up in Lakeview, a few years in LA made it feel like the whole world must be jam-packed with people, all squashed up against each other like sardines. The police station was in the same building as City Hall, so the cops and city officials all shared the same parking. With the news of the senator's daughter's death spreading rapidly through the region, there was more activity on the streets than usual, but it still wasn't a fraction of the bustle she'd experienced out West.

As she swung her legs out of the car, her phone pinged with a text from her dad. "Checking in. Did you sleep last night?" it said. She smiled. Being the only girl in a family with three boys, her parents had always doted on her. While they were proud of her career, she knew they had hated her being so far away for all those years.

She fired off a quick, "Kind of. I'm good. At the station to give my interview," before silencing her phone and shoving it back into her bag.

Standing up, she straightened her jacket. Damn, it was cold. Was she ever going to readjust to these Midwest winters? As she entered the first set of glass doors, she pulled her gloves off, rubbing her hands together and blowing into them in a vain attempt at warming herself up. Then she pulled open the second set of doors and stepped into the waiting area. The Lakeview Police Station was spacious and modern-looking, thanks to a recent renovation funded by a large donation from the Oldham family—specifically, from Mrs. Oldham's family. While Clinton Oldham had done very well for himself, Annelise Oldham came from old, old, old money, more money than Josie would see in five lifetimes.

The building had needed that renovation. Although it had good bones, the old police station had been drafty, dirty, and dated. The upgrades made a huge difference, and the station was now actually a pleasant place to be. Well, as pleasant as a police station could be.

Crossing the large marble-floored hallway to the sergeant-on-duty's desk, Josie was greeted with a warm smile from the receptionist, Martha Johnson. Martha was a short, squat woman of about sixty with the kindest face Josie had ever seen. She was a childhood friend of Josie's mother and had spent many an evening at Josie's family home over the years.

"Hey there, sweetie," Martha said. "Sean is expecting you."

"Thanks, Martha," she replied, smiling back.

"Josie," Martha said, lowering her voice, "Is it true that you found the body of that poor girl?"

Josie looked down, nodding, the image of Amber lying on the ground, all twisted and broken resurfacing.

"Oh, hon," Martha replied, getting up from her desk. She quickly emerged from the door separating the lobby and wrapped Josie in a hug. "That must have been terrible."

"I'm okay, Mar," Josie said, enjoying the warmth of Martha's hug for a moment. Martha gave the *best* hugs, like being wrapped up in a big, soft pillow. "Really," she said, pulling away. "I just feel so horrible for her family."

Martha nodded sympathetically. "Let me buzz you back."

"Thanks," Josie replied.

Martha used her keycard to unlock the inner door to the station, holding the door open behind her for Josie to pass through. Josie had always thought of the lock as more of a formality than something Lakeview needed. The town had always been safe, so a locking inner sanctum of the police station felt like overkill.

The large room contained neat rows of metal and plastic desks without cubicle dividers, with some partners' desks facing each other. Nearly all the desks were overflowing with papers, files, and assorted office supplies. A rolling chair squeaked at each station. Filing cabinets and bookcases filled with various tomes and binders flanked the walls. Several large bulletin boards displaying maps, photos, and other documentation decorated the room, along with plaques recognizing officers or the station for one honor or another. The fluorescent overhead lights buzzed and blinked, casting a kind of sickly hue. The whole setup looked very similar to the set of Josie's TV show—except for the bad lighting and lack of hair and makeup people buzzing about.

This wasn't her first time at the Lakeview Police Station—far from it. She and Sean had lunch every couple of weeks, and that often meant Josie had to show up and tear him away from the office. Sean's desk was third in the row, with the interview rooms and three offices off to the right and a couple of cells—mostly used for the occasional public intoxication or rowdy teenager—off to the left beyond a solid cinder block wall.

As she made her way to Sean's desk, she noticed Annelise and Clinton Oldham being led out of one of the interview rooms by Chief Sullivan. Clinton's eyes were rimmed with red, and he looked as if he'd aged a decade in the last twenty-four hours. Annelise looked elegant as usual, but her face was stoic, her eyes haunted. Trailing behind them was Peter Williams, Senator Oldham's chief-of-staff, looking characteristically unflappable in a dark, expensive suit. He flashed Josie a perfect smile as they passed by, which she ignored.

Her coolness didn't deter him. "Ms. Ashbury?" he called.

"Crap," Josie said under her breath, turning around. "Yes?"

"Ms. Ashbury, Peter Williams, Senator Oldham's chief-of-staff," Peter crooned, holding out his soft, perfectly manicured hand. She shook it as though it were a dead fish.

"Hello," she said awkwardly. She waited a moment for him to speak, but he just stood there grinning at her. "Is there something I can help you with?" she said finally.

"Oh, my, I'm sorry, of course," he stuttered, his perfect façade cracking ever so slightly. He cleared his throat. "I understand that you're the one who found Am-, er, Miss Oldham yesterday morning?"

"That's right," Josie answered.

"Such an awful, *awful* tragedy. Please, take my card," he said, holding out a small, black rectangle. Of course, his card was black. "And let me know if there's anything—anything at all—that I can do for you."

Was he flirting with her? She started to respond, but Peter Williams had already turned on his heel to hurry after the Oldhams. Considering that his boss' daughter had just died tragically, he was eerily composed. Certainly, this was not the time to be picking up women.

Josie shivered. She couldn't imagine losing a child. And suicide? Annelise and Clinton would probably blame themselves, however outrageous that was. How do you ever recover from that kind of loss?

"Josie," Sean called out to her. She blinked and shook off the chill, realizing she had been staring after the Oldhams. Lowering her eyes, she continued back to Sean's desk.

"Hey," she said. "How are you doing?"

"About as well as can be expected," he shrugged. "My dad was in there with the Oldhams all morning, and this place has been like a tomb since yesterday. Well, a tomb with phones ringing off the hook. These reporters are unbelievable."

Josie nodded sympathetically. Nikki was probably one such reporter trying desperately to get something—anything—to put in the paper. "Has Nik been bugging you?" she asked.

He smiled, "Yeah, but she's nowhere near as bad as the others. At least she seems like she gives a damn. You wouldn't believe the nerve of some of these other jerks. We had to fight 'em off like a pack of wolves from the scene yesterday."

"Ugh, gross."

"Understatement of the century," Sean sighed. He motioned to the interview room closest to his desk. "Why don't we go in there so I can take an official statement?"

Josie followed him into the room, suddenly feeling nervous. She didn't know if it was because of the one-way glass or the enclosed space, but the interview room gave her the creeps. Taking a deep breath, she shoved her irrational feelings down as Sean closed the door behind her.

"Do you need a water or anything?" Sean asked.

She shook her head and gestured to her bag. "Thanks, but I've got some." An old habit bred from spending hours stuck in LA traffic, she always carried a large bottle of water with her.

"Okay then," Sean said, pressing a button on the digital recorder and flipping open his notebook. "So why don't you start by telling me what happened yesterday before you found the body of Amber Oldham."

She winced at Sean, referring to "the body." "Well, my alarm went off at five, as usual. I got up, got dressed, and was out the door for my run by around five-ten, five-fifteen. At the end of my run, I took the back streets around Rose Avenue like I always do to cut through the fields in the back of the high school. When I looked out into the grass near the water tower, I saw something red—I thought it was a backpack—so I jogged over to take a closer look. That's when I realized I wasn't looking at a backpack. I called 9-1-1 and, well, you know the rest."

"Mmm," Sean said, scribbling on his notepad. "Did any time elapse between when you found the body and when you called 9-1-1?"

"I don't think so. Why?" Josie asked.

"Well, you said you started your run around five-ten, and you usually run, what, five miles?"

"Right."

"Right. So assuming you do ten-minute miles, that puts you in the field behind the high school by about six o'clock, right?"

"I suppose."

"The 9-1-1 call didn't come until six-thirty-two," Sean said, his brow wrinkling. "Are you sure you called 9-1-1 immediately after you found her?"

Josie thought for a moment. "I think so," she said slowly. "Maybe I've got my start time wrong. Maybe I thought it was five-ten, but I really didn't start until five-forty."

"Mmm-hmm," Sean said again. "Do you always bring your phone with you on runs?"

26

"Yes," she replied. "My house has a smart lock, so I need it to get back in. Unless I leave the house unlocked."

Sean snorted. They'd had many conversations about Josie's home security—or lack thereof. He didn't think the wireless lock was strong enough to secure her house and had protested her having one installed, but she insisted. She'd had one in LA that worked perfectly fine, plus she had a security system—when she remembered to use it, that is. Lately, she forgot to arm it more and more often. The safety of a small town had lulled her into a less responsible mindset; in LA, she had always locked her doors and armed her security system. Sean liked even less her recent tendency to leave her door unlocked, but they were in small-town Ohio, not South Central.

"Do we have to have this conversation again *right now?* I think there are bigger issues at hand than my home security," she said pointedly.

"What happened then?" Sean asked. He was being unusually impassive. Of course, she had never seen him from the perspective of an interviewee before. "What happened then?"

"Then I waited for the police," she said. "I think I hyperventilated or something while I was waiting; I got kind of dizzy, so I leaned up against the leg of the tower to steady myself. Then it seemed like I blinked, and you guys were there."

"We work pretty fast around here," Sean replied sharply. He was quick to remind her how much safer she was in a small town where the police response time was around three minutes. Josie had what she referred to as a "mild stalking" situation back in Hollywood. This fan had broken into her property a couple of times. As far as Josie was concerned, everything had been fine. She'd alerted the police, and they came...eventually. But it would never be good enough in Sean's eyes; *he* would have handled it better.

"Anyway," she said, "I believe I was leaning against the tower when you all arrived."

"Have you had any other dizzy spells recently?" Sean asked, frowning.

"No, not really."

"What does 'not really' mean?"

"No, okay? It means no."

Sean paused. "Did you touch the body?"

"Are you serious?" she exclaimed. "*Of course not.* And once I realized it was Amber…no, I didn't touch her or any of her stuff."

"Hey, I have to ask," he said. "There are protocols, even for friends and family. Even if they are big TV stars."

"Sorry," she sighed. "I don't mean to be snippy. I didn't sleep well last night."

"Oh? Still with the insomnia? Is that why you're having dizzy spells?"

Josie nodded. "It's not terrible, but I'm having trouble sleeping through the night."

"Are you taking anything for it?"

"No. My doctor prescribed a sleeping pill a few months ago and it was awful." Awful was an understatement. The medication had Josie up and doing things that she had no recollection of the next day. Friends sent her copies of long-winded emails she had written, and she had even driven to the drugstore one night. As soon as she realized she had driven with no memory of doing so, she immediately stopped taking the meds.

"Make sure you take care of yourself. I wouldn't want you getting hurt."

"I am taking care of myself," Josie said.

"All right," Sean said, clearly unconvinced. "So you said you're having trouble sleeping through the night. Did you get up at all on Sunday night?"

"I know I got up at one point," she answered slowly, trying to remember. Her mind was so blurry during those midnight interludes where she was up and down. "Yes, I remember. I was up around eleven. I got up and made tea."

"Huh," he said, making a note. "So you were in the kitchen. Did you happen to look out that back window, see anything unusual?"

"No. At least, not that I remember. I looked out the window while waiting for the water to boil, but…no, I don't think I saw anything particularly unusual." Josie didn't want to tell Sean that she wasn't entirely sure of what she saw in the middle of the night. There was no point in worrying the police over what might have been her memory filling things in.

"Okay," Sean said. He picked up the manila folder on the desk and slid a

28

couple of stapled pages across the table to Josie. The top page was blank except for the words "Amber Oldham: Preliminary Autopsy Report."

"Wow, that was fast," Josie remarked.

"It usually takes about twenty-four hours for a prelim, especially when the ME has a politician breathing down his neck," Sean replied.

Josie flipped to the second page and scanned the report. When her eyes reached the middle, she stopped, her blood running cold.

Cause of Death: Fentanyl Toxicity

Manner of Death: Undetermined

"This can't be right," Josie said, shaking her head.

"Keep reading."

As Josie reached the end of the page, she gasped. The small box was checked next to "IF FEMALE: Pregnant at time of death." She gaped at Sean, unable to find words.

"That's how I felt when I saw it," he said. "I spoke to the ME. He said Amber had enough fentanyl in her system to kill a rhinoceros."

"And the pregnancy?" Josie asked.

"Thinks she was in her first trimester, maybe eight weeks along," Sean answered.

"So the fall didn't kill her."

Sean shook his head. "That's unclear. But the fentanyl absolutely would have killed her even without the fall."

Josie chewed her lip. The Midwest was in the midst of a massive opioid crisis—hell, the whole country was—but they hadn't seen much of it in Lakeview. Sure, there were murmurings that some kids were dabbling in OxyContin, but their community had seen no hard drug use and certainly no overdoses. Nearby towns hadn't been as lucky. Across the U.S., hundreds of thousands of people had died from opioid overdoses during the last two decades. Doctors across seven states had recently been indicted for illegally prescribing more than thirty-two million opioid pain pills altogether, some trading sex for prescriptions while others even unnecessarily pulled teeth to get patients hooked.

The larger problem was that fentanyl, a drug measured to be fifty to one hundred times more potent than morphine and prescribed for patients in extreme pain, was making its way into street drugs like cocaine, heroin, and ecstasy. Synthetic fentanyl was being produced in labs and sold illegally as powder, on blotter paper, or even put in eye droppers and nasal sprays, which dealers then mixed with other drugs. In some cases, people didn't even realize they were taking the highly addictive, very powerful drug until it was too late.

Because of the epidemic, Sean, as well as his fellow officers, had to carry a nasal spray called Narcan, or the generic naloxone in case they encountered an overdose. Naloxone had even made its way into the schools, with counselors and other select faculty members required to have it on hand. Essentially, naloxone was designed to rapidly reverse opioid overdose; but even naloxone was being abused now. Since some states allowed dispensing of Narcan without a prescription, people were arguing that the availability was making the opioid problem worse. By being so readily accessible, some argued, it led to more people abusing opioids because they had an "antidote" at the ready. Any way you sliced it, the opioid problem was a huge mess—a mess that Lakeview had found itself right smack dab in the middle of.

Was Amber so desperate to hide a pregnancy that she took her own life? Or had she been addicted when she found out she was pregnant and knew she couldn't give birth, so she ended her life? Amber was not yet eighteen, so even if she had wanted to terminate the pregnancy, she wouldn't have been able to do so without one of her parents signing off. Did she think they wouldn't grant her permission? Josie's mind swam with possibilities.

"Josie? Jose?" Sean's voice cut through her reverie.

"Sorry, I…I'm just…" she stammered.

"Yeah, tell me about it," Sean answered, standing up. He smiled tensely. "That's all I've got for now. If you think of anything else, you know where to find me."

"Back atcha," she said, rising from her chair.

"You got plans for the rest of the day?" He asked as they exited the interview room.

"I'm meeting the girls for a late lunch," she said.

"Ah," he smiled. "Well, tell them I said hello. And tell Fox to quit calling me."

Josie laughed. "You got it, Chief," she replied, giving a small salute. She knew Sean liked Nikki, but she did tend to overstep even the bounds of friendship when she wanted a story.

Chapter Eight

As Josie exited the building, she wrapped her coat around her, shoving her hands into her pockets. She wondered if the school board would cancel the Homecoming football game and dance, which was set to take place this weekend. The board had to be in a serious panic.

When she got home, she hurried up her front steps, tapped the Bluetooth lock, and waited for what felt like an eternity for it to click open. As she stumbled in, a rush of warm air enveloped her like a hug, and she heaved a sigh of relief. Making her way into the dining room, she plopped her laptop bag on the table, glancing at her watch. It was just after noon, which gave her time to do some digging on social media and snuggle with the kitties before heading to lunch with the girls.

Josie was not a fan of social media—too many Internet trolls hiding behind their computer screens saying things they would never say to a person's face. However, she knew that high schoolers' social lives were documented completely online, and she wanted to at least look at Amber's pages and see if she could find some clues about what led to her death. She brewed a mug of coffee and settled onto the couch with her laptop. Presley jumped up and curled himself around her feet, and Monroe sat on the back of the couch, chirping at birds outside the window.

The more Josie poked around on social media, the more she understood why people were obsessed with it. You could learn so much about a person just by looking at their Instagram posts. After nosing around Amber's profile, she decided to check on Amber's three closest friends: Morgan Taylor, Lexi

Smith, and Charlotte Burnes. Amber had mentioned these girls in passing during their talks, and they reminded Josie of her friends when they were in high school. The girls were seniors this year, and they had been inseparable since they were little kids.

Josie was surprised to find that all three girls' accounts were not private, leaving all their photos and information exposed. She started with Morgan Taylor. Morgan seemed to be the most responsible and grounded of the three. A small girl with dark blonde hair and almost violet-blue eyes, she dressed like an '80s punk rocker and was always on the computer. Apparently, she was a computer whiz and a brilliant hacker. She attracted lots of male attention but appeared disinterested. Her focus was getting into an Ivy and then working for a tech company in Silicon Valley, if she didn't start one herself. Nothing could break her focus. Her feed was made up mostly of selfies (many with her tongue hanging out and her hand clenched in a rocker-style pose), cover art of her favorite bands and pictures with her friends. Nothing remarkable caught Josie's attention.

Lexi Smith, though slightly less intense than Morgan, was also fairly quiet and serious. Josie wasn't sure exactly what her ethnicity was, but she was of Asian descent and resembled a young Lucy Liu, with jet-black hair and a smattering of freckles. Amber had mentioned that Lexi was set on med school, and a boatload of science classes was keeping her busy. Josie thought she recalled Lexi having a medicine-related internship for the year, but she couldn't remember where. Lexi's feeds were full of selfies, again, but hers were either in school or in a white lab coat. Josie wondered if she had an internship with a hospital or some sort of medical lab.

Last was Charlotte Burnes. Charlotte came from an equally wealthy family as the Oldhams, and her family lived a few houses down from their estate. Tall and statuesque, she reminded Josie of Naomi Campbell, with cocoa skin and honey-colored eyes. By reputation, she had what other teachers referred to as "an attitude problem." She had been the one Amber fought with most in their group, but she was also the closest to Amber. Frank Burnes, Charlotte's father, was a prominent defense attorney, amassing his fortune representing high-profile clients in a law practice he had built from the ground up.

Charlotte's feed was different than the other girls. Yes, she had selfies and photos of the group of friends, but recently, photos in her feed looked as though they had all been taken in the same place, somewhere with lots of dark wood and expensive-looking decor. The photos reminded Josie of a cigar and bourbon bar she had once been dragged to by her ex. Was that Charlotte's house? Josie made a note of this as she scrolled. Charlotte, though she could easily pass for twenty-five, was only seventeen. More surprisingly, there were photos of Charlotte with a few famous athletes and local celebrities. That was interesting. Where was Charlotte meeting these high-profile people? True, her family did have money, but all the photos were taken in that same dark location.

The girls were an eclectic bunch, so much so that Josie wondered what held them all together. But she knew that childhood friendships in a small town were often inexplicable—you chose people as a kid, and those were your people. Sometimes those friendships lasted into adulthood, others fizzled out once graduation came, and everyone realized there was a much bigger world out there.

Several hours later, Josie glanced at the clock on her phone, which read 2:22. "Oh no!" she said aloud. She was going to be late to meet the girls. Maybe if she ignored the speed limit *just* a little, she could make it there almost on time. She grabbed her purse, stuffed her phone into it, and flew out the door. She headed east down Main Street, gunning her engine. Then she flipped on the radio, settling on an FM radio station with The Traveling Wilburys crooning their dulcet tones.

When the song ended, a brief news report came on. "Breaking news in the Amber Oldham story, WKSS has received a report that the preliminary autopsy found fentanyl in her bloodstream and also revealed that the teen was pregnant. Amber Oldham was found dead at Lakeview High School yesterday in an apparent suicide. Former Hollywood actress and Lakeview resident Josephine Ashbury reportedly found the body. Ms. Ashbury appeared in the long-running crime drama *Order & Justice* before leaving the show after a nervous breakdown following—"

Josie flipped the radio off and sighed. A kid was dead, and all the media wanted to do was sensationalize it and talk about who found the body. Typical. She wanted to give the press the benefit of the doubt, but they were predictable as ever.

As she stepped out of the car, she felt her phone buzzing and saw a text from her mom. "How are you, sweetie?"

"All good. Going for lunch with the girls. Call you later," Josie wrote back.

"Tell the girls I said hello," came the response.

Tucking her phone away, she glanced up and saw a couple of guys walking down the street, ogling her Tesla. She smiled. That car was great for pulling focus away from her. Bracing herself against the wind chill once again, she hurried around the corner and down the row of shops, finally entering the wood door with "Second Street Pub" emblazoned on the small window. She put her hand on her ear to massage some warmth back into the lobe and looked around.

"Hey, Josie," the bartender called. A small woman in her mid-fifties, Shana had long curly hair and a big smile to match her big brown eyes. She strolled over to Josie, "Boy, you've had one heck of a start to your week," she said in her gravelly voice, pointing to the TV above the bar.

The scene showed the parking lot of Lakeview High School still packed with news vans, now reporting the announcement of Amber's autopsy. Josie wondered if the police had put out a formal statement or if someone had leaked the info to the press. It seemed awfully early for these outlets to have all the details.

"Yeah, not exactly what I expected on my morning run," Josie said.

"I bet," Shana said. "You all right?"

"Oh, I'm just fine. Thanks for asking. Are the girls here?"

"Back in the 'loge,'" Shana said, gesturing towards the back of the bar with her head as she polished a glass. The 'loge' was what the girls had affectionately nicknamed their big, round booth. With high wooden walls and a big, squishy seat, the booth was the perfect spot for the girls to debrief, as they liked to call it, without calling too much attention to themselves. Josie made her way to the back. She could see her three friends tucked into the corner booth, animatedly talking over each other. As she approached, Nikki, who was facing her, jumped up and ran to greet her.

"How are you?" she said, throwing her arms around Josie.

Josie smiled and hugged Nikki back. "Good. You know," she said. "Ask me later, though, when I'm trying to sleep."

"Seriously. It's just one thing after another. Sorry, Jose," Alex said.

Alex Ziebranowicz looked like a Disney princess. With her big brown eyes, cascading auburn hair, and perfect upturned nose, she looked like a cross between Belle and Ariel. Alex was a bartender at Twin Oaks, an upscale bar and restaurant located just outside of Lakeview. She was also in the fledgling stages of a romance with Josie's middle brother, Tommy.

"Are you still seeing that counselor? The one I recommended?" Heather piped up. Heather Spooner, a prominent doctor at Lakeview Hospital, was Josie's most rational and pragmatic friend. Her pale greenish-gray eyes, blonde hair, and alabaster skin made her a frequent subject of ghost-related ribbing by the rest of the girls. The voice of reason, Heather had kept the girls out of trouble many times in their teenage years. After completing her undergrad degree at Tulane, Heather had gone on to medical school at Case Western Reserve University, where the school had a partnership with The Cleveland Clinic. Heather graduated at the top of her class and was quickly offered a position at the Clinic. When presented with an opening to join a practice at Lakeview Hospital, a partner of The Cleveland Clinic, she jumped at the chance to work closer to home. Heather had connections to the best medical help in the area—maybe even the world.

"I am. I just haven't been getting a whole lot of sleep these days," Josie said.

Alex snorted. "You can call me anytime. Or Nik. We're boring. The doc, on the other hand," she said, gesturing at Heather, "she's responsible for people's lives and stuff."

"I think you're being a bit hyperbolic," Heather laughed. "I'm in internal medicine. I mostly see adults with colds this time of year."

Alex opened her mouth to speak, but Josie cut her off before she could continue. "It's all right, but thank you. I will call if I'm feeling wonky, okay? I promise."

Shana popped her head around the side of the booth. "How you ladies doin'? Can I get anyone a glass of wine, margarita? It's five o'clock somewhere."

Josie glanced at her watch. 2:46. The women shook their heads, laughing. "Iced teas then?" Shana asked.

"Yep," Nikki said. "And onion rings, potato pancakes, and spinach and artichoke dip. And mozzarella sticks."

"Jeez, Nikki, leave something for the other customers," Josie joked.

"Hey, I figured we needed some comfort...appetizers. What, you got a TV show to be in shape for or something?" Nikki shot back, winking, her face falling when she realized her misstep. The other girls exchanged glances.

"Har-har," Josie replied, smiling. "Actually, all of those sound fantastic."

Once Shana returned to her post behind the bar, Alex turned to Josie. "So what's going on at the school? Are they shutting down for the whole week?"

"I don't know," Josie said. "They closed yesterday and today. I'm waiting for a text from the Board of Education about what's next. They convened an emergency meeting today to figure out next steps."

Shana reappeared and plunked four iced teas in front of them. "Here ya go. I'll be back in a sec with the food."

"Thanks, Shana," Nikki replied. Then she turned to Josie. "So do you really think Amber Oldham committed suicide?"

Heather almost spit out the iced tea she'd been sipping. "Nik! Give the woman a chance to breathe. This just happened yesterday! Besides, how would Josie know?"

"It's okay, Heather. I don't know, Nik. Do you mean, do I think it was an accident?" Josie asked, choosing her words carefully.

"What I mean is, what was she doing up there *alone* in the middle of the night?" Nikki asked. "And now the drugs and the pregnancy. I get that the city has tried to make that water tower inaccessible, and I understand that kids still go up there—that'll be another story in and of itself. But a high school girl up there *alone*?"

"Point taken," Josie responded. When they were in high school, the water tower was a popular spot for kids to party, but she thought that had fallen out of style with low-rise jeans and camo pants. Maybe Amber's death would be enough of a reason to make city officials finally tear it down. Josie was about to speak, but Shana came and dropped the food, and the girls dug in.

"I hadn't considered the possibility of foul play," Josie admitted after they had all taken a few bites. "Of course, I haven't had a lot of time to think. I just found out about the pregnancy and the drugs this morning when I gave my statement to Sean."

The women fell silent for a long moment. Then Alex asked abruptly, "So have you gone on any more dates with that hot teacher?"

"Nice transition," Heather said under her breath.

"'Hot teacher's' name is Jake, and I'm seeing him on Saturday," Josie said. "This will be our third date."

The girls took turns making suggestive noises and giggling like teenagers. "Oooh, third date, you know what that means," Alex teased.

"Good!" Nikki said loudly, "He's so cute!"

"I know." Josie couldn't stop herself from grinning. "And he is so sweet. He's helping me coach the kids with their Shakespeare monologues for that ESU competition. It's a good thing, too—Shakespeare is *not* my forte."

"Not a lot of Shakespeare in network crime shows?" Heather asked.

"Or Bond movies?" Nikki chimed in.

"Ha-ha-ha," Josie replied.

"You haven't dated anyone since…." Nikki trailed off, looking down into her lap.

"Since," Josie repeated. Her tumultuous relationship with James had been a disaster of epic proportions. They had been young, successful, and stupid together, spending nights out drinking and dancing until dawn with the rest of the young Hollywood crowd. Some nights were spent getting into atrocious fights when the booze took a turn. Their chemistry had been amazing, but their fights had been equally explosive. They would repeat these vicious cycles, breaking up and making up, drawn back to each other like magnets. This continued until one particularly embarrassing incident when the police were called as they screamed at each other outside of a bar on the Sunset Strip. The fight landed them all over the tabloids, and rumors of abuse and violence ran rampant. In a rare moment of clarity, they both agreed that it would probably be best if they went their separate ways, though they still had to work together. Unfortunately, this all happened just before Josie's breakdown and exit from the show, so James took a lot of heat from their fans about causing her departure.

Jake Johnson, or "hot teacher," was an English teacher and freshman football coach, with dark hair and beautiful hazel eyes. He was smart, sensitive, and calm, a nice departure from what Josie had grown used to in her relationship with James. Although they had only been out a couple of times, they had a great time together. After the breakup with James, Josie had been skittish about getting into another relationship, but Jake was different. He had a calm energy, and she enjoyed the absence of drama.

"Please tell me you're giving him a fair shot. A *real* fair shot," said Alex, looking at her pointedly.

"I am, I am," Josie swore.

"Mmm-hmm," Heather chimed in skeptically, giving Josie the side-eye.

"Honestly. I'm giving him a fair shot. I really like him," Josie promised, holding up three fingers in a Girl Scout salute.

"Woman, we all know you weren't a Girl Scout. Put those fingers down," said Heather, laughing.

"Doesn't a Brownie count?"

"Could you survive one night in the woods alone?"

"Um..."

"Then, no."

They all burst out laughing. Josie was notoriously "indoorsy." The closest she had ever come to camping was renting a cabin in upstate New York, and even that was a stretch.

"We'll expect a full report," Alex said wryly.

Heather's cell buzzed. "Is that work? I thought you were off today," said Nikki accusingly.

"I am, but I'm on call," Heather said. "Just a sec, I'm gonna step outside and call the office."

The girls rotated to let Heather exit the booth. She returned a few minutes later. "I'm afraid I've got to run, ladies."

"Everything okay?" asked Josie.

"Oh, it's fine. One of my older patients was just admitted to the hospital with a raging kidney infection. I told you, Nik, the excitement never stops."

Nikki guffawed, choking on the potato pancake she had been wolfing down.

"Seriously, Nik, I'll never understand how you eat like that and still look so good," Josie said. Nikki had a ferocious metabolism, and to this day, she could eat pretty much anything she wanted and stay a size four.

"Magic," Nikki said, waving a mozzarella stick like a wand at Josie.

"Bye, ladies. Next week?" Heather said, pulling on her coat.

"Maybe this weekend," Alex said. "I think we all could use a *real* drink."

"This weekend it is. See you all then," Heather waved and was gone.

"I've gotta go too," Alex said apologetically. "I'm opening the restaurant tonight."

"No worries," said Josie.

Alex threw some bills on the table, then shimmied her way out of the booth. After putting on her coat, she blew the remaining two women a kiss and turned on her heel.

"And then there were two," Nikki said. "You want some company for the rest of the afternoon?"

"Thank you so much, but I'm going to try to grab a nap before my date," Josie said gratefully.

Nikki narrowed her eyes. "How long has it been since you slept a full night?"

"Um, a few weeks, maybe?" Josie lied, waving her hand. "I'm dealing with it."

"Okay. But have you been talking to your therapist about it? Does she know your history?"

When Josie didn't answer, Nikki sized Josie up with her huge blue eyes. Josie met her gaze, then looked away. Like Sean, these women had seen her in some of the worst moments of her life, and Nikki knew exactly how bad things could get. Fortunately, Shana chose that moment to come by with

40

the bill and save her. Josie handed Shana her credit card without looking at the bill.

"You can't do that forever."

"Why not? You guys all left cash," Josie pointed out.

"For the bill, but you're going to turn it into a fat tip for Shana," Nikki argued.

"So what? It's not like it's hundreds of dollars. Seriously, Nik, I don't want to have this conversation again," Josie said wearily.

They had the same argument every time Josie paid for something or Nikki thought she was being too liberal with her finances. She was worse than Josie's business manager. The girls didn't know exactly how much money Josie had in the bank, but they had their suspicions. A booming career in Hollywood was nothing if not lucrative, especially as successful as Josie was.

"Fine, I'll back off," Nikki said, raising her hands in surrender. "Just don't come cryin' to me when you're broke."

"Noted," Josie said, smiling.

Both women clumsily exited the booth and put their coats on. Josie put on a hat, just for good measure.

"Seriously?" Nikki laughed. "It's like fifty degrees outside. That's summer here. Those years in LA made you soft."

"Truth," Josie said. She often snuggled under a blanket when the temperature dropped below seventy degrees. When the girls had been lifeguards at Lakeview Pool together as teens, the rule had been that the pool didn't close unless the temperature dropped below sixty-five degrees. They spent many mornings teaching swimming lessons to groups of rambunctious kids, freezing their butts off in the barely-sixty-five-degree weather. She couldn't imagine that now.

Nikki and Josie shouted their goodbyes to Shana, who was at the back of the bar, tending to another patron, then swung the wooden door open and stepped outside. True, it wasn't that cold, but the wind had a bite.

As they reached the parking lot, Nikki turned to Josie and repeated, "Are you sure you're okay?"

Even now, with a huge story on the line, Nikki was worried about Josie.

Josie couldn't imagine her life without these women. "I'm fine," she promised. "I told you, nap. That ought to catch me up on my sleep. Then Netflix. But no chill."

"Never say never," laughed Nikki. "It is your third date. But call me if you need anything. I'm going back to The Press office, but I'm happy to bug out if you need me."

"I will," Josie said, opening her car door.

"And I want a full report after your date on Saturday. Or maybe Sunday morning," Nikki teased.

"'Kay," said Josie. "Love you."

"Love you more," Nikki responded. Over the years, this had become the women's parting line whenever they left each other.

Josie put the car into gear and backed out, waving as she drove away from the lot. Being with her friends was always fun, but between lunch and her interview this morning, her energy was depleted. She was looking forward to a nice, long nap.

Chapter Nine

After teaching two periods on Wednesday, Josie was ready for a break. The fentanyl overdose and pregnancy were all the kids could talk about, and she had a hard time keeping them focused during class periods. Understandably, the kids in her morning classes had been either rowdy and uncontrollable or anxious and distant. The school board had decided Tuesday evening that they wanted to get the kids back to normal—or as normal as they could be—ASAP, so they decided against canceling any further school days. Since it was Homecoming week, the board hoped that the anticipation of the weekend's festivities would provide the kids with a much-needed distraction.

The school brought in extra counselors for those who needed to talk, and had a special assembly planned for later in the week that would run the gamut of topics Amber's death had dredged up—teen suicide, drugs, pregnancy. Teachers frantically adjusted their schedules, and board members huddled together in the teacher's lounge, planning for the presentation. In other school districts, when a student took their own life, the administrators worried about a rash of students following suit—as though it was contagious. Did they think it would become a trend, that kids would suddenly think suicide was a "solution" to their problems? Josie didn't fully understand the reasoning behind that line of thinking.

During her free period, she decided to look up Tony Burgess' schedule and was happy to find that he had a study hall block. Tony was Amber's boyfriend of about a year. As a senior, he was the quarterback and captain of the football team. He should have been on cloud nine, still enjoying the attention from last Friday's victory and prepping for the big game against Cedar Creek; instead, he was grappling with the death of his girlfriend. Josie didn't know Tony well, but Amber had introduced them early in the school year.

She strode down the hall to the classroom where the study hall was scheduled, but upon talking to the monitor, found out that Tony used this hour to go workout in the weight room. She thanked the monitor, headed for the gym wing, and found Tony in the weight room alone, music blasting.

Tall and well-built, Tony had light brown hair and a dimple in his left cheek when he smiled, which was often. He was a sweet kid from a middle-class family. His dad worked as a factory foreman, and rumor had it that his mother took off years ago. Tony was the oldest of three, with a brother who was a freshman and a sister in middle school. Amber had confided that Tony shouldered a lot of the responsibility at home, since his dad worked long hours and his mom was gone. Though he was looking at a full ride to Ohio State on a football scholarship next fall, Amber had confessed that he was having anxiety about leaving his siblings.

As Josie entered the room, Tony caught a glimpse of her in the mirror and gave her a shy smile, standing up from the weight bench. "Hey, Ms. Ashbury," he said.

"Hey, Tony," she replied, "How are you doing?"

"Okay, I guess." He shrugged.

"Got a few minutes to talk?"

"Yes, ma'am," Tony said, walking over to turn off the music. Josie smiled. He always "yes, ma'am-ed" her. He was one of the most polite kids she had come across at Lakeview High, and his politeness kind of surprised her. With his good looks and impressive athletic ability, he had reason to be arrogant, but he had maintained a sense of humility.

Josie sat on a plastic chair against the wall, and Tony sat on the weight bench facing her. "I'm sure the last few days have been really hard on you," she said, unsure of how to begin.

"Yeah, it's been pretty surreal. Like, I feel like I'm having a nightmare, but I just can't wake up," Tony said, his candor catching Josie off guard.

"I know what you mean," she replied. "I won't drag you through too much, but I just wanted to ask, have you—?"

"Heard about the autopsy? It's total bullcrap," he said, cutting her off. "Sorry," he amended quickly, realizing that he was speaking to a teacher.

"It's okay," Josie said. "We're all a little on edge."

"It's just…." Tony began, getting up from the bench to wander over and organize the hand weights, as though by force of habit. "Like, first of all, I…I don't believe she would jump off the water tower. And now the drugs, like, Amber didn't do drugs. Especially that drug."

"So how would you explain the fentanyl they found in her system?" she asked, studying him.

"I dunno," he said dully. "Like, I know they say addicts can hide things really well, but Amber wouldn't touch that stuff. We all know what it's doing to people. She's too smart for that…was too smart for that," he finished, his gaze falling to the floor.

"I know. I'm just as surprised as you are. But you know, sometimes smart people do stupid things."

"No, she wouldn't," he said, shaking his head firmly. "My cousin OD-ed a couple of months ago, and Amber saw what my family went through and what the drugs did to him. There's no way she would ever. No way."

"So if you don't think she ever would've touched it, how do you think the drugs got in her system?" Josie pressed.

Tony's face fell. He looked down at the floor again, shaking his head. "I don't know. Maybe someone slipped it to her," he said, his voice catching. As he said it, Josie could tell he knew he was reaching.

Josie was quiet, letting Tony compose himself before speaking again. "I think Amber was awesome, and I really enjoyed the time I spent with her. She had a good head on her shoulders and a really bright future. I was as shocked as anyone to hear about the drugs, trust me. But we have to look at the facts here. I know we might never get answers, but I'm going to try. I think I owe her that. We all do."

Tony looked at her for a moment. "Amber really liked you, Ms. Ashbury. She thought you were, like, amazing. And she trusted you, which is saying a lot. Honestly, I think if she was going to, like, tell anyone what was going on, it would've been you." He paused for a moment, "Or her friends, I guess."

"Right, her friends," Josie repeated. "Was something going on with the girls before Amber—or..."

"There was always drama with those girls," Tony shrugged. "Like, there's always drama with girls. With four of them, how could there not be?"

"Right, I know how that goes," Josie smiled. "Do you remember anything, I don't know, out of the ordinary happening recently?"

Tony took a moment to think. "I don't know if it was out of the ordinary, but something was going on for a couple of weeks before...ah, you know. I hadn't seen her much, but with football and everything, I didn't really, like, think about it. But I know she was having some sort of, like, thing with Charlotte."

"Thing?" Josie asked.

"Fight, maybe?" Tony said. "I dunno. They just weren't, like, hanging out as much as usual. Amber only said something once. She didn't really talk about it, but I guess I didn't really ask. I just figured it was, like, girl stuff, you know."

"Makes sense," Josie nodded. "And what about you two? Was everything... okay?"

Tony looked uncomfortable for a second, but recovered quickly enough that Josie thought she might have imagined it. "Naw, Amber and me? We were good. I mean, like I said, it's football season, so we didn't have a whole lotta time together. Plus, she had some, like, job."

"Oh," Josie said, surprised. She didn't remember Amber mentioning anything about a job. "Do you know what she was doing?"

"Uh, waitressing or something, I think," he replied, squinting thoughtfully. "I didn't really get it. I mean, like, she didn't need to work. Her family's loaded, and it's not like they were making her do it. But she said she was bored, wanted some independence or something."

"Gotcha," Josie said. Knowing she was about to get into delicate territory, she chose her next words carefully. "And what about the pregnancy?"

Tony seemed suddenly nervous. He stared at her for a moment, then blurted, "Uh, I—I mean, like, did Amber even know that she was, you know, pregnant?"

"I guess there's no way to know for sure," Josie answered. "But she didn't say anything to you?"

Tony shook his head.

"I assume the baby was yours?" Josie pressed, watching him closely.

"I guess," Tony said after a long moment. "I mean, like, yeah, it had to be. So..."

"You seem unsure. Was Amber—were you guys seeing other people?"

"No," Tony answered quickly. He looked like he was about to say something else, but then stopped himself.

"But you're not sure if you were the father of her baby?"

"No, I...I am, it's just, it's weird, that's all, you know," Tony stuttered.

"I get it." Josie nodded sympathetically. She stood up to leave, then turned back to him. "How was your relationship with Amber?"

"How was it? Uh, like, normal, I guess," Tony said, looking confused.

"Any fights or anything recently? Were you two having problems?"

"No! She was, like, my best friend." Tony choked, his eyes growing bright with tears. "Why? Did Amber say something like that to you?"

Josie shook her head, inwardly chastising herself. She needed to remember that Tony was just a kid, and he was grieving a loss. "I'm just trying to think of any reason why she might want to—"

"She was happy, as far as I knew," Tony sighed. "I don't know why she did, you know, what she did."

"Would anybody want to hurt her?" Josie asked, lowering her voice as other boys filed into the weight room, looking at her curiously. Before Tony could answer, she said, "You know what? Never mind. I'll let you get back to it," she said. "But I appreciate you talking to me. And if you need anything, please, you know where to find me."

He nodded, lying back down on the weight bench. As Josie left, she could hear some of the boys teasing him about being alone with her in the weight room. She shook her head; not even death could stop teenage hormones.

Chapter Ten

Around the same time that Josie was talking to Tony, Sean arrived at Lakeview High School. After receiving Amber's autopsy, Sean decided to request a search of Amber's school locker. He also requested to search her boyfriend, Tony Burgess' locker. Working under the assumption that Tony was the father of Amber's baby, he may have had a motive to harm her if he was unhappy with the pregnancy. Being that he was a senior and on his way to play college football, Sean could not imagine that a baby would fit into his future plans. Tony's was the locker he really wanted to see. To be thorough, Sean also ordered locker searches of Amber's three closest girlfriends: Lexi Smith, Morgan Taylor, and Charlotte Burnes.

He had spoken with Principal Tom Crandall earlier that morning, and they agreed that Sean should head over around nine o'clock, and Tom would have a custodian ready with the locker skeleton key. When Sean pulled into the high school parking lot in his squad car, he could feel the students' eyes burning through the windows. There were a few kids on the lawn, taking a break from classes or studying in small groups, who craned their necks like giraffes reaching for leaves on a tall tree. Sean strode into the school and headed straight for the office, purposely avoiding the English wing. The last thing he wanted right now was to run into Josie. She was well-meaning, but he knew she would probably not approve of his actions; he had enough to worry about today.

Tom Crandall greeted Sean with a warm handshake. Mr. Crandall had been Sean's physics teacher when he was in high school, before he became Principal Crandall, and he was one of Sean's favorites. His gentle demeanor and genuine enthusiasm for teaching made him a favorite of many students over the years, and kids would often go to him outside of class with non-academic problems. When the last principal had announced her retirement five years earlier, Tom had been the obvious choice for her successor.

"Thanks for indulging me, Tom," Sean said, awkwardly shaking Tom's hand. Calling Mr. Crandall "Tom" still felt wrong.

"Of course, anything I can do to help," Principal Crandall replied.

The law covering searches of school lockers was a gray area; basically, a precedent referred to as "reasonable suspicion" had to be met. A student's unexplained death certainly fit the bill. Sean had considered asking each of the students' permission to search their lockers, but ultimately decided against it. The girls were all friends, and they could notify each other via text to remove items from their lockers before he could get there. His safest bet was to do the locker searches unannounced.

Sean wanted to search Amber's locker first, since what he was doing wouldn't be kept under wraps for long. The janitor popped her locker open and, after pulling on latex gloves, Sean began sifting carefully through the books and papers piled on the shelves. Pictures of Amber with her friends as well as clippings from fashion magazines, hung inside the door of the locker, and as Sean looked at them, he felt a pang of sadness for this girl whose life had been cut short. He didn't find anything on the lower shelves, but when he reached past some books and a sweater was shoved up on the top shelf, he discovered a small, tattered jewelry box. It looked like something that might belong to a little girl, and as Sean gently lifted the lid, a song he didn't recognize began to play as a small ballerina popped up, twirled, arms stretched overhead. Sean lifted the top tray and unearthed a small Altoid tin in the bottom of the box. Pulling it out, he set the music box down on the shelf. As he opened the tin, he felt dread settle into the pit of his stomach; it was filled with about a dozen small, round, blue pills.

Principal Crandall's mouth dropped open in shock. "Are those what I think they are?"

Sean nodded grimly as he carefully placed the small baggie into an evidence bag and tucked it into his inner jacket pocket. They moved next to Amber's friends' lockers. The first two, Charlotte's and Morgan's, turned up nothing. In Lexi's locker, he found a note with "Amber" scrawled on the outside of it, which he placed in another evidence bag. By this time, word had spread like wildfire that the police were conducting locker searches, and as Sean, Principal Crandall, and the custodian approached Tony's locker, they had an audience.

"I think it's time to get to wherever you need to be," Principal Crandall called sternly to a group of students down the hall, trying unsuccessfully to look casual as they watched them. They began dispersing quickly like a cloud of bugs bouncing off a car windshield, hurrying away from one another and then coming back together as they scurried down the hall.

In Tony's locker, they found a photo of Tony and Amber inside the door, several books on the middle shelf, and Tony's purple and white letterman jacket hanging on a hook. Sean flipped through the miscellaneous papers and supplies on the top shelf, coming up empty. However, when Sean moved the books around on the middle shelf, he saw a gap where the metal locker wall had warped and separated on a seam. He took out his flashlight and, holding it in his mouth, squeezed his fingers through the small opening. They clamped down on something plastic, and as he pulled it out, he realized it was a plastic baggie that closely resembled the one he had found in Amber's locker. Sure enough, the baggie contained a handful of round blue pills with the "M" identifier that matched what he had found in Amber's locker. Along with the pills, there was a small cylindrical container with white powder dusting the sides and bottom.

"Terrific," Sean muttered. He had hoped to come up empty-handed. Sean and Tony's father, Brad, were friendly, and they grabbed a beer every now and then. Tony was a good kid, and his arrest would devastate Brad.

Principal Crandall simply shook his head, looking white as a ghost.

"I need to find Tony Burgess, right now," Sean barked, shaking himself out of his momentary paralysis.

They rushed back to the office to look up Tony's schedule in the school's computer database. Once they had the location, Sean took a breath and steeled himself for the task he now faced. In his decade on the police force, he had never had to arrest a student at school. Hell, he had barely had to arrest anyone, save for a few drunk drivers whizzing through town after the bars closed at two or while breaking up the occasional rowdy party. Although Tony was eighteen and not technically a minor, Sean knew the backlash from the community upon hearing that a student was arrested during school hours would likely be intense.

Principal Crandall paged Lyle, the school security guard, and they accompanied Sean as he marched towards Tony's calculus class. Sean felt as though he was having an out-of-body experience, and time slowed as they walked down the hall. When they got to the door, Principal Crandall knocked and exchanged a few words with the teacher, who went back into the classroom and retrieved Tony. The other kids in the class stared, eyes like saucers. Like mini oracles, they all seemed to sense what was about to happen.

Tony loped casually out into the hall, appearing confused when he saw Sean waiting for him. "Hey, Officer Sullivan, it's been a minute," he said affably, extending his fist for Sean to bump. "How are you? Did you find out something about Amber?"

"Turn around and put your hands on the wall, Tony," Sean replied grimly.

"Wha-, what? Are you joking?" Tony sputtered.

"I'm afraid not, son. Hands on the wall."

"What the fu—...why?" Tony cried, turning slowly and placing his hands on the lockers beside him.

Sean patted him down, grabbed one hand and then the other and wound them behind Tony's back to handcuff him. "Tony Burgess, you are under arrest for possession of a controlled substance," he began.

"No, n—no, I don't know what you're talking about!" Tony exclaimed, his eyes wild. He bucked against Sean's grip, looking up and down the halls for help, but found only Principal Crandall and Lyle, watching them sadly.

Sean went through the rest of Tony's Miranda rights quickly, eyeing the clock as he knew they were rapidly barreling towards a bell. He needed to get Tony out of there before the hallways flooded with kids. Fortunately, Tony stopped struggling and let Sean get through the speech without any further interruption. However, when Sean finished, Tony began again.

"Officer Sullivan, please! You know I didn't do anything!" he said, his voice growing increasingly loud.

"Son, please, calm down," Sean said, pushing Tony, gently at first, then more roughly as the teen struggled, towards the front door to the school.

Tony, his voice now at a fever pitch, caught sight of Lexi down the hall. He began shouting at her. "Lexi, tell him he's got this all wrong! You know. Tell him!" But Lexi cast her eyes down to her phone and scurried away as though she hadn't heard him.

Sean finally managed to wrangle the kid out the front door, down the sidewalk, and into his squad car. As he helped Tony into the backseat, putting a hand on his head to prevent him from hitting it, he glanced over at the school. Small faces peered back at him from every window, all the kids craning to get a look at the excitement. No doubt, before sunset, the entire community would have heard the news of Tony Burgess' arrest. The rumor mill would make everything worse, as usual. As Sean drove back to the precinct, he tried to brace himself for what would come next.

Chapter Eleven

The students in Josie's afternoon class were more distracted than usual during their scene work, and with a few minutes left until the bell, she ordered them all back to their seats.

"Would someone like to tell me what's going on?" she asked. "You're all so preoccupied. Did I miss something? Is there some new TikTok challenge that I don't know about?"

The kids glanced around, meeting each other's eyes and then looking downwards. For what felt like an eternity, nobody spoke. Then a freshman named Gabby raised her hand slowly.

"Finally," Josie exclaimed. "Yes, Gabby, what is it?"

"Um, like, I didn't see this?" Gabby began in her signature teen lilt that made every sentence sound like a question. "But I heard—well, I didn't just hear, there's, like, a video? Yeah, like, a video of Tony, um, Burgess getting arrested?"

After a moment, Josie realized that her jaw was hanging open, and she hadn't said anything for a good five seconds. "Are you sure?" she demanded.

"Yeah, like, that cop? The tall one? Like, he was here earlier?" Gabby continued, but the other students started talking over her, adding their own flare to the story.

"Yeah, that Sullivan cop…"

"I heard Burgess tried to punch him…"

"Shut up, you dumbass, that's not true…"

"Found drugs…"

"Pills and worse stuff…"

"He killed…"

"Okay, okay, okay, okay," Josie said, putting up her hands. "So Se-, erm, Officer Sullivan *arrested* Tony Burgess? Are you guys sure?"

Gabby raised her hand again, her cell phone clutched tightly in it. "Somebody, like, sent me the video?"

Josie beckoned her to the front of the class. Sure enough, when Gabby pressed play, footage of Sean arresting Tony began rolling. Someone had shot it from a distance through the glass on one of the classroom doors, but was clear enough. She saw Tony struggling and yelling, but couldn't make out what the two of them were saying. The video cut off when Sean wrestled Tony out the front door of the school.

"Thanks," Josie said faintly, waving Gabby back to her seat. Fortunately, the bell rang, and she didn't have to deal with whatever else the class was going to drop in her lap.

Arrested? *Tony?* The three long minutes between the bells went by agonizingly slowly, and when the second bell rang, Josie bolted for the English office, swooped up her stuff, and raced to her car. She made it to the police station in about nine seconds flat. She didn't even bother with her coat as she strode into the building, trying to maintain her composure. When she arrived at Sean's desk, she could feel it sliding away.

"You arrested Tony Burgess? Do you even have any evidence—" she whispered angrily, but he cut her off.

"This way, Ms. Ashbury," Sean said loudly, gently taking her arm and pulling her towards the interview room. "I found drugs in his locker, Josie. Not that it's your business."

"You arrested one of my students. One who's never so much as stepped one toe out of line."

"Did you hear me?" Sean asked, looking genuinely bewildered. "Drugs. In. His. Locker. I'm sorry, Josie."

"So, did you arrest him on murder charges?"

"No. Just possession of a controlled substance. *For now,*" Sean emphasized as Josie tried to cut in again. "Between that and the pregnancy, though, Tony looks guilty as hell."

Josie stopped, letting this information fully absorb. "Why were you searching the lockers?" she finally asked.

"Josie, I can't get into this with you. It's an active case," Sean said wearily, turning his back and rubbing his eyes. After a moment, he stepped back towards her. "You think I wanted to arrest that kid?"

Josie took a moment to compose herself before continuing. "You found drugs?" she asked quietly. Sean nodded in response. "Fentanyl?"

"I think so. I sent the pills and the powder to the lab to confirm, but they look like fentanyl," he said.

"Was there something in particular that prompted you to search the lockers?"

Sean stood up. "Josie, enough. I cannot give you any more details. Please stay out of this and let me do my job."

"Fine," Josie snapped, also standing. "Can I at least talk to him, see if he's okay?"

"Go ahead," Sean said. "He's over in the holding cell waiting for his dad."

Josie rushed out of the conference room towards the cell, but stopped short when she saw Tony's father enter the station. In the time since Josie had run into him at the coffee shop a few months earlier, Brad Burgess seemed to have aged a decade. Josie knew Brad from Lakeview High alumni events, though he had graduated before Josie attended school there. His eyes were wild as he approached the front desk and demanded to see his son. Josie was about to go talk to him when Sean pushed by her. The two men exchanged a few words, the volume of their voices rising as the exchange became more and more heated. Josie decided the best course of action was to get out of there and let things settle down. As she passed them, she could hear Sean explaining the arrest and see Brad's face falling. Her heart broke for him.

There had to be some reasonable explanation. Yes, of course, the drugs could be Tony's; but after her conversation with him, she couldn't believe that that was true. People who lose relatives to overdoses don't usually dabble in the drugs that killed them. So if the drugs weren't Tony's, how did they get into his locker?

Chapter Twelve

J osie's head was spinning as she drove away from city hall. Yes, something had seemed a little off with Tony during their conversation earlier, but she felt deep in her bones that he wasn't responsible for Amber's death. Learning about his cousin who had died of the fentanyl overdose and seeing Tony's reaction when he talked about the death, she didn't believe that he would ever go near the stuff. On the other hand, there was definitely something that wasn't quite right with Tony. He had seemed hesitant to accept that the baby was his, so he must have thought that Amber was cheating on him. But he didn't seem very upset. Why not? Did they have some sort of an arrangement? Amber had never said anything about seeing other people. Then again, it was looking like Amber kept quite a bit from Josie.

Then there were Amber's friends. Could one of them have planted the fentanyl in Tony's locker? But why frame Tony? It's not like the evidence pointed to one of them being responsible. Would the police find something different if they looked more closely? Perhaps one of them wanted to urge the police in Tony's direction to deflect attention. Or maybe they had planted the drugs knowing that Tony would be exonerated eventually. But that seemed like a risky play; if the plan didn't work, they would be sending an innocent kid to trial for premeditated murder. Ohio still had the death penalty, and killing an unborn child? Tony would be convicted in the court of public opinion before he ever set foot in front of a jury.

After driving around aimlessly chewing her lip, Josie decided it was time for a visit to the Oldhams. If she couldn't get Sean to listen to reason, maybe she could appeal to the family's sense of justice. Tony was such a nice kid; she couldn't imagine that Amber's family didn't like him. And even if they didn't, surely, they wouldn't want to see an innocent man—not man, *boy*—prosecuted for a crime he didn't commit. Josie swung a U-turn and sped toward the Oldham estate, pulling up to the gate at the same time as Peter Williams. He flashed his toothpaste-model smile and gestured for her to go ahead of him. She rolled her eyes when she got past his field of vision. Something about that guy that made her skin crawl. He reminded her of one of those Hollywood agents that would say anything to sign you, then three months later, an email chain from them trashing you would get splashed all over the tabloids.

She feared this meeting would not go well. One of the things that Amber *had* mentioned was the distance between herself and her parents, basically being raised by nannies, her relationship with her parents stiff and formal. Still, maybe they had noticed something, anything, that could point Josie in the right direction.

"Oldham residence," a voice crackled through the speaker at the driveway entrance.

"Hello, Josephine Ashbury, here to see Mrs. Oldham," Josie replied with more confidence than she was feeling.

There was a pause on the other end. "Do you have an appointment?" The voice said finally.

"No. But Amber was my student at Lakeview High, and I would like to speak with Mrs. Oldham. It won't take more than a few minutes," Josie added quickly.

There was another pause. Then to Josie's surprise, the large wrought iron gate swung open, and she drove up the winding driveway, watching the horses grazing in the field beside her. She pulled her car into one of the open spots at the top of the driveway. As she got out of the car, Peter Williams pulled in beside her and grinned at her once again. She hurried towards the door, hoping he wouldn't follow her. Fortunately, when she looked over her shoulder, he was gone. He must have gone through another entrance, she thought, ringing the doorbell. The door opened before Josie had a chance to knock, and a pretty, dark-haired girl in a gray maid's uniform stood before her. Josie wondered if the entire staff lived on the property.

"Mrs. Oldham is in the parlor," she said, gesturing to her right.

"Thank you," Josie replied, entering the beautiful sitting room. Annelise stood next to a bookcase that encompassed the entire east wall of the room. She was dressed head to toe in off-white and was the kind of woman who could wear all white without ever spilling so much as a drop of anything on herself. The room was impeccably decorated, with beige and leather furniture accentuating the dark wood bookcases and trim. Annelise was looking absentmindedly at the books before she turned to greet Josie.

"Josephine Ashbury," Annelise said, sizing Josie up with her ice-blue eyes. "You're the actress, correct?"

"I'm an actress, right," Josie replied, taking a seat on the large leather couch that Annelise gestured towards.

"Mmm," Annelise said, her face as unreadable as her tone. "What can I do for you, Ms. Ashbury?"

"Josie, um, you can call me Josie, if you like," Josie said. "First, I wanted to tell you how deeply, deeply sorry I am about Amber. She used to come and visit with me in the English office during her free periods, and we'd gotten close during the last couple of months. I—it's just such a shame."

"You're an English teacher?" Annelise asked, arching her perfectly sculpted brows in surprise.

"Ah, no, I teach an acting class. They stuck me in the English office because there was room, I think."

Annelise sniffed. "I see. I didn't realize Amber was taking an acting class."

"Yep," Josie said lamely. She had dealt with plenty of ultra-wealthy people in Hollywood; it was unavoidable in the entertainment industry. But there was something about Annelise that she found unnerving. They sat silently for longer than Josie found comfortable.

"Well, I'm sure my daughter enjoyed your class. Amber always did have a... *flair* for the dramatic," Annelise said.

Josie thought the statement was a little strange, but she brushed it aside as she said, "Oh, yes, Amber was wonderful. Truly talented, although I don't think she had any professional acting aspirations."

"I should hope not."

Josie chose to ignore the put-downs Annelise was lobbing her way. "Do you know Tony Burgess?"

"Of course," Annelise said. "We met him several times. He's a lovely boy, for—"

"For?" Josie pressed.

"For what he is," Annelise finished.

"I'm sorry?" Josie said, hoping she was inferring the wrong meaning from Annelise's tone.

"My daughter was on a path to do great things, Ms. Oldham," Annelise began. "This boy, this Tony, he was fine for a high school fling, but it was never going to last. And now that we know what he was capable of, well, it appears that I was right in my assessment."

Now it was Josie's turn to squint at Annelise. "You didn't like Tony?" she asked.

"Like is neither here nor there," Annelise said stiffly.

"And you've heard about Tony's arrest?" Josie demanded, undeterred.

"Yes, of course, the news is covering it quite thoroughly. As I understand it, the police found drugs in his locker. The very same drugs," she continued more loudly as Josie opened her mouth to argue, "That were found in my daughter's system during the autopsy. I assume a murder charge will follow shortly."

"But Mrs. Oldham, don't you know Tony? Does he really strike you as the drug addict type? Or worse, the *murdering* type?" Josie could feel her frustration rising.

"I've lived long enough to know that people are often not what they seem. You lived in Hollywood, Ms. Ashbury. Surely you understand that," Annelise answered, waving her hand up and down at Josie with obvious distaste.

"I do," Josie said, throwing up her hands. "But I can also still recognize the good in people. Tony Burgess is a *good kid*."

"Mmm. Tell me, if he is such a good kid, why were there drugs in his locker?" Annelise said with dark skepticism. "And let us not forget that he impregnated my daughter before any of this mess began. In fact, that seems to have been the catalyst for this entire fiasco. His arrest makes perfect sense. Is it a shame? Yes, absolutely. But at least now there will be justice for my daughter."

"Justice?" Josie said incredulously. "You think imprisoning an innocent kid qualifies as *justice?*"

"I'm not sure where you're getting the 'innocent' part, Ms. Ashbury," Annelise said coldly.

"I don't think those drugs were his," Josie said quietly.

"Thankfully, that's not up to you to decide," Annelise sniffed. "It appears that my daughter did not take her own life, but that it was taken from her. The responsible party must be held accountable."

"Come on, Mrs. Oldham—" Josie began.

"No, that's quite enough. I am certain the police know what they're doing, and if Mr. Burgess has been arrested, they must have good reason. Now if there's nothing else," Annelise plowed ahead as Josie tried once again to interject, "I need to get back to my evening. You know the way out."

"And the pregnancy? Didn't you take that seriously, either?" Josie blurted, unable to stop herself.

"I don't believe that's any of your business, Ms. Ashbury," Annelise snapped, her eyes flashing.

Josie jumped up, blocking Annelise's exit. "Please, Mrs. Oldham, I'm trying to put together what happened—"

"You'd better watch your step, Ms. Ashbury," Annelise snarled. She caught herself and straightened up, smoothing a hand over her sweater. "It's best to let the police sort these things out."

"But—" Josie began.

"Ms. Ashbury, we are dealing with a family tragedy. Please have the tact to allow us to mourn in peace. We're finished here," she stated firmly.

"I—" Josie tried again, but Annelise put her hand up.

"Enough, Ms. Ashbury. Now I want you off the property before I notify the authorities," she said loudly, causing several staff members to appear in the foyer, their fingers practically dialing the police already. Annelise pushed past Josie and disappeared around a corner.

Josie stared after her, stunned. Turning on her heel, she stormed out the front door. Clearly, she was going to get no help from Annelise Oldham. She clearly didn't care if the correct person was charged in Amber's murder, as long as someone took the blame. Where was Clinton? She looked down at her watch, which read 4:56. Clinton had one office downtown and one at the house, and Peter Williams had gone in a back entrance when they arrived. There had to be a direct route to the offices around back. Looking around and seeing no one, Josie turned left toward the back of the house instead of getting into her car. There were probably some sort of security cameras, but she didn't care. As long as no one was physically stopping her, she would worry about being caught trespassing later.

Josie trotted under several rose-covered trellises lining the path around the house. Stables and a tennis court came into view, as well as a moderately sized outbuilding that was large enough to hold offices. For a moment, she was stunned by how breathtaking the property was. She had forgotten how much land the Oldhams owned, but was reminded immediately by the rolling green hills that seemed to stretch on for miles. A large swimming pool and hot tub sat just outside the house, accompanied by a beautiful teak deck that rose to the third story, allowing for rooftop views of the lake and land as far as the eye could see.

Josie made her way past the tennis court to the stables, casually wandering in as though she had somehow gotten lost on the property. She peeked into a few stalls, hoping she would get lucky and find Clinton Oldham getting ready to ride, but didn't find him. When the stable manager stepped out of the office and demanded to know what Josie was doing, Josie muttered an apology and backed out of the building as the man picked up the phone to call security. As Josie hurried back in the direction of the house, she thought she caught a glimpse of Peter Williams peering at her through one of the back windows.

She was interrupted by two large, burly security guards in matching black jackets hurrying towards her. Josie picked up her pace and practically dove into her car, quickly starting it and putting it into gear as the guards were closing in on her. One of them knocked on her window and yelled, but Josie simply made a shrugging gesture before hitting the pedal to reverse out of her spot and speeding away. She didn't have the patience to deal with these goons right now. She needed to focus on Tony, and, more importantly, on finding the real killer. While she knew all the signs pointed in Tony's direction, something in her gut told her he was being framed.

Chapter Thirteen

From her brief interaction with Annelise, she had gotten some important insight. Still, Annelise's reactions had been really...odd. Everyone grieved in their own way, but Annelise's grief seemed different, like she had a prized possession ripped away from her instead of losing her daughter. It actually seemed almost as if Annelise didn't like her daughter. And she couldn't have cared less about Tony Burgess' predicament. When Sean heard about their visit, he was going to rip her a new one.

"Call from: Sean. Sullivan," her car announced, punctuating each syllable like it was deliberately trying to get under her skin.

"Crap," she muttered, ignoring the call. That was fast. She needed some time to regroup before she dealt with Sean. As she retreated from the Oldham estate, she mulled over the conversation, making a mental note to call Alex later and get her input. Alex volunteered with an organization that worked with the families of addicts, so she might have a little insight into what might be considered "normal" behavior from a grieving mother. Her phone buzzed with the notification of a new text, the home screen only identifying that it was from an Unknown number. She pulled into her driveway, shut off the car, and pulled up the text.

"Need to talk about Amber. Important. Meet at Twin Oaks at six o'clock tonight," the message read. Josie scrolled to see if there was a number associated, but nothing came up.

"Who is this?" she wrote, waiting for the three dots that indicated the other person was writing back. They never appeared.

Looked like she was going to Twin Oaks tonight. She fired off a quick text to Alex to see if she was working (she was) before going into the house to grab a sweater and feed the kitties. Josie always wore layers when going to Twin Oaks, where the two roaring fireplaces could make the restaurant pretty toasty. She also wanted to jot down a few notes about her meeting with Annelise, and she had left her notebook on the dining room table last night. At least, she thought she had. As she looked around, she didn't see her notebook anywhere. Odd, she thought she had left it right there on the table amongst the bills and other miscellaneous papers.

Her phone buzzed with a text from her mom. "Sorry it didn't go well with the Oldhams. Hope you catch a break soon. Love you," it read.

"Love you too," Josie wrote back. "Call you later."

Searching the house, she finally located the notebook in her office on the lounge chair. Having no recollection of putting the notebook in there, or sitting in that room making notes, she again questioned whether or not her sleep habits were affecting her memory. Had she even sat in this chair recently? She could have sworn she always sat at the table, and maybe in the living room, but perhaps she was wrong.

Jotting down a few quick lines about her encounter with Annelise, she snapped the notebook shut and left it on the dining room table, making a specific mental note of it this time. She hurried into the kitchen to pour food and fresh water for Presley and Monroe who, she noticed for the first time, were strangely absent. She made kissing noises, calling, "Pres? Monroe? Dinnertime!" She heard a faint mewing and realized that the kitties were locked in the basement.

"Oh, no!" she exclaimed, throwing open the door. Presley ran out immediately and wound his way through her legs, purring. Monroe, clearly upset about being locked in the basement, trotted past Josie with her head in the air indignantly, making a beeline for the food bowls. How had they gotten locked down there? She had gone to the basement to clean the litter boxes this morning, but she always left the door open. Could a breeze have blown it shut? She looked around to see if any windows were cracked, but none were.

"I'm so sorry, my babies," Josie said, reaching down to pet Presley, who joined Monroe at the food bowls. When she reached for Monroe, the little cat slumped her body away from Josie's hand, eating the whole time. "Lots of treats later, okay?" she said soothingly as though they could understand her. She looked at the clock. It was 5:57, which meant she was going to be late for her mystery date. Satisfied that the cats were safe and the basement door was open, she threw her coat back on and ran out the door.

Chapter Fourteen

By the time Josie got to Twin Oaks, parked her car, and ran inside, it was almost six-fifteen. She hoped her mystery date hadn't left. Running to the bar, she threw herself down on a barstool.

"Hey," Alex said, pouring her a glass of cabernet. "I think you might be looking for him."

She gestured to a sandy-haired man with his back to them. He was seated at one of the low bar tables in the corner with a view of the creek. Josie craned her neck, trying to catch a glimpse of who it was before picking up her glass and joining him. As she made her way around to the front of the man, she was surprised to find it was Andrew Oldham, drinking a dark beer. Andrew was about twenty-two years old, with the same lovely dark blue eyes as his sister. He stood about six-one with the fit frame of a man who had ample time to go to the gym, and dressed like a cross between a surfer and Jeff Lebowski. He bore a striking resemblance to her ex, James, especially when he flashed his slightly crooked grin.

He held his hand out. "Josephine Ashbury? I'm Andrew Oldham."

"Hi. It's—you can call me Josie," she stammered, feeling herself blush. What was wrong with her? She had been around some of the most attractive men in the world. But Andrew had his father's natural charm and social ease, something that always threw her a little off balance. Talking with strangers had never come easily to her, and she was always impressed when others did it gracefully.

He gestured to the seat across from him. "Please," he said as though he owned the place, waiting until she was ready to sit before taking his seat

66

again. Despite his purposely disheveled appearance, Andrew had the distinct manners of a man brought up in an affluent home.

"So you're the one who texted me from the unknown number," she began awkwardly, making a mental note not to take her terse interaction with Annelise out on her son.

Andrew smiled, "Yes, sorry, my number is unlisted. I overheard your conversation with my mother today and figured you wouldn't be too stoked about talking to another member of our family after the way she treated you."

"It's okay," Josie said as she waved her hand. "Your family is under an enormous amount of pressure right now. It's only natural to lash out."

"Yeah, no, I'm pretty sure that's my mother's natural state," Andrew laughed. "I could blame it on stress, but that's really just her personality."

Josie nodded. "Well," she said after a moment, "you had something you wanted to talk about?"

"Yes," he said, his laughter fading. He ran his fingers through his thick, wavy hair. "Look, I haven't told my parents any of this yet, but there was definitely something strange going on with Amber in the last few months."

Finally, some real information. Josie tried to keep her excitement under control as she nodded calmly. "I see."

"The thing is, I don't know exactly what. But I do know something, like, changed at the beginning of the summer. She asked me to hook her and her friends up with fake IDs. I gave her the name of a guy I know who runs a website for that kind of stuff, and I know she and the other three—Morgan, Lexi, and Charlotte –used his services."

"Are you sure that's all they got from him? No drugs?" Josie demanded. Getting a fake ID wasn't that unusual for high school seniors, but the guys who dealt in that sort of thing usually had their hands in other more nefarious activities.

"I called the guy Monday afternoon and was ready to take his head off. I was pissed because I thought he had hooked her up with the fentanyl. But he swore to me that the IDs were all he did. Drugs aren't his scene. He's got connections to people who deal some stuff, but never fentanyl—too many

ODs, too messy, too many questions."

"And you believe him?" Josie asked dubiously.

"I've known the dude for years. He's really not interested. I would never have hooked it up if I thought those girls were going to do anything except get fakes for, like, buying beer for parties and stuff. I had no idea…" His eyes misted a little, and he looked out over the creek and took a swig of his beer.

"No idea that what?" Josie asked, a little too loudly. Alex glanced up at them, and Josie gave her an almost imperceptible head shake, indicating that everything was fine. Alex gave her a thumbs up.

"No idea that things would end up this way, I guess," he sighed.

"I'm not sure that a fake ID—presumably for buying beer—contributed to what happened to Amber," Josie said gently. "If she was looking for illegal drugs, it's not like an ID would have helped her."

"Yeah, I guess you're right," he said sullenly. "But that's the thing—I'm not sure that's all they were doing with the IDs. I saw them sneaking around, whispering a lot. Like, I know that sounds like just something teenage girls do, but this was way more than usual. And once they got the IDs, Amber was around less and less. The three of them almost never hung out at the house anymore, and they used to be there all the goddamn time. I probably sound crazy, but it seemed like something was up."

"Up…like maybe a drug addiction?" Josie asked carefully.

"Up, like they were doing something more than going to keggers," he said. "The addiction thing doesn't track for me. Amber was too smart for that. And she didn't show any of the signs of an addict. Trust me, I've had plenty of friends go to rehab. I know the signs."

"Lots of smart people fall prey to addiction—" Josie started, but Andrew cut her off.

"Yeah, but she didn't have any interest either. I get why she might lie about the stuff she was doing, but we were pretty close, you know? Whenever we talked about drugs, she never mentioned anything harder than weed."

"M'kay," Josie nodded, sipping on her wine.

"Anyway, like I said, I dunno if it helps anything," he said with a shrug, slugging back the rest of his beer and signaling to Alex for another one. "But since you cared enough to talk to my mother, which is not easy, I thought I'd give it a shot. Plus, I know Amber liked you. She talked about you all the time. My parents," he stopped himself. "Ah, well, I think my parents just want this to be over. With the pregnancy and the drugs, they're freaking out about how it's going to affect my father's career. The 'optics' aren't good," he laughed bitterly. "Whether their daughter committed suicide while pregnant, or if she was doing fentanyl and overdosed, she's a baby murderer to his constituency. Don't get me wrong, they're plenty shook up about losing Amber, but this all is making it ten times worse."

Josie nodded again. She felt like all she could do was nod along, trying to absorb all of the new details that were thrown at her. Andrew was clearly in tremendous pain.

"I don't know what I'm gonna do," Andrew said, slumping back in his chair. "How do you get over something like this?"

"I wish I had answers for you," Josie responded with a weak smile. "Everyone grieves in their own way. I think it just takes time. Therapy probably wouldn't hurt, either. It's certainly helped me when I've lost loved ones."

"Yeah, well, if you find something out when you're digging around, let me know, 'kay? I need to know the truth about what happened to her," he said, his dull tone clashing with the pleading behind his eyes.

"I will," she said, waiting a beat before standing up. "Nice meeting you, Andrew."

"Oh, there was one more thing," he said, putting his hand on her arm as she passed him. "You know my dad's chief-of-staff, Peter Williams?"

"Yes?" Josie said.

"Yeah, well, things had gotten kinda, I don't know, weird between him and Amber in the last few weeks," Andrew said, his brow knitting.

"What do you mean weird?"

"Well, they were always, like, cordial and stuff, you know. But the last few weeks, she was, like, avoiding him, it seemed like. Nothing major, but just like he would come into a room, and she would leave type situation."

"I see," Josie answered. "Did she have a problem with him?"

"Not that I knew of?" Andrew shrugged. "Like I said, her avoiding him seemed like a recent thing, like, in the last few months. I mean, it could be nothing, but…"

"Interesting. Thanks for the tip."

"No problem," Andrew said, sitting back down to tuck into his new beer, gazing at the creek. Josie wondered what it did to a twenty-two-year-old to lose their sibling, especially one they were close to. She couldn't imagine losing one of her brothers; the grief would swallow her whole.

She approached the bar where Alex stood, eyeing her. "So…?" Alex said.

"I'll fill you in later," Josie said quietly, putting down her wine glass. "I've got to go call my mom."

Alex looked at her strangely, then said, "Okay. Call me later—I want to know details."

"I will," Josie said, pulling her phone out of her bag as she walked toward the exit.

Chapter Fifteen

Once at home, Josie settled into the leather recliner in her front room and flipped on the news. Monroe had forgiven her and nestled in tight to Josie's side. She couldn't believe it was only eight o'clock—this day had been one for the books. Every local news station had covered Amber's death; it was possibly the biggest news story ever to hit Lakeview and had made national news because Amber was Senator Oldham's daughter. Tony's arrest had dumped more chum into the water, and the sharks were circling.

"Coming up, an exclusive interview with Senator Oldham's Chief of Staff, Peter Williams," Darren Jenkins' day-glow teeth flashed as he spoke. This guy again? Although after the arrest, a statement had to be issued somehow. The vultures weren't going to let up for even a minute. After a commercial break, an interview with Peter Williams from earlier in the day began rolling. It looked like the interview had taken place outside Congressman Oldham's office downtown, and Josie wondered if Peter had been returning from this interview when she encountered him at the Oldham house.

Williams was young and handsome, with a shock of dark hair, hazel eyes, and freckles that made him look younger than his age. He looked like the kind of guy you'd find working on a campaign in Washington: expensive suit, perfectly groomed hair, white teeth, but not Hollywood white. Feeling restless, Josie began listening to the interview as she got up from her chair and straightened up the den.

"Of course, this is devastating," Williams said grimly, looking steadily at Jenkins. "Tony Burgess was like a son to Senator and Mrs. Oldham. The news of his arrest was shocking to all of us. This is a time of great sorrow and stress, and we ask that the press respect the family's privacy and direct all inquiries through me."

Jenkins then attempted to probe him about Amber's mental state prior to the death, but Williams brushed him off smoothly. He was good. He managed to swat away the reporter's questions without offending him, all the while maintaining a properly somber demeanor. But there was definitely something about him that seemed off to her. Though he was subdued and appropriately sad when speaking about Amber, she thought she could sense an undercurrent of excitement in his voice, like he was enjoying the spotlight. Was she imagining it?

How gross would that be? She shuddered and flipped the TV over to a rerun of *Friends* as she finished tidying up. Once in her pajamas, a pair of soft fleece lounge pants and a camisole, she tucked into the couch with a cup of tea and a book and attempted to quiet her brain for a few moments before heading to bed.

Chapter Sixteen

Josie raised her head groggily and blinked the sleep from her eyes. She looked around the living room, vaguely aware of a noise pounding in her brain. Wait, that wasn't in her brain, someone was banging on her front door. How long had she been asleep? She glanced down at her watch, seeing it was almost seven a.m. She had missed her morning run. It didn't occur to her last night to set the alarm on her watch, but she hadn't made it to bed at all, instead falling asleep on the couch with her book in her lap and the kitties snuggled up with her.

Attempting to rub the sleep out of her eyes, she stumbled over to the door and flung it open to see Sean standing there.

"Hey," she said, "Were we supposed to—"

"Josie, what the hell?" he interrupted, pushing past her into the house.

"I...I...I...," Josie stuttered, trying to pull her thoughts together. Sean didn't get this angry often, but when he did, it was best to be in a different ZIP code.

"Why the hell did you think it was a good idea to go to the Oldhams' and talk to Annelise? *And* go snooping around the property?" he demanded, turning to face her. "And by the way, do you always just open the door for anyone who knocks? No 'who is it,' nothing?"

"I just thought maybe, if I could talk to Annelise or Clinton, maybe talk some sense into them..." she began.

"Yeah, well, you did something, all right. And what did you say to Nikki? After you girls had your lunch yesterday, she starts hounding me about the possibility of foul play," Sean said. "Any idea where she might've gotten that idea?"

"God, no," Josie said. "Honestly, Sean, I didn't say a word to her."

"She cited an 'anonymous source,'" he said, making air quotes with his fingers. "Saying someone might've said that this wasn't a suicide or an accident. So you're telling me you didn't plant that idea in her head?"

"No, Sean," Josie snapped, feeling more awake now. "You know Nik. She's got weirdos she talks to all around the county. It could have been any nut job off the street who happened to watch the news this week."

"It's the timing, Josie," Sean said quietly. "We hadn't even announced a formal murder investigation. Nik called me right after she had lunch with you."

"Sean, I swear I didn't say anything of the kind to her. The only thing…" Josie trailed off, shaking her head.

"Ah, of course. The only thing," Sean said, gesturing for her to go on.

"I mean, she just asked me if I thought Amber committed suicide or if I thought there was more to the story. She pointed out that Amber being up on that tower in the middle of the night, pregnant, with drugs in her system, was pretty weird. Which I agreed with," Josie said. "I asked her if she meant did I think Amber jumped or fell, and I told her I didn't know. That's where we left it. Honest, Sean, that's all I said."

Sean sighed, rubbing his eyes.

"You know how Nikki gets," Josie continued. "She's like a dog with a bone; once she's got an idea, she doesn't let go. And she's obviously got it in her head that there's something about Amber's death that doesn't sit right."

"Yeah, well, none of this matters now anyway," Sean said.

"What do you mean?"

"The investigation has been called off."

"What the hell are you talking about? After the fentanyl and the pregnancy? What—how?" Josie demanded.

"All I know is I got word from the chief that I'm to shut down the investigation and close the case immediately. Hell, we had barely even opened an investigation. Word came down straight from the commissioner. Which means—"

"Which means he's being leaned on by someone higher up. Unbelievable," Josie breathed.

He looked at her for a second, then stood up. "I've got to get back to the station. Just do me a favor, Jose," he said, grabbing her shoulders and looking into her eyes. "Don't add fuel to this fire of Nikki's, even speculation. We're being watched like hawks by every person in the area. Hell, the whole country is watching. And now we have to shut down. The last thing we need is the press running wild with a bunch of half-cocked theories."

"I got it," Josie said. "And what happens to Tony?"

"He's out on bail. Even if he's not guilty of murder, I still found fentanyl in his locker. I can't just ignore that," Sean spat. "I know you think he's innocent, Jose, but something stinks here. When there's a murder—*if* there's a murder—nine times out of ten the significant other is the guilty party."

Josie nodded, not wanting to fight with Sean. She was just relieved that Tony had been released.

"The city is going to have a lawsuit on its hands as it is. You and I both know that water tower should've come down years ago. Those historical protections can't protect it now."

"Assuming Senator Oldham is the one who ordered the investigation called off, you've got to admit that's fishy, considering the autopsy results."

"It's over, and there's nothing we can do about it. Get back to your normal life," Sean said, looking at his watch.

Josie snorted. "It's fine, Sean. If you need to know anything else, let me know. Otherwise, I'll keep my mouth shut."

"You know it's not personal," he said, suddenly seeming weary.

"I know," she said, walking him towards the door. "And I'll talk to Nik, try to get her to back off."

"Thanks," he said.

She watched him walk down her steps, get into his squad car, and pull away. She couldn't believe the investigation had been called off. Didn't the Oldhams want justice for their daughter? It was fairly obvious that Amber didn't take her own life. Somebody else was involved. Somebody was with her that night. Somebody had to know something.

Chapter Seventeen

On Friday, the excitement about the Homecoming game and dance that weekend was palpable, despite the events of the week. Emotions were running high, and the kids needed a break. Homecoming was a big deal in Lakeview. The committee had spent hours picking a theme and putting together the decorations. Everyone had been looking forward to the big game against Cedar Creek and the dance on Saturday night since the beginning of the school year, and the powers that be decided that the tragedy should not completely override the festivities. Josie knew there was sure to be a somber pall over the game and the dance, but it was important to try to get back to normal.

Since Monday, Josie had continuously adjusted her schedule so she could devote time to helping the kids work through their feelings. She knew that the show must go on, as it were, with their other classes, but she had the freedom to be able to give them a respite from their class loads to regroup and address whatever they needed to deal with. Though counselors were available, and Josie was relieved that the school was offering support in the wake of Amber's death and Tony's arrest, she knew not everyone would feel comfortable talking to a stranger. Lakeview was lucky; in a less fortunate district, tragedy was often swept under the rug due to lack of funding and resources.

Josie couldn't figure out why Senator Oldham had called off the investigation. His office had released a statement that basically said the family wanted to move on with their lives and that they were "confident that no foul play was involved." Peter Williams had been all over the news spreading the same message to any news outlet that would listen. After talking to Sean, Josie was not convinced, and she didn't think he was, either. Alarm bells were sounding in her head. If the police weren't convinced that this was either a tragic accident or a suicide, why was the family so eager to move on? If Amber was murdered, why wouldn't they want justice for their daughter? Unless they knew something that Sean and Josie didn't, which could very well be the case. In a situation like this, the parents didn't usually get to make the call about stopping a police investigation. But when a powerful politician made up his mind, he could do things that ordinary people couldn't.

After debating with herself all week, Josie decided she was going to attend the Homecoming football game. She didn't go to all the football games, though she got a kick out of being able to hear the cheering crowd and the marching band from her living room every Friday night. She had only been to a few games this year, and she had attracted a lot of attention, which she was trying to avoid. However, the more games she attended, the more accustomed to her presence the residents of Lakeview became. It was now the visiting team's bleachers that buzzed when they caught sight of her. Plus, she was hoping to run into Lexi, Charlotte, and Morgan there. Even though the investigation was closed, Josie was determined to keep looking for answers.

As she showered and blew her hair dry, she listened to the tap, tap, tapping of the marching band drums as they began their warmups about an hour and a half before the game. One of the things she remembered most fondly about high school were those Friday night football games. She had been on the kick line, and every Friday came with an exhilarating performance, as the girls felt like they were on a huge stage in front of thousands of adoring fans. Sean had been a football player back then, and it had been fun to sit on the sidelines and cheer on her boyfriend while also getting to feed her performance bug.

She dressed in jeans and a white Henley, slipping a puffy jacket over it and pulling on wool socks before putting on her biker boots. The Weather Channel predicted temperatures in the high thirties to low forties tonight, with a chance of snow, and Josie wanted to be prepared. She stepped through her back door onto the beautiful redwood deck, complete with sunken hot tub, thankful once again to have so much space in her yard. Her home in the Hollywood Hills had been lovely, but no matter how gorgeous the houses were in that area, it still felt cramped.

As she trekked her way across the nearly one-acre backyard, she pulled her jacket more tightly around her, reaching in the pockets for her gloves and hat. It was too cold for her tonight. She exited her yard, ensuring that the alphanumeric lock on her gate engaged behind her. The parking lot was brimming with cars as students, faculty, and fans from both the home and away teams packed it in. Tonight's game was sure to be a good one. The rivalry between Lakeview and Cedar Creek was legendary, and both football teams were neck in neck in their stats for the year.

Josie made sure to arrive for the pregame festivities. Ordinarily, she might have skipped this part of the evening and just come for the start of the game. But there was a special moment at the beginning of every Homecoming game for alumni to come out on the field and be recognized, and Principal Crandall had requested that she be present for that. He thought the Lakeview residents would enjoy seeing Josie there and had confided that he hoped it would tear the focus away from the tragedy for a bit.

Josie strode across the parking lot quickly, shielding her face against the wind. Ohio had the most beautiful skies, and tonight was her favorite kind—heavy with bluish-gray and white clouds, shielding the sun and ushering a chilly breeze across the sprawling fields. It was still light out, but the sky was darkening rapidly as the lights blazed over the football field. Josie paid for her ticket and made her way around the track to the home team stands. She could hear the band marching over from the practice field to perform the opening show. Turning around, a sea of purple and white polyester gushed towards her, the flag girls flanking the band as they performed their choreography. In their short skirts and knee-high white boots, they looked like go-go dancers from a bygone era.

Josie moved along the chain link fence surrounding the track and field, greeting students and other faculty passing by as she made her way toward the fifty-yard line. She'd get a seat in the stands later; for now, she wanted to stay down on the track for the alumni ceremony. Craning her neck, she looked around for Amber's friends, but didn't see them anywhere. That didn't necessarily mean they wouldn't show up; a lot of the kids that weren't involved with the Friday night activities arrived after the game started.

As both teams warmed up, Josie admired the athleticism of some of the kids. There were a few who would probably go on to play college ball, and maybe one or two that were even on track for the NFL, if they didn't get injured. She caught sight of Jake on the sideline near the benches, talking with the varsity coaches. Even though Jake was the coach of the freshman football team, he attended all the varsity and JV games to support the kids.

Jake had played football through high school, but an ACL tear ended his career his sophomore year of college. Since he had been attending college on a partial football scholarship, the injury had derailed his plans. But he hadn't let it stop him from finishing school. He got two jobs and worked hard, earning an academic scholarship for the next two years. On their first date, they had talked about it at length, and Josie had been amazed at the ease with which he discussed it. She didn't think she would cope quite so well if something out of her control had screwed up her plans. He winked and waved and she returned the gesture.

"Hey, stranger," said a gruff voice behind her. She spun around to find Tom Jacobs, one of her father's oldest friends, standing there. At around five foot eight, Tom was stocky, with dark hair and the kindest blue eyes she'd ever seen. Tom and her father grew up together in Lakeview and reconnected after college when both moved back. Their families had spent many a night together barbecuing, having game nights, and even vacationing together. Tom had been like a second father to her and her brothers growing up. Josie knew she could count on Tom and his wife, Helen, for anything.

"Hey, old man," Josie joked, allowing herself to be pulled into a warm hug. "I thought I might run into you guys here."

Tom's kids were a few years younger than Josie, but one of his daughters lived in Lakeview with her husband and their two kids. "Rachel likes to bring the kids for the Homecoming game every year," Tom said. "They're too young to really appreciate it now, but they get a kick out of the band

and the cheerleaders. Any of your brothers here?"

Josie shook her head. "No, Kevin's working, Tommy's not really into it, and John's daughters, well, they don't particularly care for football."

"No surprise there," Tom laughed. John's daughters were six and four, and just about the girliest little things on Earth. "Saw the news," his tone shifted, striking a more somber note. "That poor girl. They said you found her?"

"Yeah," Josie said, feeling like the air was being sucked out of her lungs. "It was pretty awful."

"I bet," Tom said, his brow furrowing. "And the senator's daughter? That family isn't going to get a moment of peace for a while."

"Hopefully, it'll quiet down now that the investigation has been closed. But the press has been crawling all over this for the past few days. They've been camped out just off school grounds. Hell, they're probably out there right now."

Tom nodded. He knew about Josie's personal struggles with the press, and her deep dislike for sensationalized news. "I hope they're doing what they need to keep themselves together. Has anyone been bothering you?"

"Fortunately, no, not since the day of," Josie said.

"Well, you let me know if they start. You can always come and stay with us for a few days," Tom replied.

"Thanks," Josie said.

An announcement boomed over the loudspeaker. "We'd like to invite our alumni down to the field for the opening ceremony."

Tom held the gate open for Josie, and they made their way onto the field. Tom's daughter, Rachel, came down from the stands to join them, and Josie could see Rachel's husband and kids up in their seats, waving down at them. She waved as Rachel grabbed her other hand and squeezed it.

"Hey," Rachel said. "Lunch soon?"

"Definitely," Josie smiled.

They got to an empty spot on the quickly filling field and faced the stands. A good number of alumni showed up for Lakeview's Homecoming, especially since there were so many graduates who returned to raise their families in the community. The field was packed with people of all ages, from recent grads to senior citizens, all smiling and greeting one another.

The voice on the loudspeaker boomed again. "Now we'd like to take a moment of silence for Amber Oldham, a student Lakeview recently lost."

A hush fell over the crowd, and even the visitor's side fell silent. People bowed their heads, some clasping their hands in prayer, and when the moment was over, Josie could see several people around her whose eyes were bright with tears. The untimely death of anyone in their community was hard to fathom, but the death of a kid was especially heartbreaking. Tom and Rachel, who flanked her, moved in a little closer, and she smiled appreciatively at them.

Tony's situation still nagged at Josie. He had shown up to watch the game with his family, which was a surprise, but he looked like he'd been through hell. The school wouldn't even let him sit on the bench for the game, so he was up in the stands with his brother and sister. She'd hoped the police would have figured out where the drugs came from by now, maybe issue an apology for making a spectacle of arresting him at school just days earlier, but no such luck.

The crowd was eager for the game to begin, so the alums quickly exited the field. Josie said goodbye to Tom and Rachel, deciding to stay on the sidelines outside the fence to watch the first part of the game. As she posted up near the fence, she saw Brad Burgess exiting the field further down the track. He had joined the alumni, but stood far on the edge of the crowd. Stares and whispers followed him as he made his way up into the stands to join his two younger children. Josie felt a rush of sympathy for Brad. Though Tony was out, the ordeal was far from over. Although his arrest wasn't technically for Amber's murder, people were able to fill in the blanks. Some people in town probably thought, as Josie did, that foul play was involved; unlike Josie, however, they likely thought Tony was the culprit.

Brad sat down between the kids, wrapping an arm around each of them. They all looked miserable. Part of Josie was surprised that they had shown up. Then again, it was the Homecoming game of Tony's senior year, and he was the quarterback. Despite the events of the last week, Josie could tell that Brad felt immensely proud of his son. She hoped that this mark on the family's reputation wouldn't cast a shadow on the rest of their lives. Now she had even more incentive to find out what happened to Amber.

* * *

Josie wasn't a huge football fan, but she liked the feeling of comradery at the games. She was more interested in watching the students tonight, seeing how they were coping with the loss of their classmate, but also seeing if anyone was doing anything out of the ordinary. Although the mood seemed markedly more subdued than usual, she was happy to see that the kids were allowing themselves to have a little bit of fun this evening.

After the first quarter, the Lakeview Lions were winning seven to zero, and the temperature had dropped several degrees. Light snowflakes were slowly starting to fall. Josie decided to get herself a hot chocolate and go sit in the stands with Tom's family. Near the concession stand on the far side of the bleachers, there was an open grassy area where kids and adults were milling around, socializing. A few teens had formed a hacky sack circle and were skillfully flipping a bean bag ball back and forth. To the left of her, she could see a few kids sneaking under the bleachers. That area was policed pretty strictly by security, but the kids still went under and found places to make out, smoke cigarettes, and engage in the usual teenage debauchery. As she wandered over to the concession stand, she finally saw Charlotte. Morgan and Lexi were not with her, which was odd. It was Homecoming, after all, and most students were clustered around in their groups of friends. But Charlotte was alone, scrolling through her phone.

Josie started to make her way over to Charlotte, but stopped abruptly as a man appeared and grabbed Charlotte by the arm, pulling her away from the crowd near the concession stand. At first, Josie thought it was Frank Burnes, Charlotte's father. The man had a similar slender, tall build to Frank and the same silver-flecked dark hair. But Josie had never seen Charlotte's father at a football game. Plus, this man was wearing a leather jacket and jeans, and Josie had never seen Frank Burnes in anything but a power suit.

Josie casually inched over to them. As she did this, Charlotte broke away and started striding towards the area under the bleachers, but the man caught her by the fabric of her sleeve and yanked her back. Josie fought the urge to intervene, instead trying to get within earshot. As Josie grew closer, she heard the man growl, "You can't just do whatever you want."

"And who says I have to listen to you?" Charlotte scoffed. "Jesus, this isn't, like, a big deal."

"It is a big deal," the man replied, grabbing Charlotte's other arm and turning him to face her. "Those photos need to come down *now*."

"Ugh, whatever," Charlotte said. "I'll talk to Matt tomorrow and get this all, like, fixed."

"Who do you think sent me down here?" the man laughed. "You think I want to spend my weekend chasing girls at a high school football game?"

"I don't know what you do with your social life," Charlotte replied coolly, taking out her phone. Let's see what Matt says."

The man sat back on his heels, smirking at her as she waited for whoever was on the other end to pick up.

"Matt? Hey, it's Char….," She fell silent as she listened to the other person. "Yeah, but—" she argued, but was obviously cut off again. Her face fell, and she went pale, and she looked at the man in front of her with fear in her eyes. He didn't move, but simply folded his arms and continued to smirk.

"Okay," she said quietly. "Yeah, I understand. I—" Whoever was on the other line had hung up, and Charlotte took the phone away from her ear and stared at it.

The man took a step closer to her. "You see? What did I tell you," he sneered. "You follow instructions from now on, got it? This conversation will go very differently next time. Clear?"

"Yes," Charlotte whispered, her voice barely audible. Her hands trembled as she began tapping furiously on her phone.

The man, satisfied that his job was done, stalked off under the bleachers, disappearing into the darkness. Charlotte looked around to see if anyone had heard them. Her gaze locked with Josie's for a moment, and her eyes widened, then she took off in the same direction as the mystery man. Josie waited a beat before following them, but by the time she got under the bleachers, they were gone. She wound her way through the unhitched trailers parked under the stands, finding nothing except a few clumps of smokers who immediately extinguished their cigarettes and hurried away when they saw her.

Returning to the side field, Josie digested the scene she had just witnessed. Who was that man, and why did he care about Charlotte's photos? And why did Charlotte seem so afraid of whoever was on the phone? Josie had a nagging feeling that somehow, the answers to those questions were related to Amber's death.

Chapter Eighteen

The Lions managed to win fourteen to seven, running in the winning touchdown in the last seconds of the game. When the game ended, fans flooded the field, surrounding the players and congratulating them. As Josie looked up into the stands, she saw Tony finally crack a smile, and his siblings were on their feet, cheering. She was glad to see they were getting a moment of sunshine amidst the storm clouds.

Their happiness, however, was short-lived. Josie hung back after the game ended to say goodbye to Tom and Rachel, and when she exited the field into the parking lot, she saw a crowd gathering around something in the center of the lot. As she hurried over to see what the commotion was about, she could hear a male voice shouting.

"Which one of you little jerks did this? Huh?" came the unmistakable voice of Brad Burgess.

The crowd was around his Ford F-150, and Josie could see Principal Crandall standing a few feet from Brad, talking to him in a low voice, trying to calm him. Brad swung around wildly, stepping closer to the crowd as he shouted. Each time he stepped forward, the crowd moved back. Tony's brother and sister were huddled near the car, looking like they wanted to sink into the ground. As Josie pushed her way to the front, she finally saw what Brad was so worked up about.

The paint job on Brad's black pickup truck was destroyed, with the words "murderer" and "faggot," along with some obscene illustrations, spray painted in bright red all over the vehicle. For a second, Josie felt stuck in place, stunned that someone in their community could be so cruel. When she caught sight of Tony moving forward through the crowd, her heart sank. Then she saw Jake step forward and put a hand on Brad's arm.

"Brad, you've got to calm down," he said quietly.

"Calm down? Look at my damn truck!" he shouted, looking incredulous. "Tony didn't do anything. He's a *good kid*."

"I know," Principal Crandall had gotten to the other side of Brad. "And we'll find out who did this. There are security cameras in this area of the parking lot. Our kids know that."

At that moment, Brad Burgess caught sight of his three children; Tony, standing just inside the circle, looking totally defeated, and his other two, huddled miserably against the car.

"I want to see that security footage," he spat, shaking off both Jake and Principal Crandall. "Let's go," he said to the kids, nodding his head at the car.

Tony looked at Josie with such sorrow in his eyes, she swore she felt her heart break into pieces. Jake stepped towards her and wrapped her into a bear hug, and she allowed herself to be comforted, just for a moment. As Brad started the truck, Principal Crandall addressed the crowd.

"Show's over, folks. Get to where you need to be," he said, sounding exactly like he did in the halls at school.

"Tom, are there really security cameras that might have caught this?" Jake asked, his arms still around Josie.

Tom nodded. "We've got a few cameras aimed in the lot and on the field to monitor for illegal activity. And before you ask," he said, seeing Josie open her mouth, "No, we don't have footage of the water tower. Fortunately, Brad parked right in the line of the camera." Tom pointed up at one of the huge streetlights and, sure enough, Josie saw a small camera pointed down at them. "They run on a loop that erases every twenty-four hours, but I'll go in now and get the footage from this evening." He dropped his voice, "Our kids know where those cameras are. My money is on someone from Cedar Creek."

"That makes sense," Jake said.

"Take care, you two. I'm going to go get that footage right now," he said, then took off towards the building.

Josie sighed and buried her face in Jake's chest as he stroked her hair. Whoever was responsible, it was a terrible prank to pull. And while she hoped this would be the last of it, she had a sinking feeling that the trouble was not over for Tony Burgess.

Chapter Nineteen

On Saturday, Josie gave herself permission to relax. She knew she needed some self-care or she was going to completely come apart. She booked a mani-pedi, facial, and massage, and spent some time prior to her appointments in the steam room and sauna at the Sacred Tree Wellness Center. By Saturday night, she felt like a new person—just in time for her date with Jake. He was picking her up at seven for a seven-thirty dinner reservation. Around six, Josie got ready for the evening. She hated to be late.

Once she had applied her makeup, she went into her closet to inspect her wardrobe options for the night. Monroe and Presley were both stretched out on the bed, and when Josie opened the door Monroe promptly jumped up and ran in. She loved snuggling on the shelves with Josie's sweaters, and Josie didn't have the heart to stop her, even if it did mean her sweaters were covered in fur.

After selecting a pair of dark jeans and a white top, she slipped on camel-colored boots and gold accent jewelry. She transferred items from the black Chanel purse she had been carrying to a bag that matched her boots as Presley woke up and watched her sleepily. Once the transfer was complete, she spritzed herself with a cloud of perfume, which caused Presley to squint at her accusingly. As a training technique when they were kittens, Josie had used a spray bottle to deter unwanted behavior, and whenever Presley heard any sort of spray bottle, he gave at least a disapproving glance.

Her phone dinged with a text notification from her mom, "Have fun on your date tonight!"

Had she told her mom about her date? She must have. With her insomnia and the chaos of the last week, she was losing track of things. She jotted a quick, "Thanks! Call you tomorrow ☺," and tossed the phone onto her bed.

Looking herself over in the full-length mirror in her bedroom and finding her appearance satisfactory, she wandered into the living room to wait, scrolling through Instagram to see if anything interesting was in her feed. Earlier in the week, when she was digging into Amber's case, she had created a fake Instagram account from which to follow Amber and her friends, just in case any of them decided to make their accounts private. Fortunately, they had all accepted her follow requests.

When the doorbell rang, Josie looked at her gold watch, which read seven on the dot. She appreciated that Jake was punctual; it didn't hurt that he was also easy on the eyes. She swung her front door open to find Jake, looking gorgeous in a black pea coat and dark gray slacks. They were going to a nice restaurant downtown with a dress code. She held up a finger to indicate she needed a moment and grabbed a long coat that matched her purse and boots out of her coat closet. As she exited the house, she pulled the door shut firmly behind her and tapped the lock once, twice, three times to engage the mechanism before pulling on her gloves. The ring on the edge of the device lit up, and she heard the mechanism click into place.

"That thing's pretty cool," Jake commented, leaning down to greet her with a soft kiss on the cheek.

"It is," Josie replied. "I can do everything through the app, including sending people e-keys. Comes in handy for pet sitters or when one of my brothers or girlfriends pops by while I'm out. I've got so many e-keys out there, I may as well just leave the door unlocked. Well, actually, sometimes I do forget and leave it unlocked. It's a bad habit I've been trying to break."

Jake's brow creased. "Josie, you should be careful. Didn't you have a problem with a crazy fan in LA?"

"Yes," she admitted, looking down at her gloves. "But everything is fine now."

"Still, I'd feel better if you made sure your doors were locked. You can never be too careful, even in a place as safe as Lakeview," he said. He followed

Josie to the passenger side of his black Lexus and opened her door.

"Thank you," she murmured.

Jake was a true gentleman, one of the many things she liked about him. She had been in his car a couple of times now, and it was always spotless. The car was several years old, and he had bought it used, but he kept it in great condition. The first time they went out, Josie had wondered how he could afford such an expensive car on a teacher's salary. She learned later that he had inherited some money from an uncle who passed away—so much, in fact, that he didn't have to keep working. But he loved teaching, plus he said he didn't know what to do with all that wealth. He had grown up middle class, and his parents struggled to make ends meet sometimes, so he was taught from an early age to save. The car, though an older model, had been a splurge for him.

The ride downtown flew by, and the conversation flowed easily between them. Josie was again surprised by how comfortable she felt with Jake. She had learned the hard way to protect her privacy. Her many public fights with James had landed them on the cover of tabloids, and rumors about their relationship were splashed all over the Internet. But with Jake, things were different. While she and James had had an immediate physical connection, she and Jake seemed genuinely well-matched. She and James had fallen in love while filming, but sometimes onscreen chemistry simply didn't translate into a well-adjusted relationship. It wasn't until she and James were deep into their relationship that Josie realized that their physical chemistry, like their relationship, was explosive.

Jake pulled up to the valet at Chop & Vine, a steakhouse that everyone had been raving about since its opening last year. The valet opened Josie's door and helped her to her feet.

After getting the ticket, Jake sidled up to Josie and offered his arm. "Shall we?"

She took his arm, though not for long, as Jake quickly stepped in front of her to open the door. The restaurant was stunning, put up in an old warehouse on Sixth Avenue. The exposed brick and high ceilings told the story of the building's prior life, but the dark wood tables, roaring fireplaces, and giant wall of wine had transformed the once vacant building into one of the most beautiful restaurants in the area. The hostess led Josie and Jake to their table, a large booth along the perimeter of the restaurant, and Jake helped Josie out of her coat and hung it on the hook positioned on the partition. Once they settled and ordered a bottle of cabernet, they both started to speak at once. After a couple moments of, "You go ahead," "No, no, I'm sorry, you go," back and forth, Josie spoke.

"I'm glad we got to do this," she said, suddenly feeling shy.

Even though they had been out a few times, Josie still got nervous on dates. She felt a lot of pressure to live up to people's expectations of her. Last spring, she had tried an online dating app with disastrous results. All the men she had been out with seemed to think she was her character from *Order & Justice*, or asked her endless questions about her life as a celebrity. That was when they got as far as a date; a lot of men on the site didn't even believe it was her. She'd deactivated her account after a few weeks, vowing never to use a dating app again.

"Me too," Jake smiled.

The waitress brought the wine and went through the ritual of pouring a small amount for Jake to sample. He swirled it while winking at Josie, tasted it, and gave his approval. Then the waitress poured them each a generous glass and disappeared.

"So," Jake said.

"So," Josie replied. "The wine is good. Good choice."

"I have a secret," Jake whispered. She leaned in closer. "I know nothing about wine. It was a shot in the dark."

"Good guess," she laughed. "It's one of my favorites."

"Next time, I think you should pick," Jake smiled, taking a sip. "So, how are things? Are you holding up okay?"

"Okay. I'm still in shock, but okay," Josie replied, taking a gulp of her wine. "I keep going over and over Sunday night and the days leading up to it in my head, trying to figure out if I missed something."

Jake frowned. "Sunday night?"

"Yeah, I was up around the time that Amber…" Josie swallowed hard. "I

91

couldn't sleep, so I went to the kitchen to make some tea. I was looking out the back window at the water tower. I thought I saw something, but now I can't decide if I remember seeing her or if my mind is just filling in blanks because I know she was up there." She paused. "I guess it doesn't matter now."

"Of course it does," he said, taking her hand across the table. "This is a terrible tragedy, and I'm sorry you're going through this. I can't believe they haven't torn that thing down," Jake said, shaking his head. "I know it's a landmark, but haven't they been having problems with kids going up there for years? That chain link fence doesn't seem to be much of a deterrent."

"No, it isn't. It's a battle that's been going on for years, at least as far back as when I was a kid, and probably longer than that. That water tower's been there since the late nineteenth century—there were a few of them around the county that were all built at the same time. But you probably know all this," Josie said, blushing.

"All I know is what's on that plaque at the base of the tower, which isn't much. Besides, I like hearing it from you," Jake said, his eyes twinkling as he sipped his wine.

Josie laughed. "So anyway, all these towers were built, and the towns kind of grew around them. Once modern plumbing made its way into the area, there was no use for them anymore. Some of them got torn down. Others were turned into funky apartments or artist studios. Lakeview is the only city that kept theirs up—the historical society pitched a fit when the city started talking about tearing it down or converting it, so they stepped in and saved it."

"I guess there's no way they could have predicted this," Jake said as the waitress appeared to take their orders.

"There's always been a battle between forces in town—parents want the tower demolished because kids are always messing around on it, the city still wants to turn it into some sort of trendy lofts, but the historical society won't budge," Josie continued after they ordered. "Kids have always gone up there and screwed around, and an injury every decade or so gets the argument going again. Surprisingly, no one has ever died. Maybe now they'll finally do something about it."

"Did you and your friends ever go up there when you were in school?" Jake asked.

Josie shook her head. "I was around when other kids went up, but heights have never been my thing. Neither has breaking the rules." She stopped, blushing again. "I sound like a nerd."

"A little. But I like it," Jake laughed. Now it was Jake's turn to blush.

Josie was about to say that she liked him, too, but the waitress popped up again with a basket of bread and their salads. As they ate, their conversation shifted away from Lakeview, and they traded stories about their childhoods, growing up in small towns, their dreams, and aspirations. They had discussed it previously, but Jake, too, had been raised in a small town in Utah and began his teaching career in a neighboring city. Their steaks came, and they continued to chat. Since this was their third date, Josie was feeling more and more comfortable with Jake. By the time they had finished dinner and polished off the bottle of wine, they had moved on to past relationships, a topic that was usually touchy for Josie, but felt natural to talk about with Jake. He, too, had had a long-term relationship that ended a few years ago, before he left Utah, and it was one of the reasons he had jumped at the chance to get a fresh start in Ohio.

"I just needed to get away from all the memories, you know? I felt like everywhere I turned, I was reminded of her. And, well, my heart was broken," he said.

"I know what you mean," she responded quietly. "It's like the weirdest things will spark a memory."

"Exactly," he said. "And I'm glad I came to Lakeview. If I hadn't, I wouldn't have met you."

He caught her eye, and they both smiled. She could feel the warmth from the wine and the dinner and the flush of new love flowing through her body. When the waitress returned, they both passed on dessert, opting instead for coffees before Jake drove them back into the suburbs. When they arrived at Josie's house, he walked her to the front door.

"I had a really nice time tonight," Jake said, taking both of her hands as he moved in close.

"Me too," she replied, biting her lip. He leaned in to kiss her, and almost immediately, they were swept up in a passionate embrace, with her back pressed against the door. When they finally broke, she said, "Do you want to come in for a nightcap?"

Jake hesitated, and Josie immediately felt stupid for rushing things. "I—you don't have to, don't feel like you have to—" she began, but he cut her off.

"No, I do," he said firmly. "I just don't want you to feel any pressure."

Standing on her toes to kiss him again, she whispered, "I don't."

He smiled down at her and allowed her to pull him inside, swinging the door shut behind them.

Chapter Twenty

Sunday morning, Josie got up slightly later for her morning run and left Jake snoozing in her bed, looking peaceful. When she returned, she was disappointed to find that Jake's car was no longer in the driveway. Had she scared him off? Maybe she had moved too quickly last night. It *was* their third date, the generally accepted time for two people who are dating to sleep together, but he had hesitated. She scolded herself as she sat down on the living room floor to stretch, Monroe winding around Josie and getting in the way whenever she could.

As she was finishing her cool-down, the doorbell rang. Puzzled, she looked at her watch, confirming that it was way too early for a drop-by from either her brothers or her friends. She opened the door to find Jake standing there, a tray of coffees in one hand, a paper bag in the other. A wave of relief crashed over her.

He grinned at her, holding out his hands as he said, "I thought I'd go get bagels and coffee. I would've cooked breakfast, but you don't seem to have any actual food in the house."

"Nope, I'm a terrible cook. I never picked up the skill from my mom," she laughed, stepping back to let him in.

She cleared some space on the table, which was laden with papers and notebooks. Jake unpacked the bagels, cream cheese, lox, and fresh fruit while Josie got plates and flatware.

"I also didn't know what kind of coffee you like, so I just got regulars for both of us," he called into the kitchen.

"Any coffee will do," she quipped, re-entering the dining room.

After they had their plates, she patted her leggings and looked around the table, prompting Jake to ask, "Phone?" Josie nodded, her mouth full of an everything bagel with plain cream cheese. "Nightstand," he replied, gesturing towards the bedroom with his bagel.

She nodded again but didn't make a move to leave the table. Once she had swallowed, she said, "I don't need it, but if I don't keep track of where it is, I'll lose it somewhere in the clutter." She gestured to the pile of papers and books.

"I hear you," Jake replied. "School stuff?"

"Some. Others are journals of one kind or another, keeping track of my thoughts or ideas for class, anything, really," she said, feeling suddenly vulnerable. "I prefer to write things down as opposed to typing them into a phone or computer. I find I remember things better."

"Same," Jake said through a bite of pineapple. "I'm the same way with books. I prefer to have a book in my hand rather than read on a device."

"Me too. I've been keeping track of all my notes on Amber's case in this one," she said, pointing to a blue notebook. "Although I'm not sure what good it'll do me, now that the investigation has been shut down."

"Yeah, what happened with that?" Jake asked.

Josie shrugged. "Who knows? The family wanted it stopped, and Senator Oldham has enough pull to do it. On one hand, I'm pissed off because I don't think her death was an accident or suicide; but on the other hand, I'm happy Tony Burgess is out. I don't think he was involved."

"You think the drugs were planted?"

Josie nodded.

"Yeah, he seems like a good kid," Jake said. "I don't have him in class, but I've only heard good things. Friday night was nuts."

"Yep," Josie answered. "People can be just awful. At least it wasn't our kids, though. Crandall emailed me and told me it was some Cedar Creek punks who obviously didn't realize there were cameras."

"Trying to psych out their competition?"

"If they were, they were pretty stupid to do it during the game," Josie replied. "We'd already pummeled them by the time everyone saw it."

"It's still a damn shame," Jake said, shaking his head. "And now they have to pay to get the car fixed."

"At least the parents of the little jerks will be paying for that. And the kids will probably be suspended."

"I'll never understand why kids try to get away with stuff like this. Nowadays, there's surveillance everywhere. They're practically guaranteed to get caught," Jake commented.

Josie just shook her head. She didn't understand why people spewed such hate at each other in the first place, even without the threat of being caught. She wondered if Tony had had prior issues with the Cedar Creek boys. She picked up her phone to check Instagram for any chatter about the incident. A few kids had posted photos of the defiled truck, while others were posting photos in support of Tony and lashing out at the Cedar Creek kids. She checked Amber's friends' accounts and saw nothing unusual until she got to Charlotte's page. Nearly all the photos from June through the present day had been removed. She must have made a noise because Jake said, "What's up?"

"Look," she said, passing him her phone. "All of Charlotte Burnes' posts from this school year and last summer are gone."

Jake's brow wrinkled as he scrolled through. "Are you sure she hasn't just been inactive?"

"I'm positive. I looked at her feed the other day, and there were tons of photos from the last six months. Now, zilch."

"So what does that mean?" Jake asked, passing the phone back.

Josie hesitated. She hadn't told him about the interaction she witnessed between Charlotte and the mystery guy at the football game. They'd been having such a good time the night before, she had nearly forgotten about it. She quickly filled him in on the scene.

"Huh," Jake said. "You think she cleared her Instagram account because this guy threatened her?"

"Certainly seems like it."

"That's interesting. Charlotte Burnes doesn't strike me as the type of person who likes being told what to do."

"I know. That's why it worries me," Josie said. "If she caved to this dude, there's obviously a reason."

They both chewed in silence for a moment, then Jake said, "Well, I know you've already gotten your workout in, but I need to hit the gym before practice this afternoon."

Josie walked him to the door, and he planted a light kiss on her lips before saying in a low voice, "Try not to worry about this too much. I'll call you later."

Josie spent the morning texting with the girls and catching up on work. Her agent had sent over several scripts, which she browsed through without much enthusiasm. Her family usually did a Sunday dinner when her mother wasn't working, but Josie couldn't remember the last time they did one. She made a mental note to get something on the books soon. The rest of the day, she dug around on social media and read the local news coverage of Amber's case. She noticed a small article on one of the web pages for The Cleveland Press about a couple of young women who had recently died of a fentanyl overdose. Both had only been in their early twenties—so young, so much wasted potential. It was interesting that two other young white women had OD-ed at almost the same time as Amber, but then again they were in the middle of a drug crisis. She thought a lot about Amber, how her life, and the lives of these two other women, had been cut unfairly short. Imagine having your life reduced to a few hundred words casually strewn on a webpage. At least Amber's death was getting recognition. People who hadn't previously been paying attention to the fentanyl problem in their city were definitely taking notice now. But these three girls were only a small sample of the many, many lives that were being lost in their community, and until they got it under control, no one was safe.

Chapter Twenty-One

On Monday, the mood at school was somber once again in spite of the weekend's festivities. Since Josie only taught a couple periods of classes, she didn't have a class first thing in the morning. Thank goodness, too—with the way she had been sleeping (or not sleeping), it was a miracle she made it in to teach at all. Josie knew the kids counted on her, though. She tried to make her classes fun while also teaching them some technique. There were so many people out there in the world who wanted to be famous, and far fewer who actually wanted to learn the craft of acting. Ultimately, she wanted to show the kids who were serious what it was like to truly work and study as an actor, but also make it fun for the kids who didn't take it quite as seriously. It was a hard line to toe sometimes, especially given that she was only in her first months of teaching. But she liked it. The kids were fun, and it was better than just sitting around trying to figure out her next move.

Plus, being a teenager these days was stressful, and she was happy to provide some lightness to their days. Many kids at Lakeview were overachievers looking to land at Ivies. On top of a full load of schoolwork, there were the pressures of extracurriculars, volunteer work, and jobs that many balanced. Add in trying to make everything look pretty on social media, and Josie couldn't imagine being a teenager today. But as much as Josie loved being home in Ohio and teaching at Lakeview, she wasn't sure that her move back was permanent. She'd left LA in a hurry, heartbroken and needing time to recover. Now that she had some distance, she realized that her decision had been hasty and not very well thought through.

Tony Burgess wasn't in school on Monday, and Josie heard through the teachers' grapevine that the school board wasn't sure how to handle the situation, despite him being out on bail. After all, they had found drugs in his locker, which warranted suspension at the very least and was grounds for expulsion. Josie believed Tony's claim that the drugs were not his, as did most faculty members. But there was no way to prove that the drugs had been planted, aside from simply taking his word. Tony had a good record, excellent grades, and near-perfect attendance, so Josie was hopeful that the school board would consider not expelling him.

Jake dropped by with flowers and a bottle of wine on Monday night, much to Josie's delight. She loved that people still "dropped by" in Lakeview—in Los Angeles, unless you lived close to someone, a visit was a carefully choreographed event. Jake and Josie had some wine and talked about Tony's undetermined fate, which Jake found just as unsettling as Josie. They then decided it was time for a break and watched *Better Off Dead*, a John Cusack film from the '80s, on Netflix. Since they both had to be up early for school, Jake ducked out afterwards.

On Tuesday, as Josie trekked across her backyard, she glanced up at the water tower and shivered, flashing back to that terrible moment when she found Amber's body lying in the field. Pausing, another series of images appeared from the recesses of her mind. A flash of red on the water tower? Then suddenly, Josie was looking out over the town from the top of the tower, the moon shining as the sky began to grow lighter with the sunrise. As she looked down, she grew dizzy, and her dizziness snapped her back to reality. No, none of that could be real, she told herself, shaking it off. She was just imprinting the color of Amber's blouse onto the tower now that she knew what happened. Plus, she had never been up on the water tower, so how could she know what the view looked like from up there?

Blinking back to the present, Josie walked to the back entrance of the high school, glancing at her watch. She hurried along as she realized she was now somehow fifteen minutes behind when she had planned to get to school. The parking lot was filled with cars already, sedans, SUVs, trucks, and compacts of every size, shape, and color. Some parents in their affluent community did hand over the keys to a BMW or Mercedes when their kid turned sixteen, other parents gave their kids more modest vehicles, and a few made the kids buy their own. In another town, that might sound ridiculous, but Lakeview was filled with lawyers, doctors, politicians, former pro athletes—the money in town flowed like a river, and parents made sure their kids had the best of the best.

As she passed by the gymnasium, she saw kids running circles in their gym uniforms. The kids were allowed to bring their own gym clothes to school these days, and thank goodness, because the gym uniforms when she was in school were just awful. "LHS!" they screamed in purple iron-on letters, as if there were any doubt about where they were or what they were doing. The mood in the gym, as well as the halls, was markedly subdued. Kids who would normally be goofing off, temporarily granted a leave from class with a hall pass, stayed in their classrooms. No noise floated down the corridor where the orchestra and band classes were held, and that hallway was usually a cacophony of different instruments warming up.

When she passed Jake's classroom, she peeked in and waved, which he returned with a smile and a wink without breaking the stride of his lecture. Sitting down at the extra desk in the English office, she opened her laptop and pulled up her agenda for the day. After last week's debacle of trying to continue teaching her unit on Chekhov Technique—the kids had all been too distracted to absorb anything—she decided to try something different today.

Opening a browser window, she typed "handling grief through humor" in the search box. She thought maybe they could talk about grief in a more unexpected way, discuss how people like comedians tended to have some of the darkest dispositions, and how they worked through past traumas with their art. Looking at the clock, she realized she only had a few minutes to hit the bathroom before the next bell rang. She jumped up and walked quickly out the door, turning right down the corridor of English classes.

When Josie arrived back at her desk, she grabbed her computer bag. Before she could close her laptop, she noticed that a Word document was open. Strange, she didn't remember opening one before she left. There were two words typed in the center of the page that made her blood run cold.

KEEP LOOKING

Josie whirled around, scanning the room for other bodies, but saw no one. She ran out into the hallway to see if she could catch someone turning a corner, but found a vacant corridor, the fluorescent lights flickering. The bell rang, and she nearly jumped out of her skin, throwing her hand to her chest and trying to slow her heart rate, which had skyrocketed at the jolt of the bell. As Jake strolled out of his classroom and turned to head towards the English office, he spotted her immediately. His face filled with concern as he quickened his pace towards her.

"Josie?" he said. "Are you okay? You look like someone just walked over your grave."

Chapter Twenty-Two

Josie faced Jake, feeling dizzy from lack of sleep, trying to blink herself into a rational state.

"Did you see anyone come out of the office? Run past your classroom?"

Jake looked at her strangely, then said, "No, but...I was teaching. I didn't look out the door until after the bell rang."

"Mmm-hmm, mmm-hmm," Josie said, craning her neck to look down the hallway over his shoulder, no easy feat as Jake towered over her. The hall was flooded with kids now, rushing to get to their next class before the bell. There were too many of them, making it impossible to tell if one of them had run out of the English office.

"Josie," Jake said, waving a hand in front of her eyes.

She blinked up at him. "Sorry, I'm a little distracted."

"Yeah, I can see that. I called your name three times before you heard me," he laughed. "Did you happen to see my wallet at your place? I think I might have left it last night," Jake said, lowering his voice so as not to be heard by the deluge of teenagers. "I couldn't find it anywhere yesterday. I usually leave it in my glovebox, but it wasn't there."

"I didn't notice, but I guess it could've fallen out onto the floor, right?"

"Exactly. And I kind of need it," Jake said, looking at her sheepishly.

"Yeah, no, of course," Josie said. "I've got a class right now, but you've got a free period, right? Let me just send you an e-key, and you can go look."

"Thanks. I panicked when I couldn't find it, but I think it might have fallen off the coffee table under the couch," Jake said, relief washing over his face.

He smiled down at her. "I was actually going to see if you wanted to go out this weekend."

"I'd love to go out with you again, Jake. I had a really great time on Saturday, and last night," Josie said, blushing. She didn't know what it was about him that made her so nervous. "Why don't you call me—"

Josie was interrupted as the second bell rang, signaling that time to switch classes was over, and everyone should be in their classrooms.

"I should go," she said, realizing she had a roomful of students waiting for her.

"Yeah, you should. Oh, wait—how do I lock the door once I'm out?" he called after her as she bolted away.

"Just tap it three times," she replied.

"Great, thanks. I'll call you later."

"'Kay," she said.

God, things were so awkward at school. When she and Jake were out together, it was like they were in their own world; here, it felt like they were under a microscope. But she should be better at dating by now. She was thirty-one years old; she should probably have a handle on it. Having all the kids staring at them like they were aliens definitely didn't help. She picked up her pace, and "KEEP LOOKING" glowed behind her eyes as she raced toward her class. Whatever that note meant, it would have to wait until later. She had a roomful of grieving students to attend to.

Chapter Twenty-Three

Nicole Fox sat at her desk at *The Cleveland Press*, hands clasped behind her head. She leaned back and closed her eyes, deep in thought. There had to be more to the Oldham case. Her anonymous source had suggested that Amber's death was more than a simple fall or suicide, but they wouldn't say anything more concrete. Nikki didn't actually even know who the source was, but she had her suspicions that it was someone from the Lakeview Police. Whoever it was used a voice masking app whenever they called her and refused to reveal who they were. But that wasn't unusual; she'd had anonymous sources in the past, usually on stories that turned out to be huge.

Officially, the Lakeview Police stated that they were satisfied that the teen's death had been either an accident or suicide, and the family just wanted to find peace and move on with their lives. The Oldhams believed that Amber either took her own life or overdosed, and did not think there was foul play involved. But Nikki knew they weren't telling the full story. The police already had Tony Burgess in custody when the case was shut down, and although he had only been held on drug possession charges, the police had gone looking through his locker because they had reason to suspect that Tony had something to do with Amber's death. Nikki had hoped that the county prosecutor might go ahead with an indictment, even though Josie was loudly protesting Tony's innocence, but even the prosecutor buckled to pressure coming out of Senator Oldham's camp. So the question then became: why would a family not want justice for their child who the police clearly believed was murdered?

Nikki pulled up the email she'd received last week, the one with the subject line that read "PA—AO." Nikki got several emails a day with tips about stories, but when she saw Amber Oldham's initials in that subject line, she knew this was going to be good. Nikki scanned down the page to cause and manner of death. Amber Oldham had been high as a kite when she plunged off that water tower and pregnant to boot. But jeez, the amount of fentanyl in this girl's system—a little research told Nikki that it was enough to kill a horse, and Amber was tiny.

Her eyes flicked up to the email address, but whoever had sent it had done so from an anonymous email address. Even if she traced the IP, she was sure it had come through a VPN or one of those websites that allowed you to pay to send anonymous messages. People sending this kind of sensitive information generally didn't do it from their work computers.

At the bottom of the page were two words: KEEP LOOKING.

She was on the right track, she could feel it in her bones, but this email confirmed what she suspected. Someone else out there thought there was more to the story. She jumped up from her desk and walked quickly to the editor-in-chief's office, closing the door behind her.

Sharon Sykes, Editor-in-Chief of *The Cleveland Press*, sat behind her large walnut desk, overflowing bookcases covering the wall behind her. In her mid-fifties, Sharon was a tall, elegant woman with bobbed light brown hair and expressive blue eyes. She began her career as a writer at *The Press* and worked her way quickly onto the editorial staff before claiming the EIC position ten years prior. Sharon was tough as nails, but there was a kind soul beneath her rough exterior. Her desk was organized but stuffed with papers, stories lying in wait, all clamoring for their chance to be told. Nikki took a seat in one of the chairs and looked intently at Sharon.

"Okay, Fox, spit it out," Sharon nudged, pounding away on her keyboard. "I can tell you're bursting at the seams."

"Amber Oldham," Nikki began, "I think there's a story."

Sharon peered at Nikki over her half-moon reading glasses. "Oh, yeah? The case is closed. You want to go the teen suicide angle?"

"Maybe," Nikki lied.

Sharon stopped typing and sat back in her chair. "So if not teen suicide, what? Another article about fentanyl overdoses? Sorry, Nik, but we're saturated with those already. We just ran a piece about those two young women who were found downtown earlier this week. And we did a whole special feature section on the epidemic last month."

"I forgot about those women," Nikki replied. "What was the story there again?"

"Couple of young women, suspected prostitutes, OD-ed and were found in an alley over by Playhouse Square. Looked like they might have been dumped there," Sharon said after pulling up some notes on her computer.

"How old were they?" Nikki asked.

Sharon scanned the page. "Mmm, says here early twenties, but no details on their exact ages. Why?"

"Just curious. No, look, I think something happened with the family, or Clinton Oldham's campaign—something caused them to lean on the police to shut down the investigation. The police thought Amber was murdered, basically had a suspect in custody, and suddenly Oldham puts pressure on them to shut it down. Why would he do that?"

Sharon looked around the room thoughtfully for a moment. "Maybe they found a note. Maybe they knew she was an addict and didn't want to release it to the public. Maybe they didn't want to ruin another young person's life when they were certain their daughter had taken her own life."

"Yes, but—"

"Sorry, Nikki, it's a non-starter," Sharon interrupted. "We can't run a story based on a bunch of maybes. Even if I wanted to, we'd have to call around to get confirmation of facts, and the story might get shut down at that point. That's a whole lot of work for nothing."

"I'm willing to accept that risk," Nikki said.

Sharon paused, taking off her glasses and wedging the arm into the corner of her mouth. "You're sure you want to do this?"

Nikki smiled. "Absolutely."

"Any other news outlets covering this?"

"Not that I know of. I've got an anonymous source. 'Far as I can tell, they've only come to me."

"Good, good," said Sharon, putting her glasses back on. "Okay, stay on this, Nikki. But Nik," she said, as Nikki started to rush out of the room, "Nothing's getting printed until we have a solid story. Clinton Oldham's attorney would have me for breakfast if we published anything unsubstantiated about that girl. And with Forestview owning the paper—you know that they're huge supporters of his campaign. If we're going to publish, we need solid, confirmed *facts*, not sensationalist gossip. And I don't have to tell you what would happen if they caught wind of us sniffing around this when the investigation has been called off, so keep it on the QT."

"Gotcha. I'll play this one close to the vest," Nikki said calmly, but inside, she was bursting. This story could make her career. Now to figure out how the hell this kid ended up lying dead in a field instead of getting ready for her senior Homecoming celebration.

Chapter Twenty-Four

That night Josie slept less than usual, which she didn't think was even possible. When she did manage to doze off, her dreams were filled with images of Amber's cold, white face staring up at her from the bright green grass in the field, and visions of the girl tumbling, unconscious, to her death. In her dream, she saw Amber and another figure leaning against the railing of the water tower. She couldn't make out the person's face, and she jolted awake in a cold sweat after every one of these brief nightmares. Finally, around four a.m., she decided to give up on trying to sleep and start her day. Monroe and Presley were sound asleep on the opposite side of her king-sized bed, and they barely stirred as she got up, put on her slippers, and began to pace.

Eventually, she made her way into the kitchen to start a pot of coffee and shake herself awake for her run. Maybe a jog would clear her head. Although her watch told her it was only thirty-five degrees outside, normally too cold for a run by Josie's standards, she knew she needed to go if she was going to clear the fog of last night. She got herself into her running tights and thermal top, strapped into her shoes, put on her outdoor gear, and was out the door.

Although she wasn't a morning person, Josie had always loved the stillness of the early morning hours. Los Angeles was always running at full speed, with people everywhere and no space to breathe. But in the wee hours of the morning, between three and four, there was a slight respite from the breakneck pace. Those were the hours when the city was at its most quiet and serene, although there were still a few cars on the road here and there and the occasional party breaking up. But usually, she could count on that early morning time before she was due on set to run and reset her brain.

Lakeview was not so different, except that everything fell absolutely silent during the early morning hours. Los Angeles always had a buzz to it, some low level of noise no matter how quiet the city got, but not Lakeview. It was so quiet Josie felt as though she was jogging in a vacuum where sound didn't even exist. The night sky, with its inky blackness stretching out onto the horizon, became a blanket, and the absence of stars was the only way to distinguish the sky from where it met the lake on the horizon. And my goodness, were there stars. Josie remembered going outside as a kid with her dad, him pointing up at the sky and teaching her where to find the Big and Little Dippers, Orion's Belt, and even some planets at different times of the year.

Her watch buzzed and startled her, and she was surprised to see a text from her dad. He was an early bird and had always made a point of getting to the FBI office every morning by six, but she usually didn't hear from him. "How you sleeping?"

She held down the button and spoke into the watch. "Okay. On a run, call you later."

As Josie jogged, she tried to work the tension out of her neck, rolling her head and swinging her arms in large circles. Frustration and stress were taking their toll on her body, and she felt like a rubber band stretched to its breaking point. She ran most of her usual route, skipping the shortcut through the school field and running the extra half mile around the school property to avoid passing the water tower. The thought of running the same way as the day she found Amber filled her with unease. Tacking on the extra mileage was worth it if she could save herself the discomfort.

By the end of the run, Josie's body felt a bit looser, even if her mind was still a tangled spider's web. There was a flier taped to the glass on her screen door that read, "I buy houses. Call 866-333-2525." Josie flipped it over, and on the back, there was a single phrase written in block letters: "Trust the Process."

"Weird," she muttered, looking around to see if any other houses had a similar flier taped to the door. She could see none.

Once inside, Josie stripped off her outerwear, threw the flier on the table, and went to get some water. As she walked into the kitchen, she noticed Monroe and Presley sitting on the kitchen floor on full alert, their gazes fixed on the back door.

"Aw, is there a bug?" Josie asked, peering at the back door.

She saw nothing out of the ordinary at first glance, but as she was about to close the curtain, she saw a flash of headlights in the school parking lot. She looked at the clock and saw that it was only five-sixteen. Not an unheard-of time for a teacher to be reporting to school to get in some extra work, but still pretty early. It could have been one of the night janitors leaving, but she had been up to see them leave before, and it usually happened around three a.m. Even as she tried to rationalize the sight of the headlights, she was getting that feeling again where all the tiny hairs on the back of her neck felt like they had been raked over with static electricity. As a reflex, Josie reached down to make sure the lock on the back door was still engaged, and was alarmed to find that it was not. She could have sworn she checked the back door last night before she went to sleep.

She turned to look at her home. Were the cats acting strangely because someone had been in here? Monroe and Presley, startled by her sudden movement, bounded out of the room. Moving around the kitchen, Josie tried to determine if anything was missing. Should she call Sean? And what, tell him that she had forgotten to lock her back door when she went on her run, and her cats were acting weird? Nope, couldn't do that; that would just invite another lecture about the dangers of leaving her doors unlocked. She looked over near the coffee pot and saw the Sleepytime tea box sitting next to it. Had she even made tea last night? Josie rubbed her eyes, trying to remember, then began laughing. Yeah, someone broke into her house just to take tea out of the cupboard and put it on the counter. Right.

"Get a grip, Jose," she chastised herself, grabbing the box and shoving it back in the cabinet.

Determined to pull herself together, Josie marched into the living room and flicked on the TV. A preview for the six o'clock news was playing, featuring a storm headed for the Midwest. She left the TV on as she stretched for a few minutes, then after making sure all the doors in the house were locked, went to shower and get herself ready for school. Around six-thirty, she decided she couldn't handle being alone with her racing thoughts any longer and dialed Nikki's number. She didn't expect Nikki to pick up at such an early hour and was surprised to hear her friend's chipper voice bouncing over the phone line.

"What's up?" she barked.

"I-, I-, sorry, I didn't expect you to actually pick up. Did I wake you?" Josie stumbled.

"Nah, I've been up for an hour," Nikki practically yelled. "I'm already at the office on my second cup of coffee. You still having trouble sleeping?"

Josie felt herself nodding, then realized she hadn't said anything and quickly answered, "Yep."

"You really need to see someone about that," Nikki clucked.

"Can we get together tonight? I need to decompress," Josie answered.

"Sure. You want me to call the girls?" Nikki asked. Josie nodded again. "I'm going to assume you're over there nodding since you haven't said anything," Nikki said finally.

"Jeez, sorry, yeah," Josie said. "Yes. Yes, please call the girls."

"Roger that," Nikki said. "Gotta go. My editor just walked in, and I want to grab her before she gets busy. I'll text you later with a time, 'kay?"

"Okay," Josie answered a bit too loudly, determined to break her nodding streak.

"Right," Nikki laughed. "Just...don't do anything that requires too much brain power today, all right?"

Josie laughed, her tension finally easing. "You mean like shaping the young minds of our future?"

"Exactly," Nikki said. "But seriously, maybe take the day off and just rest. I'll call you later."

With that, the line went dead. Josie took a deep breath. She needed to take better care of herself, but she was afraid if she slowed now, she would lapse into a coma. Which is exactly why she needed the girls; she needed a clear head to solve this case, and she knew she was rapidly running out of time.

Chapter Twenty-Five

During school on Tuesday, Josie continuously tried to shake off the heavy cloak of exhaustion that enveloped her. When she ran into Jake, he looked at her with worry in his hazel eyes, and when he tried to confirm details for their Friday night date, Josie had just nodded along, agreeing to whatever he asked. What had he suggested? She couldn't even remember at that point.

Her morning classes went by in a similar fashion, with the kids peppering her with questions and her sleepwalking her way through. Fortunately, the kids were all working on scenes in pairs, so once their warmups were done, they peeled off, and she sat at her desk, trying to go over her notebook for Amber's case, but having a hard time concentrating. Every noise was like a wrecking ball to her concentration, from the excited babble of the students to the click, click, clicking of the second hand on the old school clocks.

When her morning free period finally came, she was en route to the English office when she saw Morgan, Charlotte, and Lexi down at the end of the long hallway. As she strode towards them, the girls noticed her and scattered. Charlotte and Morgan rushed away immediately, but Lexi hung back for a moment. She looked as though she was about to call out to Josie, but Charlotte returned, grabbed her wrist, glared down the hall at Josie, and yanked Lexi up the stairs with her.

Josie needed to get Lexi alone. Lexi seemed like she wanted to talk, but the other girls weren't going to make it easy for Josie. From her chats with Amber, she knew that Amber turned to Lexi as a sort of confidante. While Amber and Charlotte spent the most time together, Lexi could be trusted to keep Amber's secrets. Josie waited until Lexi had her lunch period. This was going to be a little tricky, because most seniors left campus for lunch, so she'd have to just say a little prayer that Lexi would be dining in the cafeteria that day. Josie's prayers were answered as she turned the corner to the cafeteria hallway and saw Lexi settling down at a seat in the cafeteria with a slice of cheese pizza, her laptop open in front of her.

Josie approached her casually, saying, "Hey, Lexi," as she slid into a seat across from her.

"Uh, hi, Mrs. Ashbury," Lexi said as she pulled out her earbuds, her mouth half full of the last bite she had taken. A beat passed, then Lexi said, "Do you need something?"

"I hate to interrupt your lunch, but I was hoping we could have a quick chat," Josie replied. "Can you come with me?"

"Oh. Um, sure, I guess. Should I…" Lexi gestured at her food.

"Go ahead and bring it," Josie said, hoping that Lexi was a neat eater. She would hate to get crumbs all over a classroom that she wasn't supposed to be in in the first place.

Lexi nodded, scooping up her purple backpack and pizza and trailing after Josie, shuffling her boots as she walked. Josie led her to the English department hallway; she knew there was a lecture hall free this period, and was relieved to find it empty. She held the door open for Lexi and then closed it behind them, peeking down the hallway as she did to make sure no other teachers had seen her. Lexi neatly placed her backpack on one of the desks and her food on another, then took the seat with her pizza. Josie sat on the teacher's desk at the front of the room, facing her.

"So, what did you want to talk to me about?" Lexi asked, taking a small bite.

"Actually, I wanted to talk about Amber," Josie said gently.

Lexi stopped chewing. "I figured you might."

Josie looked at her for a moment, cocking her head to the side. "Why'd you figure that?"

"Oh, uh, you know, I know you and Amber were, like, kinda close and stuff. Plus, I heard you talked to Tony the other day before…" she answered, swallowing her bite.

"Right," Josie murmured.

"Yeah, well, I talked to him like right after you did. I think he was kind of star-struck, to be honest," Lexi said.

"Huh, I didn't get that impression. He seemed pretty relaxed," Josie said, narrowing her eyes.

"I'm sure he didn't, like, want you to know," Lexi said.

"Well, he hid it well. But the reason I wanted to talk to you, and I guess Tony, too, is I wanted to see what you think about all of this," Josie said.

"Like the pregnancy? Did you talk to Tony about the pregnancy?" Lexi demanded.

"Yes. It seemed like he was having some trouble accepting it."

"You have no idea," Lexi said under her breath, almost too quietly for Josie to hear.

"Sorry, what was that?" Josie asked.

"No, no-, nothing, I just said yeah, I'm sure it was, like, weird for him," Lexi said more loudly.

"Weird, yeah," Josie said. "So what do you make of it? Did Amber tell you she was pregnant?"

"I-, me? No, no, no, no, no," Lexi shook her head almost violently, picking at her pizza crust.

"But you girls were close, right? I mean, if she knew, she would have told you, wouldn't she?" Josie asked gently, sensing she had struck a nerve. "Do you think she even knew about it?"

"I-, I don't know. You know, Amber was, like, weird about some stuff. Like, one day she'd tell you every single detail of what happened to her, and the next day, like, nothing, she'd have nothing to say," Lexi said.

"Interesting. Was that a recent change in her personality, or had she always been that way?"

"Recent? No, Amber's always been like that. I think it's because of, like, her family, you know. Like, they expect her to be a certain way, and some days she, like, cares more about it than others," Lexi said, taking a swig of her soda.

"What do you mean, 'a certain way?'" Josie pressed.

"You know, like, her dad's a politician, so she's expected to act a certain way in public," Lexi said. "Especially since Ohio is so, whatever, like, conservative."

Josie nodded. "I guess a teen pregnancy and a drug addiction wouldn't look that great for a conservative senator's daughter."

"No way. Her parents would've kill…." Lexi clapped her hand over her mouth. "I'm sorry," she whispered, her eyes filling with tears. "I didn't mean it like that."

"No, no, it's okay," Josie said, grabbing a tissue from the box on the desk and handing it to her. "I know what you mean."

"It's not like they would've, like, done anything or whatever," Lexi amended, wiping her eyes and smearing her mascara. "But, you know, getting pregnant in high school wasn't exactly what was, like, expected of someone like Amber."

"Gotcha. I totally get it." Josie paused for a moment. "And what about the drugs?"

Lexi snorted, wiping her nose and then balling up the tissue in her fist. "Honestly? I have no idea. That came out of, like, *nowhere*. We all know about the whole fentanyl thing. We're not, like, stupid. That's the stuff that those people overdosed on who, like, left their baby in the car seat for, like, six hours, right? It's screwed up."

"How do you think she got all that fentanyl in her system?"

Lexi looked around, almost as if making sure they were alone in the room. Then she lowered her voice. "Look, honestly? I think—I think someone must've drugged her. There's no way she would've, like, done that to herself. Especially if she was pregnant, but even if she wasn't."

"So…does that mean you think someone killed her?"

Josie thought she saw fear cross Lexi's face, but it was gone too quickly for her to be sure. "I definitely think she wouldn't have, like, gotten up on the water tower if it weren't for the drugs. And I don't think she took those drugs herself," Lexi said, almost in a whisper.

"Who might have given them to her?" Josie asked, finally feeling like she was getting somewhere.

"Look, like, I...I don't know who could've given her drugs. I mean, like, who would do that? But..."

"Yes?" Josie said, feeling her window closing.

"But I don't think Tony was the father of her baby," Lexi said finally.

Josie stared at her. "Wait, what? Why do you say that?"

"Amber was—she was, well, I think she was, like, messing around with somebody else," Lexi said reluctantly.

"Who?"

"I don't know," Lexi answered quickly, looking around again. "Honestly, like, I don't. Amber didn't really talk about it."

"But what about Tony?" Josie asked, frowning.

"Look, Tony and Amber's relationship was just, uh, it was like, complicated," Lexi said, looking increasingly uncomfortable. "I—I really think you should talk to Tony about it."

"Lexi, I may not get to talk to Tony for quite a while. Even if I do, I'm not sure he'll be inclined to talk to me after what he's been through. Please. Don't you want to help your friends?" Josie said gently.

After a moment, Lexi heaved a deep breath and said, "Okay. So, like, Amber was cheating on Tony," Lexi said, frowning and tracing her finger along a carving on the top of the desk. "I guess you would, like, call it that. I mean, they weren't really, like, a 'couple,' so I guess it's not technically cheating then."

"Hold on. What do you mean they weren't a couple?"

"They were pretending," Lexi said. She swallowed hard. "Ms. Ashbury, Tony's gay. Or, like, he thinks he might be? He says he doesn't, like, really know."

Josie sat back. Tony was struggling with his sexuality? She had never gotten that impression from him. He always seemed so self-assured, so confident, and affectionate towards Amber. Was Lexi lying to her? Then again, there were the obscene drawings and the slur that was painted on Brad's truck, so maybe there was something to what Lexi was saying.

Lexi continued, "He didn't know, like, how he felt. He was still, like, working things out. So Amber agreed to go on, like, 'dating' him until he did. But they never even slept together or anything. Anyway, he was, like, messing around with a guy from Cedar Creek, but they, like, broke up or whatever. That's why..."

"That's why you know the baby isn't Tony's," Josie finished.

Lexi nodded. "I didn't want to, like, out Tony. Like, it's not my place. It's not my story to tell, you know?"

"But who was the father of Amber's baby?" Josie demanded.

Lexi continued as though Josie hadn't interjected. "Amber kept Tony in the picture because she didn't want anyone to, like, suspect that she was seeing someone else. Like, her parents, people at school, even us, for a while. But we figured it out."

"Who's the guy?"

"I don't know much about it, but from the stuff that she said, I think he was, like, older. She was seeing him all summer."

"Older? Like a college boy?"

Lexi shrugged. Josie didn't know what to say. She felt like someone had hit her in the chest with a sledgehammer.

"Please don't, like, say anything to anyone…at least not before you talk to him," Lexi pleaded. "I don't know if, like, his dad knows, and I know no one at school does. This could really, like, mess him up, and I don't want to be the person that outed him. He's been, like, a really good friend to me."

"Okay, I won't say anything until I talk to him," Josie promised.

"Thanks," Lexi said, her eyes filling again with tears.

Josie felt for her. Losing your best friend couldn't be easy under any circumstances, and this whole thing had to be brutal for these girls. Wanting to change the subject, she asked, "And what about the IDs? Andrew told me about the fake IDs."

Lexi looked at her worriedly for a second, opened her mouth as if to answer, then stared down at the remains of her cold pizza.

"Look, I'm not going to turn you girls in," Josie said. "Like I said, I'm trying to piece this together more for myself than anything else. Andrew seemed to think the IDs might have something to do with Amber's death."

"We—we just wanted them to, like, buy beer for parties, and to have for college next year," Lexi said lamely after a moment, not meeting Josie's gaze.

"Are you sure there's nothing else?" With the revelation about Tony, Josie felt like she was teetering on the verge of breaking through a wall, of finding one key piece of the puzzle that was just outside of her reach. But Lexi was starting to clam up.

Lexi looked like she was about to answer, but her eyes widened as she looked behind Josie to the small square window in the closed door. Josie whipped around to see what—or who—had startled her, but there was no one in the window. Then Lexi leapt up and grabbed her backpack, practically running for the door, yelling, "Uh, Mrs. Ashbury, I've got a lot of reading to do before ninth period and, uh—"

Josie countered and blocked the doorway. "Lexi, listen, if there's something you're not telling me, please reconsider. I truly, truly just want to find out what happened to Amber."

Lexi swallowed hard and nodded. "Yeah, I get that," she whispered. "But I—I have to go. I'm sorry."

She pushed past Josie into the hall and took off towards the cafeteria. Josie stood in the doorway, watching Lexi hurry away. Why was she being so cagey? She tried to collect her thoughts as she made her way back to the English office. Obviously, she needed to talk to Tony again. Glancing at her watch, she realized she had only three minutes until the bell rang, and she had a class to teach next period. The detective work would have to wait until later.

Chapter Twenty-Six

Since the girls couldn't get together the previous night due to Alex's schedule, Josie was looking forward to debriefing tonight over a glass of wine and some greasy munchies. She felt like she hadn't slept in years. This bout of insomnia had to end soon, or she was going to lose her mind. When this had happened in the past, the insomnia disappeared as quickly as it came, and she would suddenly sleep like Rip Van Winkle. She hoped that break in the clouds was coming soon.

After the bell rang, releasing her final class of the day, Josie went to the English office to gather her things, then to the office to check her mailbox. She hadn't checked it that morning (like she was supposed to do every morning) and wanted to see if there were any vital communiques from the powers that be. There was a physical printout of a memo that had already been sent around in email form addressing Tony's arrest and release on bail. The administration still printed out all electronic communication for those teachers who preferred killing trees to keeping up with technology. Not many left, but a few holdouts staunchly clung to their paper.

The memo outlined that Tony was still serving a suspension for the drugs found in his locker, but as most of the faculty believed that the drugs could have been planted, expulsion was off the table—for now. Josie hoped they would get answers to the drug question quickly; he had been through enough.

"The press are still around and will be asking questions. Please do not offer them any information or opinions. A simple 'No comment' will suffice," the paper instructed. Did they think that the teachers were itching to talk to those piranhas lurking just outside of school grounds? Some of the reporters had dispersed, but there were still a few eager ones hanging around just off school grounds, waiting to pounce. Every one of the teachers at Lakeview had had it up to their eyeballs with the press.

Josie peeked into her mailbox, noticing a small red envelope sitting on the bottom. She pulled it out and opened it, finding a pretty, blank notecard inside. Confused, she turned it over, and saw the letter "O" printed in large, scrawled font. Frowning, Josie turned the card back over. It was a plain white notecard with some silver embossed design on it, nothing particularly out of the ordinary. Glancing around to see if anyone was watching her open the note, Josie tucked it back into the envelope and carefully put the small red rectangle in her purse.

Was that envelope even meant for her? Maybe it was some sort of weird way two teachers who were hooking up communicated, and one of them had just slipped the envelope into the wrong box. She hoped she hadn't messed up someone's rendezvous. Pushing open one of the glass-paned double doors of the main office and heading down the long hall to the parking lot, she could see a few local reporters pacing impatiently just off school grounds, waiting for the school day to end. The national news outlets were no longer covering the story, so just the local reporters were left.

Darren Jenkins' grin blinded her even from a distance as he waved his arm and tried to beckon her over. Would that idiot never give up? She ignored him and strode purposefully towards her backyard, inputting the gate code and swinging open the large wood door leading to her property. He'll probably come knocking, she thought, but once inside the house she was pleased to find that none of the press had come prowling. They were likely more interested in getting the students' reactions to Tony's arrest and release. Glancing at her watch, she was relieved to find that she had just enough time to catch a quick nap before meeting the girls at the pub. She made sure to set four alarms on her phone just to be safe, then sank into her large chair. Much as she had difficulty sleeping at night, naps came easily to Josie, and she drifted off peacefully within a few seconds.

Chapter Twenty-Seven

The girls were all assembled in their usual spot when Josie came blowing into the restaurant fifteen minutes late like she was on fire.

"Whoa, slow down, tiger." Nikki mugged at her, sliding the glass of cabernet they had ordered for her away as Josie hung up her coat and flung herself into the booth.

"I'm sorry, I'm sorry," Josie said breathlessly. "I took a nap, and of course, I overslept."

"At least you're sleeping," Heather said, eyeing Josie over her vodka soda. "Have you had a good night of sleep anytime recently?"

Josie shook her head. "That's why I was napping. Sleeping during the day is much easier for me."

"Maybe you're nocturnal," Alex piped up.

"That's definitely a possibility," Josie said dryly. "It worked for me when I had to be on set at six a.m., but I also had a trailer that I could crash in and designated PAs to wake me up. This bout's worse than the one in college."

"Oh, poor you, not having a staff of PAs dancing around you," Nikki teased, sliding Josie's glass of wine back across the table at her.

"I know, right? I should've brought some back with me just to manage my sleep schedule," Josie joked, and the girls laughed merrily.

"How's my favorite group of troublemakers?" Shana said in her raspy tone, sauntering over to their table.

"Hey, don't lump me in with these punks," Heather protested.

They all laughed again, and Josie felt herself relax. After they put in orders for pretty much all the appetizers on the menu, Josie reached into her bag and pulled out the red envelope.

"Okay, we've got a lot of catching up to do, even before we get to this," Josie said, gesturing at the envelope. She filled the girls in on the appearance of the Keep Looking note.

"Wait, you found a note that said 'Keep Looking?'" Nikki demanded.

"Not a note. Someone typed it in a Word document on my computer at school when I ducked out to the bathroom," Josie replied.

"You don't lock your screen when you leave your computer at school?" Heather asked incredulously.

"Usually, I do. But I guess I didn't think about it since I was just stepping out to the restroom," Josie shrugged.

Heather clucked in disappointment. "We don't lock our doors; we don't lock our computer. How did you survive in LA?"

Josie swatted at her playfully. "I was more careful in LA. I guess I've just sunken into the comfort of a small town. I'll try to be more careful, I promise."

"You'd better," Heather said.

"Can we focus, please?" Nikki demanded. "I got an email last week from an anonymous address with Amber Oldham's preliminary autopsy in it."

"You *did?*" Josie gaped at her.

Nikki nodded. "At about the same time as it was released to the police. But that's not even the strangest part. At the bottom of the email was a line that read 'Keep Looking.'"

"Soooo, do we think it's the same person?" Alex asked. "That would be quite the coincidence if it wasn't, right?"

"Agreed. I also don't know what to make of this," Josie said as she pulled the card out of the envelope and set it on the table. The other women looked at it like Josie had just put down a bomb.

"'O'? What does that mean?" Heather asked, turning the note over in her hands and examining it.

"I was hoping you guys could help me figure that out," Josie said. "Someone left this in my mailbox in the school office. I'm not sure if it was an accident, although at this point, I'm not willing to believe that anything is a coincidence."

"Fair point," Nikki drawled, stirring her drink.

"O," Alex said, tapping her fingers on her chin thoughtfully. "Isn't there a social club downtown called O?"

Nikki snapped her fingers. "That's right," she said, a little too loudly. She lowered her voice. "It's a new VIP club downtown. Works like a speakeasy if you're not a member, *and* you have to get a member to vouch for you. I think it's actually owned by one of the social clubs downtown, but I can't remember which one off the top of my head. That place is closed up tighter than a tick," she paused to allow the girls to snicker at her use of a Southern phrase she had picked up in college. "But the members, or whatever you want to call the guys that frequent the place, are very prominent people—athletes, politicians, businesspeople, even actors, when they're in town filming. Rumor has it that everyone who works there has to sign an NDA, right down to the bathroom attendants."

"Interesting," Josie said. "I'm surprised I've never heard of it."

"Me too," said Alex. "The guys at the restaurant have talked about it for years. The place is *expensive.* Membership is in the thousands, maybe even tens of thousands of dollars."

"Okaaay," Josie said, swirling her wine. "But why is someone trying to point me in that direction?"

The girls sat pondering in silence until the food arrived. They all piled their plates high while brainstorming ideas about the note, but ultimately came up with nothing. Eventually, Nikki suggested that after they finish, they go to O.

"I can make a call, see if I can get someone to sponsor me in for the night," Nikki said, reaching for her phone and slipping out of the booth.

"What do you make of the police calling off the investigation?" Alex asked as Josie speared a potato pancake with her fork and dropped it on her plate.

"I think they're wrong, but there's nothing that can be done about it," Josie answered. "Sean wasn't happy."

"I'll bet," said Heather. "But what about Tony Burgess and the drugs?"

"I think someone planted the drugs," Josie said. "And his poor family with the vandalism of the car, it's such a shame. People can be so cruel."

Alex and Heather exchanged a glance. "But aren't they prosecuting Tony for drug possession?" Alex asked.

"I don't know," Josie admitted. "I know he was suspended, but he maintains that those drugs were not his. And I believe him. His cousin overdosed on fentanyl a while back and died. I don't think he'd go near it for a million bucks."

"You don't think," Heather began carefully, "that his cousin OD-ing on fentanyl maybe brought it to his attention? Maybe informed his...method?"

"Brought it to his attention?" Josie asked incredulously. "You'd have to be living under a rock not to know about the fentanyl epidemic in this country. I'm pretty sure they're teaching seminars on it in college now. The school psychologist has to have Narcan available in his office."

"But what about the pregnancy? Wasn't that jeopardizing his future?" asked Heather as Nikki slid back into the booth.

"Well, according to Lexi Smith, the baby wasn't Tony's," Josie said, leaning back in her seat.

"How would she know that?" Nikki demanded.

"Lexi said Amber has been seeing another guy. She said that Amber and Tony weren't really dating, but Amber was pretending to be Tony's girlfriend because Tony was...figuring things out," Josie answered.

All the girls stopped their forks in midair and looked at her curiously. "Really," Alex said. "Now *that's* interesting."

"You think someone planted the drugs in Tony's locker?" Heather said. "Maybe the mystery baby daddy?"

Josie shook her head. "Lexi says the mystery guy was older. Not a high school student."

"I don't know, Jose. Don't you think that's a little far-fetched?" Nikki asked dubiously.

"As far-fetched as someone throwing a pregnant teenaged girl off of a water tower?" Josie shot back, grabbing her water and taking a long drink. The girls clammed up at that point, and they all chewed in awkward silence.

126

Nikki finally broke the stillness.

"Listen, let's go to that club tonight and see what we can find," she said gently, reaching across the table and squeezing Josie's hand. She looked around at the other girls. "Maybe you're right. Maybe Tony is being framed. But we're going to need more than your conviction to find the real killer."

"Yeah," Alex said quickly, putting her hand on top of Nikki's. "If you say he didn't do it, then he didn't do it. I'll help however I can."

Heather added her hand to the stack. "I don't know how much help I can be with my crazy schedule at the clinic," she said. "But I'll do everything I can."

Josie looked at the hands piled on top of hers, then up at her friends, saying, "So are we going to do some kind of break here?"

The girls laughed, yanking their hands back. "No way!" Alex exclaimed. "I don't do any of that sports junk."

"Ha-ha! It's a good thing you're not dating John then," Josie teased, giggling as Alex blushed. "But really, thank you guys. I need the help. Jake's been great, but I don't want to get him all tangled up in this."

"I hear that," Nikki said, spearing a carrot stick with her fork and plunging it into some Ranch dressing. "I keep running 'em off, too. We'll get to the bottom of this, Jose. Promise."

Chapter Twenty-Eight

After another hour of talking, laughing, and much-needed relaxation, Heather and Alex waved goodbye to Nikki and Josie in the parking lot.

"Whose car should we take?" Josie asked.

"Hmmm, my Jetta or your Tesla. What will I choose?" Nikki said, tapping her finger against her temple, pretending to ponder.

"I like your car," Josie protested.

"Oh, I like my car, too. But it's no Tesla," Nikki said. "You're driving around in two years' salary for me."

"The Model 3 is reasonably priced," said Josie.

"Is this a Model 3?"

Josie didn't answer.

"I rest my case. I love your car. Besides, we're going to a fancy club, we need a fancy car," Nikki laughed.

"You win," Josie said, and they climbed in. After driving for a minute, Josie said, "You know, what you save in gas mileage alone makes these things worth it."

Nikki burst out laughing. "Right. I'll think about getting one, okay. When I win the lottery. Now just drive."

Josie loved the sweeping view of Lake Erie from the Shoreway into downtown. The city had changed so much in the last fifteen years. After graduating from college, she had moved straight to Los Angeles, but came back to visit her family and friends often. Ten years ago, Downtown Cleveland had practically been a ghost town after seven p.m., emptying itself of all the workers who would trek in from the suburbs during the day and leaving nothing but small pockets of life in an increasingly desolate landscape. However, it had been revitalized, now more resembling the thriving metropolis it truly was. Hip restaurants and boutique hotels flourished, and shops and small businesses were starting to pop up again all around. It was truly inspiring to see her hometown pick itself up, dust itself off, and thrive, much like its sports teams had a knack for doing—every decade or so.

Which is why she was surprised when her GPS pointed her towards a building just east of Playhouse Square. She would have thought if a new nightclub was going to thrive, East Fourteenth Street, with its many restaurants and proximity to several new, modern apartment buildings, would be a more reasonable choice.

"Wait, where is this place?" she demanded, turning to Nikki.

"Hang on," Nikki said, holding up a hand and looking at the map on her phone. "Okay, so I had a source of mine email me the details. The club is kind of concealed, and like I said, it's like a speakeasy. Do you see that restaurant, Lockhart?" She pointed at a chic black and white sign with slim lettering to the right.

"Yes," Josie replied, narrowing her eyes.

"Right, so there's that alleyway kind of right beside it. The entrance is there," Nikki said. "Why don't we valet at Lockhart and cross?"

"You got it," Josie said, swinging a sudden U-turn that wedged Nikki into the door.

"Hey!" Nikki yelped, laughing as she dropped her phone into the depths of the car.

"Sorry," Josie said sheepishly. "Sometimes I forget I have to be more careful when there are other people in the car."

"You should be careful even when it's just you," Nikki chided playfully from her bent position, searching under the seat for her phone. "You'd better hope I find this phone. The password's on it."

"Password? Geez, this is involved," Josie mumbled, pulling up to the valet stand.

"Got it!" Nikki cried, sitting up triumphantly, iPhone in hand. "Just in time."

Josie flashed a smile at the handsome valet as she handed over her keys in exchange for a stiff ticket. The young valet looked as though he'd just won the lottery as he gave Josie's car a once over before eagerly hopping in. She hoped her car wasn't about to succumb to a *Ferris Bueller's Day Off* scenario. She met Nikki around the back of the car and they strode across the street.

"Didn't this used to be a mall or something?" Josie asked.

Nikki nodded. "They gutted it and put in the restaurant and apartments," she said, gesturing up at the tall building with her chin. Sure enough, Josie noticed there was not only the trendy restaurant, but also what looked to be modern loft-style apartments in the upper levels of the building.

"Okay, so according to this, there's a dress code, but I think we're good," Nikki said, scrolling on her phone and looking over herself and Josie. "There, that's the entrance," she said, pointing down the alley at a small black awning. Josie had never noticed this alley before, let alone an entrance to a nightclub.

"When we get there, let me talk," Nikki said, unable to hide the excitement in her voice. "Since I've got the passphrase for tonight."

"Oh my god," Josie said, choking back a laugh.

There had to be something illegal going on down there, with this much cloak-and-dagger nonsense just to get in the door. Josie hung back as Nikki sauntered up to the huge iron door and rang the bell. The small window on the door opened, and she thought she heard Nikki say the word "rosemary," along with some other things. After the window snapped shut, they heard some heavy bolts unlatching, and the door swung open, revealing a large African American man in a black-on-black suit. The guy had to be at least six-foot-six and looked like he could have played linebacker in the NFL.

"Here we go," Nikki said under her breath, as the women smiled at the large, unflinching man and started down a long, dark hallway.

Chapter Twenty-Nine

Josie took a deep breath and followed Nikki down the narrow brick-lined hallway, her boots clicking on the beautiful hardwood floor below them. When they got to the end of the hallway, there was a coat check room on the right. To the left, the hallway opened up, revealing a large, opulent staircase leading down to a lower level. The girl in the coat check room looked like she could've been on a high fashion runway in Milan. She was tall and slender, with bright green eyes, honey-colored skin, and a full mane of kinky-curly hair. She put out her hands as if to indicate that keeping their jackets was not an option, and Josie reluctantly obeyed. She had been hoping to keep her coat in case they needed to make some sort of fast getaway. That was ridiculous, but still, this place kind of gave her the creeps.

The girl handed Josie and Nikki each an antique-looking key with a number on it and whisked their coats away. The women continued down the stairs, where they found themselves in a lounge area. The room was breathtaking, with a large, fully stocked mahogany bar, a blazing stone fireplace, and several tufted couches. The ceilings were vaulted like most of the older buildings in Cleveland. There were several doors on the right that led to other rooms. Oddly enough, this room was empty save for the one extremely handsome bartender behind the bar.

"Are you getting an Overlook Hotel kind of feeling?" Nikki whispered, elbowing Josie's ribs.

"Maybe we've been here all along," Josie responded in a hushed tone, giggling as they slowly approached the bar.

"Hello, ladies," the bartender said, flashing a perfect smile at them. "What's your poison?"

"Club soda," "Scotch, neat," Josie and Nikki said simultaneously as Nikki threw down a card and put up her hand when Josie started to protest. "Write off," she whispered as the bartender turned away to prepare their drinks.

Josie nodded, and they took their drinks and meandered towards one of the doors on the other side of the room. "I feel like Alice in Wonderland," she murmured.

"Yeah, if the white rabbit lived in The Magic Castle," Nikki muttered back, choosing one of the three doors and swinging it open.

Inside was another long hallway paneled in gorgeous wood carvings, with small, pretty chandeliers lining the ceiling and giving off a dim glow. When they arrived at the end, they were surprised to find that the establishment didn't seem like a nightclub at all. The room looked like the one they had just come from, only bigger, with several more mahogany bars strategically placed and more of the antique furniture. Upon closer inspection, however, Josie saw that there were young women in little black dresses milling around, some sitting with tables of men (and a few women), some serving drinks, and some leading people down the many different hallways that stemmed from this grand room.

It quickly became apparent that instead of waitresses, the club employed "hostesses." Josie had been to a club like this in New York once. By having hostesses in place of waitresses, the experience was more like being at a private party than a bar. The hostesses just happened to fetch drinks and expected a tip at the end of the night. The club that Josie had visited in New York had been expensive and catered to a high-end clientele, which seemed to be the same story here. From what she understood, clubs that used hostesses looked for a specific type—gorgeous, yes, but also charismatic, charming, and well-educated—the type of woman that could put anyone at ease as though each patron were a guest in their home.

"Jeez, this place doesn't end," Nikki said, taking a sip of her scotch and making a face.

"Why did you order that?" Josie laughed. "I don't think I've ever seen you drink scotch."

"Eh, it seemed appropriate at the time. Lots of wood, cigars, the smell of cologne—scotch seemed appropriate. I'm regretting my choice," Nikki choked after another sip of the dark liquid.

Josie wandered over to the bar and set herself up on one of the leather stools with Nikki in tow. She sipped her soda and looked around. The hostesses weren't wearing uniforms, but they were all wearing some iteration of a sexy black dress. As she was looking around the room, she thought she saw her father sitting amidst a group of men over on the couches. Josie was putting up her hand to wave when, after one of the hostesses passed by that table, she realized it wasn't her father, just another man with salt-and-pepper hair. She put her hand back on her drink, and she was finishing her visual sweep of the room when she saw something—or more accurately, *someone*—in the corner that made her heart skip.

"Holy crap, is that Charlotte?" she demanded in a whisper, gesturing with her head.

"I don't know what Charlotte looks like," Nikki said back through a plastered-on smile, trying to look casual.

As if sensing she was being watched, Charlotte looked up and locked eyes with Josie. Her mouth fell open, but she quickly closed it and averted her gaze. She bent down to say something to the man she had been talking to, grabbed a tray from the table near them, and took off at a brisk pace down one of the many hallways. Josie followed her, but was waylaid by another linebacker in a black suit.

"Excuse me, miss, but this is the VIP area," he said in a booming voice reminiscent of Barry White.

"Sure, sure," Josie said, pulling out her black Amex card.

"No can do," he said, shaking his head and holding up his hands. "Omega Society members only."

"But I need to talk to that girl," Josie said impatiently.

"Those are the rules, miss. You have to be a member for VIP privileges," the large man explained, more kindly than Josie expected.

Josie threw her hands up in frustration. "Okay, all right, thanks for your time," she said as Nikki steered her away from him. "Unreal," she muttered under her breath.

At least now she knew—Charlotte was hostessing at O, which meant that the note in her mailbox wasn't a mistake. Had Amber been working there, too? Once they had liberated her car from the valet and were speeding towards the Shoreway, she and Nikki rapid-fire discussed the evening. As she passed Cleveland Browns Stadium, Josie explained who Charlotte was and why seeing her at that club meant more than just an awkward situation at school the next day.

"Okay, wait," Nikki finally interrupted her. "You think Amber Oldham was working at O with Charlotte?"

"Yep," Josie said.

"Are these girls even of age?" Nikki demanded. "You've got to be at least eighteen to work at a club, right?"

"I think twenty-one, since all of them are serving drinks," Josie said. "But I don't know the ins and outs of the underground club business. Either way, neither of those girls is anywhere near twenty-one; they're not even eighteen."

"Oh, man," Nikki said, pulling out her phone and rapidly typing notes. "I'll call around tomorrow and see if I can find anything out. You would think there'd be some sort of background check before they hire girls, but maybe if you're attractive enough, management doesn't care much about that."

"Or maybe they know exactly what they're doing," Josie answered.

"Wait a second," Nikki said. "Those girls who overdosed—do you remember the article from about a month ago about the two women found in an alley, dead from a fentanyl overdose?"

"Yes, I think so."

"They worked at the club," Nikki said. "If Amber was working there—"

"That makes three," Josie finished. "Okay. I'll try to get to Charlotte as soon as I can, but I doubt she'll be eager to talk to me after what just happened."

"No kidding," said Nikki, shaking her head. "This is beyond. Can you imagine if we had tried to pull this kind of crap in high school?"

Josie laughed. "My parents would have locked me in my room until I was thirty. Actually, forget that. My *brothers* would have locked me up."

"Right? My parents were pretty lenient, but I never would have tried this," Nikki responded.

"Things are different now," Josie sighed. "You wouldn't believe what these kids get away with. Especially the rich kids whose parents are never around."

"I bet that does make it a lot easier," Nikki nodded, looking out the window. "But I think we can both agree that Amber's friends know way more than they're letting on. At least Charlotte does."

"Oh yes, she does," Josie responded, her hand twisting back and forth on the steering wheel. "And I'm going to get some answers."

"See, now you're starting to sound like a reporter," Nikki teased, taking a large gulp of water out of a bottle she produced from her purse. "Yuck, I don't think I'll ever get the aftertaste of that scotch out of my mouth."

Josie laughed and hit the gas to make it through a yellow light.

Nikki continued, "Do you mind if I crash at your place tonight? I don't feel like driving all the way back down here to my loft."

"Sure, there's clean sheets on the guest bed," Josie answered, happy to have the company. "Do you want to pick up your car from the pub?"

"Nah, I'll get it in the morning."

"I can take you before my first class."

"As long as you promise not to wake me up to run with you," Nikki said, mock threateningly.

"I swear," Josie laughed, throwing up her hands in surrender. She didn't know if she would be getting up to go running herself. Her adrenaline was pumping too hard to sleep.

As if reading her mind, Nikki said, "Not that I think I'm going to sleep anyways. I'm too wound up. Like, even if there's no connection to Amber, the fact that that club is hiring high school kids is a story in itself."

"Mmm-hmm," Josie said. "Just do me a favor and—"

"I know, I know. Sit on it for now," Nikki interrupted. "Don't worry. This is a big story, and I want to have all my facts straight before I run with it. Do you think the club owners found out that she was underage and that's what got her killed? See, *this* is why I'm not going to be able to sleep."

"That club caters to highbrow clientele. I'd be willing to bet that any of the local power players who frequent that establishment wouldn't want their name associated with a scandal," Josie said.

Nikki fired off a text. "I just sent a text to my editor asking if she knows who owns the club. Hopefully, we'll have some answers tomorrow. In the meantime, I have an important question for you," she said, wriggling her eyebrows devilishly at Josie as they pulled into her driveway, "Do you have any Ben & Jerry's?"

Chapter Thirty

After getting back to Josie's house, she and Nikki had talked nonstop about the club, the death, the drugs, and how everything could be connected until the sun came up. Josie missed her run and promised herself she would not pull any more all-nighters on school nights. With her insomnia, she should feel no different after staying up versus being kept up by her thoughts, but she could feel a difference as she walked to school on Thursday. Her body felt like she was moving through water, and each step felt more labored than the last.

However, she got through her first class and on her morning break, decided to check in on Tony. But she found that he still wasn't in school. Disappointed, she stopped in for a visit with Principal Crandall before afternoon classes.

"Knock, knock," she said as she rapped on the doorjamb.

Tom Crandall glanced up from his papers and gave her a warm smile. "Good morning, Josie. What can I do for you?"

Like Sean, Tom Crandall had been one of Josie's favorite teachers when she attended Lakeview. She had never liked science, but he made chemistry fun and accessible in ways that were unexpected. Even though it wasn't her favorite subject, she had asked Tom to write her a recommendation for college, which he found time for despite the large number of such requests he received every year.

"Do you know what's going on with Tony Burgess yet? Has the school board decided on a punishment?" she asked.

Tom sat back, removed his glasses, and rubbed the bridge of his nose.

"Well, as you may or may not have seen in the memo, they've decided not to expel him."

"Right," Josie said.

Tom smiled ruefully. "Unfortunately, he is serving at least a two-week suspension, maybe longer. The board is still debating whether suspending him for a longer period of time is appropriate. If that happens, he'll likely have to repeat his senior year."

Josie let out a forceful breath. "Oh, boy."

"Yeah, I'm fighting like hell to keep them from doing that, but at this point, I can't tell which way they're leaning. We have another meeting this evening to discuss it. And that's not even addressing the criminal charges he's facing. If he gets jail time for the drugs, this could all be a moot point."

"Okay," Josie said, nodding and turning to leave. "Thanks for the update."

"Anytime," Tom said, preparing to bury himself in the towering stack of papers on his desk again.

"Tom?" she said, stopping in the doorway.

"Mmm?"

"What do you make of all this?"

He stopped his shuffling and sat back again, cocking his head. "Well, I'm a scientist, Josie. I look at empirical evidence and draw conclusions from that evidence."

Josie frowned. The evidence made Tony look guilty, and she was a little disappointed to hear Tom's response.

"However," he called out as she turned to go. "As a human being who knows empirical evidence doesn't always tell the full story, I think there's something fishy going on here. Tony Burgess is a good kid. I know about his cousin's overdose, and Tony doesn't strike me as the type of person that would experiment with the same drugs that killed a family member."

"Right," Josie said.

"That being said, human beings do stupid things all the time. And people aren't always who they appear to be. So while I don't want to believe that the drugs were Tony's, or that he, let's say, gave them to Amber Oldham, I do think Occam's Razor applies in most cases—the simplest explanation is usually the correct one."

She nodded. "I'll let you get back to it. Thanks."

"Anytime," Tom replied.

Much as she didn't want to admit it, Tom had a point. People did things that seemed out of character all the time. Loving husbands murdered their wives, devoted executives ripped off millions—people turned on each other every day. Maybe she was being short-sighted and naïve; maybe the drugs were Tony's, and the facts actually represented the truth. The shortest distance between two points, after all, was a straight line. As she turned to leave the office, a news report playing on the TV hanging in the corner stopped her in her tracks.

"Can you turn that up?" she asked the administrative assistant, who grabbed the remote and slammed her finger on the volume button.

The reporter was on the sidewalk across the street from a house in Lakeview. Police were milling around, and an ambulance sat in the driveway. She narrated as two EMTs wheeled out a still figure on a gurney.

"This morning, police received a 9-1-1 call from Brad Burgess, Tony Burgess' father, regarding a potential drug overdose."

They played a clip of the 9-1-1 call, and Josie heard Brad pleading for the police to "please, come quick, my son isn't breathing. I think he overdosed" and to "send an ambulance!"

The reporter returned to the screen, and Josie could see Sean in the background directing his officers to different areas of the scene and trying to keep a handle on the neighbors, who were spilling out of their houses in pajamas to see what the commotion was about. The station then cut away to the two desk reporters updating the earlier story.

"As stated in the 9-1-1 call, Tony Burgess apparently suffered a drug overdose during the early morning hours. We now know that it was a fentanyl overdose. His father, Brad Burgess, carried Narcan following the overdose death of a relative earlier this year, and he administered the drug when he found his son unresponsive with powdered fentanyl next to him. Authorities say the Narcan saved Burgess' life, but he is still in critical condition at Lakeview Hospital, and we have no word on whether he will recover. Tony Burgess was recently arrested and subsequently released in conjunction with the death of Amber Oldham. Ms. Oldham died from a fentanyl overdose earlier this month before falling from the Lakeview Water Tower, and Burgess was under investigation. Amber Oldham was the only daughter of Senator Clinton Oldham, a state senator currently running for reelection. The charges against Burgess were dropped following an investigation that determined that Ms. Oldham's death was accidental. Stay tuned as we cover…."

Josie couldn't listen to any more. As she stumbled out of the office, she reached a trembling hand into her pocket and pulled out her phone, which had been in Do Not Disturb mode all morning while she was teaching. She had a bunch of missed calls from Sean, as well as Nikki, Alex, and Heather. She hit the redial button on Sean's name, but it went straight to voicemail. When the bell rang, and students flooded the halls, she realized that most of them were glued to their phones, a blatant violation of the school's no cell phone policy. Some of the kids were crying, while others looked quietly at their phones, some chewing their nails or twirling their hair to calm their anxiety. As Josie watched them, she wondered how the school was going to handle this latest tragedy in what had been an already tumultuous year.

Chapter Thirty-One

For the remainder of the day, Josie gave her classes a free period. It was technically a "study hall," but few of them were studying, instead glued to their phones. She could hardly blame them. Growing up in Lakeview, these kids were insulated from a significant amount of the tragedy that the rest of the world had to cope with. Josie knew that firsthand. For the opioid epidemic to reach Lakeview was shocking in itself, but two students overdosing in less than a month was catastrophic.

Before her final period of teaching, Josie stepped outside her classroom and saw Charlotte at the end of the hall. Even though Charlotte turned and seemingly saw Josie after Josie called out her name, she hurried away. Unfortunately, the hallway was packed with kids, and Josie was unable to wade through quickly enough to catch her. She'd have to deal with Charlotte later.

When Josie exited the building after school, she was dismayed to see throngs of reporters once again lined up on the sidewalk just off school grounds, eagerly awaiting their opportunity to pounce on passing kids and faculty. Unable to fight off the anger in her chest due to pure exhaustion, she strode over to the line of reporters hovering at the edge of the front walk.

"You ought to be ashamed of yourselves," she spat as she got within earshot. "Can't you see these kids have been through enough? Why don't you back off and do the right thing for once? They need time to process. What they don't need is their faces splashed all over the six o'clock news with an edit to fit whatever narrative your producers want to push." She realized that as she was speaking, all the cameras had been trained on her, and several of the reporters stepped forward and began shouting questions her way.

"Josie, how do you feel about the news of Tony Burgess' overdose?"

"Was Tony Burgess a student of yours?"

"Do you believe that Tony Burgess is innocent?"

The questions rang in her ears as she took a few steps back and started back towards campus. She heard a familiar voice calling her name and getting closer, and as she turned around, she saw Darren Jenkins hurrying towards her, ignoring the mandate that press stay off of school property. She took a few steps in his direction, ready for a fight, but the quick wail of a police siren in close proximity caused Jenkins to stop dead in his tracks. Sean's police cruiser appeared around the curve of the front entrance, and he leaned out the window to yell at the reporter.

"Get off school property before I arrest you, Jenkins," he warned. "You know better."

Darren Jenkins and his cameraman slunk quickly back to the sidewalk as Sean pulled up next to Josie. "Get in," he said. "I hope you didn't say anything to those hyenas."

She threw her bag on the floor and climbed in. "Unfortunately, I did. You can bet I'll be all over the evening news. I just don't have the energy to care today."

"I get it," he replied. "I'll take you over to the hospital. I assume that's where you were planning to go?"

"I can't believe it. Have you seen him since this morning? How is he?"

"It doesn't look good, Jose." Sean shook his head. "Brad administered the Narcan, but Tony already had so much fentanyl in his system that the doctors aren't sure it was enough. They gave him more Narcan in the ambulance, but I don't know if they got to him in time."

"What happened?"

"Brad said Tony didn't get up this morning. When he went to his room to check on him, Tony's lips were blue, his breathing was very slow, and his pupils were constricted. Brad bought some Narcan after they found the drugs in Tony's locker, given that his nephew overdosed. Even though

Tony denied that the drugs were his, he wanted to have it around just in case. He opened Tony's nightstand while he was waiting for the ambulance and found a bag of powder."

"Oh, my god. Poor Brad."

"Poor Brad is right. He's had an unimaginable week. Tony's in a coma. They don't know when or, ah—" Sean paused, gathering himself as he turned into the entrance to the hospital. "They don't know when or if he'll wake up."

Josie could feel tears prickling her eyelids. How had they gotten here? Just a few days ago, Tony had seemed okay, doing his best to get through Amber's death, but okay. Was he an addict, and they had all missed the signs? Did this mean Amber was an addict?

"Josie," Sean said, rapping on her window with his knuckle.

Blinking rapidly, she realized they were parked, and he had already gotten out of the car. She unfastened her seat belt and joined Sean, walking quickly into the building. Since Sean had been at the hospital all morning, he knew where Tony's room was. Josie likely wouldn't be able to see him since she wasn't family, but she at least wanted to check on Brad. As they stepped off the elevator, they could hear the alarms in the ICU going off. "Code blue" was being broadcast loudly over the PA system in the hall. As they hurried towards the unit, Josie could feel dread rising in her throat. When they rounded the corner of the nurses' desk, they could see nurses and doctors rushing into a room.

"Tony's room," Josie whispered, not needing confirmation.

Sean nodded as he stared blankly at the flurry of activity at the end of the hall. Tony's brother and sister stood just outside the room, both of them crying. Several other family members were standing in the hallway, some holding magazines, having obviously come running from the waiting room. Two male nurses dragged Brad Burgess out of the room, struggling against their grip, as a cacophony of alarms drifted out behind him. Another nurse came barreling around the corner with a crash cart, and within seconds Josie could hear someone yelling "Clear!" with the familiar, sickening jolt noise afterwards.

After what seemed like an eternity, everything slowed to a halt, with medical personnel slowly filing out of the room, looking visibly shaken. A nurse met Josie's eyes and answered Josie's unspoken question with a shake of her head. Brad Burgess entered his son's room, and Josie could feel her legs buckling as she heard him release a loud, guttural sob.

Chapter Thirty-Two

As soon as word of Tony's death reached school officials, they convened a virtual meeting and canceled classes for Friday, Monday, and Tuesday. They announced that they would reconvene on Monday to evaluate whether to cancel the remainder of the week. Since Tony's overdose was the second in less than a month, they had decided that Lakeview High was in a state of emergency, dipping into the school's bank of emergency days that were normally reserved for weather events like snow days. Since the weather was getting worse each day and the weather forecasters were predicting a brutal winter, the school board was trying to weigh those factors wisely.

Josie was happy that they were doing what was best for the students by canceling classes for the next few days, and she did not envy the decisions the board was going to have to make in the coming days and weeks. More outside counselors would be needed, and a second memo went out that day urging all teachers to go to a pharmacy and buy Narcan nasal spray to keep in their classrooms or on their person. Until this point, only the school counselors and nurses were required to carry the medicine, but considering Tony and Amber's deaths, the school decided that they couldn't be too careful. Teachers would be reimbursed for this purchase.

Once the doctor called Tony's time of death on Thursday, Sean had dropped Josie at home and gone back to the hospital. He wanted to support Brad and the kids, and Josie didn't want to crowd them. She told Sean to call her if he or the Burgess family needed anything and spent Thursday evening on the phone with the girls, Jake, and her family relaying the tragic news. Despite feeling a little dizzy and very tired by the time she got off the phone that evening, her sleep was fitful. She tossed and turned all night, visions of Tony and Amber's faces haunting her dreams.

In the morning after her run, Josie went to Lakeview Pharmacy and purchased a bottle of Narcan. It was still relatively early in the morning, and she didn't see any other teachers there. Then she went home, showered, and settled into her big chair with a cup of coffee. Around eight, Nikki showed up with pastries and fruit from the local coffee shop.

"Hey," Nikki said as Josie ushered her inside. "I wanted to check on you and see how you were doing."

"Still in shock, I think," Josie replied.

"Yeah, that's not a surprise. I'm here if you want to talk, or I've got some ideas about the club if you want to think about other stuff for a while."

"Yes, please," Josie laughed as Nikki brought the food into the kitchen and grabbed plates. "Do you need coffee?"

"Yes, please," Nikki parroted back, laughing. "I finished my first cup on the way over."

Josie poured Nikki a steaming mug of coffee, and the two women took their plates into the dining room, where Josie shoved her papers and books aside. Nikki didn't bat an eye. Josie had always worked this way, often surrounded by piles of papers when she was working on a project in high school.

"So, whatcha got?" Josie asked, spearing a grape with her fork.

"Well, I found the website for O. There's not much on there, but after a little digging I did find out the deal with The Omega Society, the owner of the club. The social club, O, is only part of the whole business. The Omega Society is in the building next door and has a restaurant, fitness club, business center, and dining parlors for special events. They even have a Michelin-star chef on staff. They also have ten rooms available for overnight accommodations," Nikki said.

"I don't know much about social clubs," Josie said slowly. "Is that normal?"

"Seems to be." Nikki shrugged. "This one is privately owned, but it says that they partner with a network of hundreds of clubs across the United

States."

"Interesting," Josie commented.

"That's not all. They hold a bunch of events throughout the year, like a Lunch with Santa, Holiday parties, a Mother's Day Brunch…." Nikki trailed off.

"Okay, The Omega Society is kind of like a country club?" Josie continued.

"I guess they used to just have the one building, but they needed more space. Once O's building went up for sale, the club jumped at the chance to buy it. The evening social club was a part of that expansion. The members wanted more nightlife, so they opened O. They wanted to be able to entertain out-of-town bigwigs, and they were looking to attract a younger demographic—athletes and other local celebrities."

"That makes sense," Josie said. "But who owns The Omega Society?"

"I have no idea," said Nikki. "Like I said, the website is sparse. Aside from a history lesson dating back into the 1800s, a description, and a membership inquiry button, there's not much else on the site."

"Damn," Josie said. "Do we know any members? Any way to get in there during the day and poke around?"

"I don't know anyone who's a member. But I have a feeling that if a famous actress who just happened to be living locally made a membership inquiry, they'd be inclined to let her in for the day," Nikki sang, her eyes sparkling.

"You crafty minx," Josie said, swatting at her. She retrieved her phone from the living room, dialed the number on the website, and left a message when she got the club's voicemail.

"Hopefully, they won't leave you hanging for too long," Nikki said.

"Fingers crossed," agreed Josie, getting up to clear their dishes. Monroe jumped up on the table and wound her way over to Nikki, purring loudly and stretching her back legs out as she walked.

"This little showoff," Nikki laughed, rubbing Monroe's head, then lifting her up and placing her gently on the floor.

When Josie returned to the table after putting the dishes in the dishwasher, she was surprised to see two voicemails on her phone. "Wow, that was fast," she exclaimed, clicking open the app to listen. However, the first message was not from the club.

"Josie, this is Dr. Gupta. I'm calling to see if you'd like to reschedule your canceled appointment from last week. I haven't seen you in a couple weeks and—" the voice boomed over the speakerphone.

"Nope, that's not it," Josie muttered, clicking the other message.

"You canceled your appointment last week? How long has it been since you've seen your therapist?" Nikki demanded.

"A couple weeks," Josie admitted. "With Amber's death and now Tony, it's just been really hectic, plus I haven't been sleeping, so I'm exhausted and—"

"You need to reschedule," Nikki cut her off, but her tone was gentle. "Make sure you do that as soon as I leave, promise?"

"Fine, I promise," Josie mumbled.

She put the next message on speaker, and a smooth male voice crooned, "Ms. Ashbury, this is Franklin Mather from The Omega Club. I would be happy to schedule a tour for you at your convenience. Please call me back at 216-555-7100."

"Wow, that was fast," Josie remarked.

"See, I told you. No matter how old and established they are, they're still thirsty for fame," Nikki teased.

Josie stuck her tongue out at her, then laughed along with Nikki. It felt good to laugh.

"Okay, I gotta go to the office for a while," Nikki said, jumping up and grabbing her bag. "But call me or text me when you set up something for the club, okay?"

"I will," Josie replied. "I'll call them back as soon as you leave."

"And Josie? Seriously. Call your therapist. Don't make me call in reinforcements," Nikki chided. She sounded like she was kidding, but Josie knew she was serious.

"I will. I'm not dodging her, I swear."

Nikki looked at Josie like she didn't believe her, but a glance at her watch told her she didn't have time to argue. "Call me later. Love you," she yelled as she flew out the door.

"Love you more," Josie called after her.

She sat down on the couch and turned on the TV, settling on a rerun of *Parks and Recreation* to play in the background while she worked. After gathering her papers and computer, however, she was asleep within minutes of plopping down on the couch.

Chapter Thirty-Three

That afternoon, Josie managed to get a hold of Franklin Mather and schedule a visit for late Monday morning. She made sure to inform him that she would be bringing a guest, and he arranged for them to have lunch in the restaurant after their tour. He asked that they please observe the dress code—a minimum of business casual—and told her that they were delighted by her interest. She shot Nikki a text that was met with a thumb's up emoji. Then she called Dr. Gupta and set up her missed appointment. She knew she shouldn't be skipping appointments with her doctor, but things had been so hectic, she felt like she had no time to spare.

The rest of the afternoon, Josie dove deep into online research about The Omega Club. Charter members of the club included some of the most prominent names in the city's history, and it was the oldest social club in the region. The club also hadn't admitted women until 1985, a fact that Josie snorted at while sipping her tea. She couldn't believe that organizations excluded women so recently in history. The country as a whole wasn't quite as progressive as it would like to believe itself to be.

While the history of the club was somewhat standard—a place where influential and accomplished people could get together and mingle and so on—the Reddit threads about the club and other similar ones were crazy. Theories about everything from the Illuminati to Satanic activity took up pages and pages of threads. Some alleged that there were clues in the murals hanging in the clubs. Others said there were underground tunnels leading from one club to another in a secret network across the United States. Still, more seemed to think that the clubs were part of the New World Order, linking them all to the Denver Airport, of all places.

While some of the ideas seemed well thought out, others were just plain crazy. In the 1980s, there was a widely circulated theory that members of such clubs were running some sort of child pedophilia ring, and Redditors attempted to link the clubs to high-profile kidnappings. Conspiracies related to the Kennedy assassination, 9/11, the moon landing, Roswell, the Catholic church—anything shrouded in even a hint of mystery—were all somehow tied back to these clubs in intricate and, in Josie's opinion, crazy narratives. There was even one about time travel, claiming that several clubs had portals that allowed members to travel through time and influence world events. More recently, threads about highly profitable drug activity, arms dealing, and underage prostitution rings had popped up.

The threads were correct that the club was a for-profit institution, and light digging did not reveal who owned or ran the club. Again, there was speculation that everyone from JFK Jr. (still alive, of course) to Elvis to Hillary Clinton owned the clubs, but no one had any actual proof or answers. Josie wondered if ownership records were kept on-site or if they were housed in some sort of clandestine warehouse that didn't show up on any blueprints or city plans.

She decided to take a break after tumbling down the conspiracy rabbit hole for several hours and check Lakeviewen-thirty Funeral Home's website to see if any information had been put up about a memorial service for Tony. His obituary ran underneath a school photo of him, and comments from friends and family were pouring in. The page confirmed that his memorial service would be held on Tuesday at ten-thirty am and that donations in lieu of flowers should be made to the American Association for the Treatment of Opioid Independence.

Josie shut the computer and put a note on her calendar, not that there was any chance she would forget. She sent her brother John, the FBI agent, a text asking if he knew anything about The Omega Club and the crazy conspiracy theories. John usually took a little while to get back to her, but he responded almost immediately with one word: "Nonsense."

Still, something nagged at Josie. She fished around in her stack of papers until she found what she was looking for. She'd printed out the article that she and Nikki had discussed about the two young women who had recently died of opioid overdoses. The article did not give their names, but did mention that both women were employed by O in some capacity before their deaths. Was that a coincidence? Was she reaching for some connection because her brain was overflowing with conspiracy theories she'd found, or was there a tie between the overdoses and the club?

Maybe she'd been on Reddit for too long and was seeing connections where there were none. She tucked the article into her notebook and checked her watch. She was supposed to have drinks with Jake tonight, but wasn't feeling very cheerful. Perhaps an evening out would lift her spirits. And Jake was pretty level-headed—maybe he would have some insights about the conspiracy theories she hadn't thought of. She tucked away her research and set about getting ready for her date.

As she was pulling her black leather jacket out of the coat closet, she was surprised to see a second black leather jacket hanging behind hers. Funny, she didn't remember buying another jacket. Had her stylist, Noelle, sent her one that she just didn't remember? She pulled it out of the closet and inspected it closely. The jacket was a small, which wasn't her normal size and not the style Josie usually liked. It looked more like a bomber jacket, and Josie preferred a more tailored, structured fit. She turned the jacket over in her hands, racking her brain to think of where it might have come from. A quick search through the outer pockets revealed no clues. Josie held it out and stared at it once more and, coming up with nothing, shrugged and hung it back in the closet. The jacket did look familiar, but she couldn't place where she had seen it before. She made a mental note to text Noelle the next day and stepped out the door.

Chapter Thirty-Four

On her date with Jake, Josie had been anxious and moody, and she could tell she wasn't very good company. They chatted about the memorial service and the school cancellation, and she told him about her Reddit deep dive. He seemed interested, telling her that he was fascinated by conspiracy theories and offering to do some research on his own. She invited him to the Cleveland Animal Protective League's annual Masquerade ball on Halloween, which she and her friends and family attended every year. He stayed the night on Friday, but was up early on Saturday morning for football practice with the kids. Even though school had been canceled, the players had expressed a desire to keep holding practices. They thought it was the best way to honor their fallen teammate, and the coaches agreed to convene for practice despite school not being in session.

Once he left, Josie made coffee and sat in the kitchen, staring out the back window at the water tower. The temperature had continued to plunge, and forecasters were calling for storms all week, but for now, a few light snowflakes softly floated past the window. Presley flopped behind Josie and began making cooing noises, so Josie bent down and rubbed his belly. When she stood up, she once again had a flash of looking from the top of the water tower down to the ground, the neighborhood swimming before her eyes.

What was with these flashes? Josie rubbed her eyes and grabbed her mug, deciding to wrap herself in a blanket and binge-watch some true crime on Netflix. She was about to turn on a documentary about false confessions when something clicked in her mind. The jacket. She knew where she had seen that jacket before. Throwing open the coat closet, she pulled it out and inspected it again. That jacket was Amber Oldham's. She was almost sure of it, she'd seen it on her so many times, and Josie could have sworn it was hanging over the bars on the top of the tower when she found Amber's body. How had it gotten into her house?

She searched the pockets, once again coming up empty, then turned the jacket over in her hands, feeling the leather as she went. Her fingers clamped down on a flat, round object on the right front side of the coat, and Josie ran her fingers over the lining until she found an inside pocket held closed with a small zipper. She unzipped it, reached in, and pulled out a single silver poker chip. The chip was heavy, obviously real silver, and aside from the grooves around the edge, had no other markings on it.

She slung the jacket over the back of her chair and held the chip between her thumb and index finger, examining it more closely. As she turned it to look at the edge, she discovered a tiny symbol carved into it, almost impossible to see with the naked eye. Holding it closer, she realized it was the Greek symbol for omega.

She sat on the arm of the chair, the jacket in one hand, chip in the other. She knew she should call Sean immediately and tell him, but how would she explain the jacket being in her house in the first place? Should she call Jake? He was still at practice, and besides, what was she going to say—hey, I found Amber's jacket, which I shouldn't have, by the way—in my closet, and there's a weird poker chip in it? Or she could call the girls, but she didn't want to embroil them in whatever trouble she was in now. No, she needed to figure this out on her own.

Her phone dinged with a message from her mom, asking how her date went last night and when they were going to get to meet Jake. She wrote, "Good! Soon!" then returned to freaking out. She sat cross-legged on her couch, placed her hands face up on her knees, and closed her eyes. The past couple weeks, all she needed was to think clearly, and fatigue was making that impossible. But meditating helped sometimes, so she tried to focus.

After a few minutes of clearing her head, she had an idea. The neighbors. She should talk to the neighbors. The investigation had been called off so quickly the police couldn't have had time to go door to door collecting statements. But it was possible that one of the neighbors had seen something on the night of Amber's death. She sent Sean a text asking if they had canvassed before the case was closed and received a "No. Why?" response from him a few minutes later.

"No reason, just thinking," she answered.

"Josie…" came his reply. Sean knew her well enough to know that "just thinking" meant a plan was forming in her head. She sent back a smiley face with flushed cheeks and got dressed. She would wait until late morning to start her door-to-door investigation to ensure that she wasn't disturbing anyone, but she could feel she was onto something. She would tell Sean about the jacket and the chip later, when she hopefully had some answers.

Chapter Thirty-Five

When picking which neighbors to interview, Josie focused on the houses that had the best view of the water tower. With any luck, somebody from one of those houses had looked out the window on the night of and seen Amber up there. Her next-door neighbors on both sides would have a clear view, and the houses across the field that jutted up against the high school property would have an even better one. She knew the people next door, but this might be a good time to capitalize on her fame with the people she didn't know, so she left her hat at home in order to look as much "herself" as she could.

As Josie trekked her way across the backyard, she noticed Jake's car pulling into the parking lot of the high school. He got out and walked around to the trunk, looking around as if to make sure he wasn't being seen. She peeked around the tree and saw him walking towards the building; Josie followed his path.

Once she reached the back doors, she looked in and gave him a second to get further down the corridor before throwing the doors open and hurrying after him. What was he doing here on a Saturday? The football teams usually held their practices in the mornings. But this afternoon, the school seemed deserted except for a few cars parked in the lot.

Josie arrived in the English wing and didn't see Jake, but she did see a light on in one of the classrooms at the end of the hall. Slowly and as quietly as she could, she tiptoed her way towards the room.

She nearly jumped out of her skin when she heard someone say, "Excuse me," in heavily accented English, as a small, older Latino man smiled at her as he passed and disappeared into the room.

Josie noticed the sign on the wall of the hallway. "ESL Class," it announced, with an arrow pointing towards the room that the gentleman had entered. Josie peeked into the room. Sure enough, there was Jake at the head of the class, unloading papers from a cardboard box and greeting the students. There weren't many of them, but they all watched him eagerly and greeted him with slow "How are yous?" over pronouncing each syllable.

She knew that the school was going to be offering English as a second language classes in the evenings and on weekends, but in the course catalog, it was still listed as teacher TBD. It warmed her heart to know that Jake was giving up his free time, for very little money, to help people. The fact that he hadn't bragged about it made her like him even more, because she knew he wasn't doing it to get praise or make people think he was a good person. She was so used to being around people in Los Angeles who always had an angle, she had almost forgotten that people did things simply out of the goodness of their hearts.

Josie watched for another moment as Jake engaged with his students, marveling at the way he took time to connect with each one and the kindness that seemed to emanate effortlessly from him. He moved to close the door, still talking to a young Russian woman about her week in a slow cadence, and Josie turned and hurried away before he could catch her spying. She needed to get going on her neighbor interviews, and she couldn't spend all day mooning over the man who she was falling more in love with by the second.

* * *

Though she wanted to continue to watch Jake teach his ESL class, Josie knew she needed to get back to her plan of talking to the neighbors. The first couple of doors she knocked on were met with no answer. The third house she tried was on the other side of the field, and the guy was no help. He hadn't been home on the night of Amber's death—he had been at the Indians game, which had gone into overtime, and had gone out afterwards.

He didn't get home until well after midnight. A shorter gentleman in his fifties with kind eyes and a burgeoning beer gut, he seemed tickled at the idea that Josephine Ashbury was knocking on his door. He shyly asked her to bring him a signed headshot when she could, which she promised she would do.

Josie went to the next house and knocked on the door, noting the lace curtains and well-kept lawn of what was probably an older resident. An elderly woman's voice called, "Coming, just a minute," and Josie prepared herself for a bit of a wait. The door opened, and a tiny woman in her late seventies stood before her dressed in a light pink blouse, khaki slacks, and house slippers. Her white hair was permed and coiffed to perfection, and she stood about five feet tall, if that. She wore a simple, but beautiful, antique diamond wedding ring on her left hand.

"Can I help you, dear?" she asked, her voice sweet as sugar and soft like snow.

"Hi, I'm Josephine. I live across the field over in that gray house," Josie said, pointing towards her house.

"Oh, yes, dear. You're the actress. I remember reading about you moving back into town. I'm Marion, Marion O'Donnell," the older woman said, holding out her hand.

"Nice to meet you, Mrs. O'Donnell," Josie said, gently shaking Marion's hand.

"Oh, please, call me Marion," the woman chuckled.

"Okay, Marion," Josie smiled. "I wish I was here under better circumstances, but did you hear about the death of Senator Oldham's daughter?"

"Oh, yes," Marion said, bringing a hand to her face. "Just awful. Just *awful*. And to think, it happened practically in my own backyard. It just makes me sick."

"I know. I feel the same way."

"Such a shame. She was a very pretty girl. Such a bright future. It's terrible what drugs have done to the world." Marion shook her head.

"Yes, it is," Josie replied. "I'm sorry for the intrusion, but I wanted to talk to some of the neighbors about the night Amber Oldham died. She was one of my students, and we were quite close. Do you remember if you were awake last Monday between eleven and midnight?"

Marion paused for a moment, then stepped back, opening her door wide and gesturing with her arm. "Please, dear, come on in and have a cup of tea. You look like you're freezing."

"Thank you," said Josie, stepping inside and running her fingers through her hair.

Marion O'Donnell's house was neat as a pin. The living room to Josie's left housed several beige couches and large glass cases filled with ceramic figurines. The carpet, also beige, was spotless and vacuumed so as not to leave any marks. Beyond the living room, Josie could see a formal dining room with a large oak table, matching buffet, and a crystal chandelier. To the right, a staircase lined with dozens of photographs of smiling children and grandchildren wound up to the second floor.

Josie followed Marion back to the kitchen, which was also immaculate, if a little dated. The linoleum floor squeaked under Josie's boots, and the cabinets looked like they had been there since the 1980s. A small, light-colored wood table sat off to the right side, and Josie took off her jacket and slung it over the back of a chair, rubbing her hands together to warm them up as Marion filled a stainless-steel kettle with water.

"You have a lovely home," Josie said.

"Thank you," Marion replied. "Not quite as full as it used to be, especially since my husband passed away a few years ago. But my children and grandchildren live just a few streets away. My kids keep telling me I should move into a house without stairs, but I can't bring myself to do it. This house holds all our memories, and I can't bear to part with it until I absolutely have to."

Josie smiled, admiring her candor. Older people who lived alone were quick to open up, especially when it came to their families. "I understand," Josie said, nodding sympathetically.

"Do you have a large family?" Marion asked.

"Three brothers."

"Sisters?"

"Nope. Just me and the boys."

Marion laughed, a tinkling, musical sound. "I bet that was a real handful growing up."

"More than you can imagine," Josie laughed. "But I never had to worry about anyone messing with me—especially boys."

"No, I'd imagine not," Marion said, stretching to get cups and saucers from one of the upper cabinets.

"Can I help you?" Josie asked, stepping forward.

"No, no, dear, I'm fine," Marion said, waving her off. Once she had the cups and saucers down, she arranged them on a silver tray with a matching teapot, sugar bowl, and small pitcher of cream. When the kettle began to whistle, she shuffled quietly to the stove and poured the boiling water carefully over the teabags in the teapot. Then she picked up the tray and brought it over to the small table to join Josie.

"What do your brothers do? Are they in the entertainment industry as well?"

"Gosh, no," Josie chuckled. "Well, I guess one of them is, in a way. My youngest brother, Tommy, owns a tattoo parlor, so he's an artist."

"Oh," Marion said, raising her eyebrows and nodding.

"My oldest brother, John, used to be a football player in the NFL, but he injured himself early in his career and had to retire. So he decided to follow in my father's footsteps and work for the FBI. And my middle brother, Kevin, is an attorney."

"Sounds like a very well-rounded family," Marion smiled, pouring them each a cup of tea, then passing one to Josie.

"Thank you," Josie said with a small smile. She loved teatime. When she was a young girl, her mother used to take her for high tea at the Ritz-Carlton. They would get all dressed up in their Sunday best and wear white gloves and pretty hats, and her father would chauffeur them down to the beautiful hotel where they would spend the afternoon enjoying tea and finger sandwiches.

"Now, you were asking me a question, dear? Something about last Monday night," Marion said.

"Yes," Josie said, blowing on her tea to cool it before taking a sip. "I was wondering if you were home between eleven and midnight. That was the approximate time Amber Oldham died."

"I was home that night, and I'm usually up until around one a.m. I've always been somewhat of a night owl." Marion chuckled, then looked at Josie curiously. "What exactly are you trying to find out, my dear?"

"Anything out of the ordinary," Josie said quickly, spooning some sugar and pouring some cream into her tea. "Like if you happened to look out the window and see kids in the field, lights in the parking lot, a car. Or if you heard something, maybe an argument. Anything out of the ordinary."

Marion looked at her strangely, then said, "Well, there's always lights in and out of the parking lot. You know how kids are; they like to go places and just hang about until someone tells them to leave." She paused. "And yes, I did look out the window that night and see someone out in the field around that time."

"Oh? Can you describe that person for me? Did you recognize them?" Josie said eagerly.

"Why yes, my dear," Marion said. "But I'm a bit confused. You see, the person I saw that night in the field was *you.*"

Chapter Thirty-Six

W hat?" Josie sputtered, nearly spitting out her tea. *"Me?"*

"Yes, you. Well, or someone who looked an awful lot like you. It struck me as odd because you weren't wearing a jacket, just a small top with those skinny straps and a pair of lounge pants," Marion replied.

"What was I doing?"

"That was odd, too. You were just standing there, in the middle of the field, staring straight ahead like you were in a trance. I went to make myself a cup of tea, and when I looked back out, you were gone."

Josie sat back, stunned. This had to be a mistake. "Mrs. O—er, Marion," she said urgently, leaning forward. "Are you absolutely sure it was me?"

"I may be old, but I'm not senile," Marion clucked. "As I said, I'm fairly certain it was you. I suppose it could have been someone with a similar haircut and build. I assumed it was you because you live so close. There was only one car in the parking lot, and it was at the other end. It would seem silly to park so far away in an empty lot and then walk out into the field."

Unless you were trying to hide your car, Josie thought. "Did you happen to see what kind of car it was? Make, model, color, anything?"

Marion shook her head. "I'm sorry, dear. I don't know much about cars. It was a dark color and parked in the shadows near the music wing."

"M'kay," Josie said, biting her lip.

The car was an interesting new development. The police had found Amber's car parked on a side street, so the car couldn't have been hers. But Josie was trying to wrap her brain around Marion seeing her in the field.

She was sure she had not left her house that night, although Marion had described the pajamas Josie slept in almost every night to a T. Could Marion be mistaken? Or had it been someone else? Josie looked at Marion's sweet face, gentle hands, and sparkling eyes. She had no motive to be dishonest.

"Well, I don't want to keep you for too long," Josie stood up, still shaken. "Thank you for the tea."

"Anytime, love," Marion said softly. "I do have dinner plans with my daughter and son-in-law this evening, so I should get ready myself. We're going to Twin Oaks. We've got a table by the windows that overlook the creek. I just love those little mallards."

Alex was always talking about how the older patrons at Twin Oaks were obsessed with the ducks. Obviously, she wasn't exaggerating. Josie pulled on her coat and gloves, heading slowly for the door with Marion in tow.

"Thank you again," she said over her shoulder, reaching for the brass doorknob.

"Please stop by anytime," Marion said warmly as Josie turned back to face her from the porch. "I'm sure my daughter and her husband will get a real kick out of hearing that I had tea with a famous actress today. They might not even believe me."

Josie flashed a quick smile and said, "Maybe we can do it again sometime? Or maybe next time you can come to my house for tea. I'll get you some autographed photos that you can give to your family, if you like."

Marion let out a coo of delight. "That would be wonderful. Thank you so much. See you soon, my dear. Bye-bye," she said, closing the door.

"Bye," Josie said to the shut door.

She was reeling. If she had been in the field that night, she had absolutely no recollection of it. How could she not remember? Could it have been someone else? She thought about Amber's close friends, but none of them fit the bill. Josie had gone to Marion O'Donnell's house looking for answers, but she left with more questions and an even bigger problem: If she had been out there on the night Amber died, did she know something more? She thought back to that night. After getting up to make the sleepy tea, she sat for a while to drink it, then went straight back to bed. At least, that's what she remembered doing. Her insomnia was still clouding her brain and making every memory appear as if through a haze.

No, she decided firmly. She couldn't have been in the field; there was no way. Marion must be mistaken. It had to have been someone else.

As she walked back towards her house, however, a small seed of doubt tugged at her. Every memory lately felt like she was viewing it through a smudged lens, every thought more muddled than the next. Although she had experienced sleepwalking when she took medication for her insomnia, she hadn't taken any recently for that very reason. Her ex, James, claimed that she did crazy things in her sleep, but he usually only brought it up when they were fighting, and she dismissed it. She assumed he was just gaslighting her to win the arguments, but now she wasn't sure. A bad feeling was creeping over her, making her second-guess her every move. She didn't know if she could trust herself anymore.

Chapter Thirty-Seven

Marion's words haunted Josie all through Sunday as she tried to prepare for her visit to The Omega Society the following day. On Monday, Josie drove downtown and picked up Nikki from The Press office, with Nikki talking a mile a minute about the conspiracies, which she and Josie had discussed at length the night before.

"I bet there's tons of clues in murals and statues and stuff all over this place. Do you think they'll tell us the history? Do you think they know about the theories? They have to know, right? It'd be stupid of them to not keep up with stuff like that, don't you think? Josie?" Nikki chattered.

"Mmm? Yeah, it would," Josie agreed, even though she hadn't really been listening to what Nikki was saying. She was so tired today. Her research into clandestine social clubs had given way to vivid, unsettling dreams, and she'd been up a few times during the night, pacing around, trying to quiet her mind.

Nikki continued to prattle on, with Josie nodding along until Nikki said, "And then I thought I'd join a commune and move to Alaska to join a sled dog racing team."

"Huh?" Josie asked.

"You're not even listening to me," Nikki accused.

"You're right. I'm sorry, I'm sorry. My head is somewhere else," Josie answered, yawning.

When they arrived at the building, Josie pulled into the parking garage on the lower level. They could have parked here the other night when they went to O, if she had noticed the lot. As she pulled in and gave her name, she admired the building's elegant sandstone exterior. Standing five stories tall, it was smaller than the eight-story structure next door that now housed O, but just as stately in its presence.

They got off the elevator, which was run by an attendant, and turned left into the lobby, where large Turkish rugs in rich reds and golds and a giant marble staircase awaited them. A tall, slim man who appeared to be in his early thirties stood in the center of the lobby near a large mahogany table with a crystal vase full of fresh lilies. He wore an impeccably tailored suit and had a slightly effeminate air about him.

"Ms. Ashbury, so good to have you. Franklin Mather the third," the man said, stepping forward and extending his hand.

"Nice to meet you," Josie said, taking his hand. "This is my friend, Nicole Fox."

"Charmed," Nikki drawled in a dramatic fashion, earning her a swat from Josie as Franklin turned around.

"I'll take you on a tour of the facilities; then I've made arrangements for you to have lunch in the restaurant."

"Perfect," Josie said.

"Please, follow me," Franklin said as he started up the stairs.

"What about these rooms down here?" Josie asked, gesturing to the hallways leading off of the lobby that housed a good number of large, thick doors.

"Offices," Franklin said, waving his hand. "This is the administrative level."

"Got it," Josie said, meeting Nikki's eyes for a moment.

"The second level houses our Reading Room, the restaurant, several meeting rooms, and a gathering room," Franklin said, leading them through the first doorway and holding his finger to his lips as a reminder to be quiet.

The Reading Room was full of stuffed leather chairs, each accompanied by a standing lamp. Grand fireplaces sat at either end of the room, which had to be the size of Josie's entire house. Paintings of what Josie could only assume were founding members covered the walls in the Reading Room, as well as the hallways they had seen so far. Several older gentlemen looked up from their papers, then buried themselves back in their work.

The restaurant had the same heavy, embroidered curtains as the library. Each table had a white linen tablecloth and four seats, and several servers were putting two tables together and shuffling chairs around for a larger party. The artwork in the restaurant was different; the portraits replaced by paintings in muted colors encased in heavy gold frames. One end of the room had a floor-to-ceiling bar with a television in the center, which was off. The chairs in the bar area were tufted red leather, with only two per table.

Franklin led them out of the restaurant and down the hall to the conference and gathering rooms. Each conference room contained an enormous table that stretched from end to end, leather chairs, and an oak and glass buffet. The gathering room was filled with large, round tables, each set with eight perfect place settings as though a "gathering" could break out any minute. They continued their tour on the third floor, which held only the Grand Ballroom. The room was truly spectacular and seemed to stretch on endlessly, crystal chandeliers and wall sconces dancing as they flickered to life. The fitness center was located on the fourth floor and was nicer than any gym Josie had ever been in. The fifth floor was where the guest rooms were located. Every room had a queen-sized bed with perfect white bedding, a desk, and a small salon area with seating. Some of the rooms even had their own fireplace. Franklin narrated as they went, talking about the founders, the history, and the perks of membership.

"Guest rooms are available for out-of-town business associates or family, and members are offered a discount to rent the party room or the main ballroom," he droned.

"And what about the newer social club in the building next door?" Josie interrupted.

"Ah, yes, the nightlife," Franklin offered a wan smile. For a younger man, he spoke with the world-weariness of someone twice his age. "Yes, entrée into the social club, O, is included in the membership package."

He led them back to the restaurant, and as they were about to sit down, Nikki said, "Thanks, Frank. Where's the loo?"

"Ahem. Franklin," he corrected. "And if you turn left, then make another left at the first hallway, you'll find the restrooms."

"Thanks," Nikki said, winking at Josie and mouthing, "Keep talking," as Franklin turned his back to her.

"So, Franklin, how does one become a member here?" Josie asked, gesturing for him to sit down.

"Well, Ms. Ashbury, the waiting list is quite long, actually," he said, hesitating and looking around for a moment before gingerly sitting in the seat. "And normally, we require that an existing member sponsor a new member's candidacy."

"Really? That's too bad," Josie said, pulling a notebook and pen out of her purse as though she was going to take notes. "And there's no sort of trial membership?"

"Mmm, no, I'm afraid not," Franklin said, and Josie thought she detected a hint of disdain in his voice. "However, we may be able to make an exception in your case. The membership board was very pleased to hear of your interest and notified me that should you desire to become a member; they would be happy to have you. With the proper initiation fees and annual dues, of course."

"Of course," Josie repeated. "Do you have a fee schedule I could look at?"

"I'll email you one as soon as I get back to my desk," Franklin said, looking pleased with himself.

"Perfect," Josie said.

She heard a familiar voice outside the restaurant, and as a group of men passed the door, she noticed Clinton Oldham amongst them. As he passed, he glanced into the room and nodded at her, then continued on his way. Franklin opened his mouth to say something more, but Nikki came barreling back into the room like a freight train.

"Josie, I'm not feeling very well all of a sudden," she belted as she approached the table.

"Okay, well, we should go then," Josie said, standing up.

"You're not going to stay for lunch? The chef told me the halibut today is truly divine," Franklin said, his brow wrinkling in disappointment.

"Nope, sorry, can't," Nikki called over her shoulder, dragging Josie by the arm out of the restaurant. "Thanks for the tour, Frank."

"Franklin," Josie could hear him calling after them, but they were already halfway to the elevator.

"Nik, what the hell?" Josie whispered as they waited for the elevator.

"Someone caught me snooping around in Frank's office. But not before I could grab this," she turned and lifted her shirt to show Josie a file folder tucked into the back of her pants. Josie smiled at her friend. She had to admit, the girl had balls. They hopped into the elevator and asked the attendant to take them to the garage, and as the doors were closing, Josie could hear Franklin's terse "She did what?!" as they sank to the lower level.

Chapter Thirty-Eight

Tony's memorial service the next morning was painful. As Josie made her way through the receiving line to give her condolences to the family, she was shocked by how much Brad Burgess had changed in just one week. He looked disheveled, like he hadn't slept in years—likely not much different than Josie herself, though she was covering her dark under-eye circles with a thick layer of concealer. When she took his hand and spoke to him, it was as though he didn't even see her; he seemed to look through her at the ghost of what was his former life. Tony's brother and sister both looked equally numb, like they had cried all the tears they had and the well had run dry.

On her way in, Josie saw Sean and some other Lakeview PD officers standing guard outside of the Lakeview Chapel as various members of the media tried to sneak by. Brad Burgess had been firm that he wanted no reporters at the service, and Josie was a little worried about what Brad would do to a reporter if one happened to get past the officers. Most of the press corps seemed content to broadcast from the sidewalk, with some attempting to stop funeral-goers as they were walking onto the chapel grounds. Thus far, not one person had stopped to give an interview.

There was a beautiful memorial set up in the back of the church with several poster boards filled with pictures of Tony, photos of him as a baby, through his school years, with his family, with Amber. A couple of trophies for the sports he played stood on the table next to the easels, along with his letterman jacket and *The Lord of the Rings* trilogy of books. In front of the books, there was a little card with an explanation: *"The Lord of the Rings* series was meaningful to Tony. His father read him the books when he was a child, and Tony read them to his brother and sister when they were growing up." As Josie flipped open the pages of *The Hobbit*, she saw some scribbles in the margins and several passages underlined in dark ink. She felt herself starting to tear up as she thought about Tony's life being cut short, the struggles his family would face in trying to recover from his death, and her own inability to help him.

The pastor made an announcement asking everyone to take their seats, and as Josie slid into a pew, she saw a woman sitting alone at the back of the chapel, a few rows behind where the crowd ended. The woman had to be Savannah Burgess, Tony's mother, simply by the resemblance to her son. Amber had told Josie that she had taken off years ago, and from what Amber said, Savannah had not communicated with Brad and the kids for years. Josie was a little surprised that she had shown up for the service, even though she was Tony's mother.

The familiar words of "The Lord is my shepherd, I shall not want," brought Josie's attention back to the front of the chapel, as the service began. A few of Tony's friends got up to read Bible passages, poems, and snippets of literature. The truly difficult part came when Brad Burgess got up to speak.

"My son was a bright light in a world filled with darkness," he read from a sheet of notebook paper on the pulpit, not looking up at the audience. "He stepped up to help when our family needed it most and never once complained. He sacrificed the end of his own childhood to help care for his brother and sister, often more of a parent to them than I was capable of being. He was beloved by everyone who met him and had a way of making anyone feel like they were at home in his presence. He always welcomed new people into his circle and was often called upon to show new kids around at school. He hated when anyone felt excluded. He fought against social injustice, attending many rallies and protests, and encouraged others to do the same. He made me—" Brad paused, stepping back from the podium to compose himself. "He made me want to be a better man, a better father, and to lead a better life. We were all blessed to have him in our lives for even a short time; I hope that his life inspired many others to follow his example. He was more than my kid, he was my friend, and he left a mark on this world that can never be erased. I love you, son." Then he folded his paper and rejoined the family.

Once the ceremony ended, the attendees stayed in the chapel and lobby, milling around and exchanging condolences and stories. The family had decided on a private burial and given the circumstances of Tony's death, had opted not to host a reception. Josie felt a hand on her arm as she made her way through the lobby, and turned to see Jake, looking handsome in a black sweater and slacks.

"Hey," he said, wrapping her up in a hug. "How you doing?"

"I'm okay," she said, embracing him back. "How are you?"

"So-so," he admitted. "I've got to run right now, but are you busy later?"

"Unfortunately, yeah. Tomorrow night?" Josie asked.

Jake nodded. "I'll call you," he said, then turned and left.

After a few more similar encounters with teachers, students, and friends, Josie had had all she could take. She made her way outside and found Sean near his patrol car, speaking into the radio.

"Sean?" she said, approaching the car.

Sean stopped speaking with an "Over," got up, and engulfed her in a bear hug. She had held herself together pretty well up to that point, but as Sean squeezed her, she felt tears overflow from her eyes.

"Can you come by tonight?" she asked, wiping the tears away and stepping back.

Sean looked at his watch. "Uh, yeah, I'm off around six o'clock. Does that work?"

Josie nodded, feeling suddenly unable to speak.

"You going to be all right?" he asked.

She nodded again.

"M'kay. I have to head back to the station. I'll see you later," he said, getting into the car.

She started to make her way to her car, which was on the other end of the parking lot, glaring at the reporters who had managed to ensnare some of the funeral-goers in their nets. When she got to the car, she heard voices growing louder from the edge of the parking lot. She peeked over the roof and saw Charlotte, Morgan, and Lexi clustered together, arguing. Lexi looked miserable, and Morgan looked numb, but Charlotte looked furious. At first, they were whispering, but their voices grew louder as Josie listened.

"You know what happened, Charlotte," Morgan said.

"Yes, I do. That's the point," Charlotte shot back.

"Come on, Char, we have to do something," Lexi joined in.

"No, we don't," Charlotte said firmly, looking around. "This is over, okay? Tony couldn't deal with Amber's, like, suicide or accidental death or whatever it was."

"You know that's not what happened," Morgan answered.

"No, that's exactly what happened," Charlotte insisted. "The police investigated. They dropped the case."

"Yeah, but you know they only did that because her dad made them," Lexi exclaimed. "Because he didn't want—"

"It's that club," Morgan snapped, sounding more assertive than Josie had ever heard her. "That's when this all started. You guys and that stupid club. Now they're both dead."

"Stop! Just *stop*. There is no conspiracy. You guys sound totally crazy," Charlotte growled, looking around again.

"Oh, what, are you scared someone is gonna hear us?" Lexi said loudly.

Charlotte grabbed her arm, but Lexi wrenched it away. She crossed her arms and looked down at the ground. Morgan seemed like she was about to speak, then closed her mouth.

"This is the way it is, okay? I know you guys don't want it to be this way, but, like, we can't go back," Charlotte said after a moment.

"Okay, you're right," the other girls mumbled, and all three of them hurried away.

Josie looked around to see if anyone had seen the exchange. There were a few reporters on the sidewalk who looked at her with interest, but with the police presence they didn't dare enter the parking lot. She heard a thump and looked up to see Nikki slapping her hand on the passenger side of Josie's car. Josie flipped open the lock, and Nikki climbed in, crying, "What was *that?"* as she got in.

"I have no idea," Josie said.

"What were they talking about? I couldn't hear them, but it looked heated."

"They were arguing about the deaths. Charlotte was insisting that they were exactly what they seemed to be—an accident and a suicide. Lexi and Morgan disagreed."

"Interesting," Nikki said, taking out her phone and tapping in a note. "They think something's rotten here, too."

"At least two of them do. But they backed down when Charlotte pressed them. You know she's got the strongest personality of those girls. They argued with her, but eventually, they backed down."

"Mmm," Nikki said.

"Do you have your car?"

"Nah, I caught a ride with Jesse. He's covering the service," Nikki responded. "I'll call an Uber from your place?"

Josie nodded and leaned her head against the cool glass of the window for a second, then put the car into gear. As interesting as the conversation was, the day was taking its toll, and she was getting a headache. She needed to go home and lie down.

Chapter Thirty-Nine

By the time Sean arrived at Josie's that night, she was a nervous wreck. She knew she had to tell him about the jacket and Marion, but she didn't know how he would react. Would he believe that she didn't know how either of those things had happened? Or would he think she was somehow involved in Amber's death? She waited for what felt like an eternity until the doorbell rang that evening, calling, "It's open," when he finally arrived.

"I really wish you'd lock your door, Jose," he chided as he entered the house, shaking off his jacket and hanging it in the closet.

She waved her hand and then brought her thumb to her mouth, chewing the skin on the side of her nail and taking a seat on the arm of the chair.

"So, what's up?" he asked after a beat.

"Okay, listen, I know the case is closed, but I have some information about Amber Oldham," she began.

"You're right. The case is closed. Have you been poking around?"

She nodded, and he sighed, sitting down on the couch.

"Okay, what have you got?"

She stopped chewing on her thumb and looked at him. "Really? You're not mad?"

"Not yet. Let's see what we're dealing with."

"Okay. Well, first, I went to talk to the neighbors," she began.

"Great."

"Just listen. I only talked to one woman, a nice older lady named Marion O'Donnell. She was awake on the night of Amber's death and looked out the window, and, well, she thinks she saw me in the field around the time of Amber's death," Josie blurted.

Sean looked at her steadily for a moment. "And did she say what you were doing in the field?"

"That's the thing; she said I was just standing there, kind of staring off into space. She said she couldn't be sure it was me, but her description of my pajamas was accurate."

"Wait, you were out in the field in your pajamas in the middle of the night? That makes no sense."

"I know, I know. I thought so, too. But that's not all."

"Oh, boy."

Josie retrieved Amber's jacket from the coat closet, laying it carefully on the coffee table. Sean looked at it for a moment and then looked up at Josie.

"What am I looking at here?" he asked, palms up.

"I think it's Amber's jacket. I can't be sure—it's not like there's a name sewn on the inside or something, but I'm pretty sure I saw her wearing it at school a few times."

"Wait, is this the jacket you were talking about on the morning after her death? The one you said was up on the water tower?"

Josie nodded.

"But how did you get it?"

"I don't know."

"What do you mean, 'you don't know'?"

"I found it in the closet the other night, Sean. I was getting ready to go out and was getting my coat, and…there it was."

"This jacket just magically appeared in your closet?"

"I don't know," she whispered. "I don't know how long it's been there. I don't remember putting it there. I don't know how I got it."

Sean raised his hands to his face and rubbed it vigorously. "Okay. Is that it?"

Josie shook her head.

"Terrific. What else?"

She went to the kitchen and pulled on a pair of rubber dishwashing gloves.

Sean looked at her like she had gone crazy as she walked to the coffee table and reached into the inside jacket pocket, pulling out the poker chip and holding it up. Sean looked puzzled, then abruptly stood up and strode out the front door. He returned with an evidence bag and latex gloves.

"Put that down," he ordered quietly.

Josie did as he instructed.

"Did you handle this without gloves?"

"Yes," she admitted. "When I first found the jacket, I thought it might be mine. I thought maybe Noelle sent it, and I had forgotten about it. After fishing around in the pockets and finding the chip, I pieced it together, but it was already too late."

Sean nodded, pulling on the latex gloves. He picked up the silver chip by its edges and examined it. Then he carefully placed it into a small evidence bag, put the jacket in the larger evidence bag, and pulled off his gloves.

"Okay," he said, taking a deep breath. "I'll run the chip for fingerprints and submit the jacket for DNA, but I expect I'll only find yours and Amber's. I'll also check around and see if anyone else on the squad has seen a poker chip like that before. That little engraving—that's the Greek symbol for omega, right?"

"Right."

Sean nodded. "As far as how the jacket got into your house, I don't know, and at this point, I don't want to know. The case is closed, so even getting these tests run is going to have to be done on the down low."

"What about the other thing?"

Sean sighed, rubbing his eyes again. "Honestly, Jose? I don't know what to think. From the description, it sounds like you were sleepwalking. If that's true, I think you've got a bigger problem on your hands. Have you seen your doctor recently?"

"I've got an appointment next week."

"Maybe you should take it up with her," he said, rising from the sofa. "It's one thing to sleepwalk in your own home, but if you're leaving the house, you're putting yourself—and others—in danger."

"But...do you think I could have seen something that night?"

"Whether you did or didn't is irrelevant. Her death has been ruled accidental, and the case is closed."

"Do you really believe that?"

"It doesn't matter what I believe. That's just the way it is. Now please, do me and yourself a favor, and get some sleep. Talk to your doc. I'll let you know if I find anything."

"I feel like I'm losing my mind," she said, back to her perch on the arm of the chair, chewing her thumb.

He came back and squatted down in front of her. "That's why it's important to take care of yourself, Josie. I don't want to see you have another breakdown, and I know your friends and family don't, either. If you still can't sleep," he posed it more as a question, and Josie nodded. "Then maybe it's time to go to a sleep clinic or something. But it's time to face reality—there's something wrong."

Chapter Forty

Late Tuesday night, in an unprecedented move, the school board sent a mass email announcing that classes would be canceled for the remainder of the week. School would resume the following Monday, hopefully giving the students the time they needed to grieve and recover. Friday afternoon, Franklin Mather called Josie and informed her that the board of The Omega Society had fast-tracked her for membership, if she was still interested. She told him that she was still thinking about it, and when he asked her if there was anything more she'd like to know about the club, she was struck with sudden inspiration.

"Actually, I'd like to do an overnight in one of the guest suites, if that's not a problem," she told him.

"Of course. How is tomorrow?"

"Tomorrow works," she said. "Can I bring guests?"

He paused. "This isn't a party, correct?"

"Oh, no, nothing like that," she laughed. "I'd like to have a couple of my girlfriends join me, if that's all right. Just so I'm not cooped up in a hotel room by myself for the night. If you can arrange it, I'd like to take them to O."

"Of course, no problem. I'll send you an email confirmation. Please respond to that with the names of your guests. I'll also send you a dues schedule and outline our vetting procedures. The board fast-tracked you, but we still have to do our due diligence, you understand."

"No worries, I trust the process," she said.

There was a brief pause on the other end of the line. "Well, lovely, we have you and your friends on the books for Thursday night. Would you care to have dinner at the restaurant before you venture down to the club?"

"Why not?" Josie said. "We'll make a night of it. Thank you very much, Franklin. I appreciate you going to all the trouble."

"Not a problem at all, Ms. Ashbury. I'll put your group down for a seven-thirty reservation. We look forward to seeing you." And with a click, he was gone.

Josie immediately got on a group chat with Nikki, Alex, and Heather and invited them all to go with her. They agreed, although Alex was scheduled to work on Saturday night, so she said she'd have to miss dinner. Heather said she'd have to check with her husband to make sure he was okay staying with the kids by himself.

The women had discussed specific parameters for the evening. Josie assumed everything was bugged with some sort of recording system, be it cameras or audio, so they weren't going to talk about any suspicions or theories while in the vicinity of the club. The goal was to get in, get a look around, see if anything stuck out or, you know, if anyone outright committed a crime in front of them.

Nikki was immediately enthusiastic and called Josie as soon as they stopped messaging. "What's the plan here?" she demanded.

"What do you mean? I thought we'd have a nice night out."

"Don't toy with me, Ashbury. You're up to something."

"I want to do some more digging, that's all," Josie said. "I know there's some sort of tie from this club to Amber. I just have to figure out what it is."

"Well, I have some news for you, if you're ready for it."

"Always."

"You know how I stole that file the other day? Unfortunately, it didn't have too much info, but I did some digging based on what was there and found out that the club is owned by a shell corporation. I tried to find the larger owner, but was routed in a million different directions and ended up looking at companies in Switzerland, Canada, the Cayman Islands, but found nothing at the top. I even talked to Sharon, who knows everything about everyone that goes on in this town. While Sharon had obviously heard of the club, she didn't know any details except that it was a favorite haunt of athletes, celebrities, and politicians and not a place she personally cared to visit."

"Ugh, too bad," said Josie.

"Wait a sec. I'm not finished. You ready for this? We already know that The Omega Society is one of many businesses owned by this shell corporation in Delaware. People set up shell corps in Delaware because it can be done same day, and Delaware has pretty relaxed laws. Here's where it gets interesting, though. According to Sharon's sources, the shell corporations are all tracking back to a company called Cape Town Ventures, which is located in Bermuda but has dealings in countries all over the world. However, Cape Town Ventures uses those shell corporations to funnel money into political campaigns, and guess who one of their biggest beneficiaries is?"

"Clinton Oldham," Josie murmured.

"Bingo," Nikki said. "Among others. But as far as local politicians go, Senator Oldham gets a lot of campaign support from that particular company."

"That is interesting."

"Sharon is as convinced as we are that there's something suspicious about the club, so she'll be stoked that I get to do an overnight visit."

"Just don't get us thrown out until we learn something, okay?" Josie laughed.

"I'll do my best," Nikki promised.

"Wait, what does it mean that the company is a big donor to the Oldham campaign? Is that significant?"

"I don't know yet. My working theory is that the club is a front for illegal activity and they're using it to launder money. Which would mean that, at best, Oldham is accepting laundered funds as campaign contributions."

"And at worst?"

"At worst, since he's a member of the club, he's directly involved in those illegal activities. All I know is I'm excited to get inside and dig around."

"Me too. I feel like we're so close to unlocking this whole thing," Josie said.

"We just need one or two more pieces of the puzzle."

Chapter Forty-One

Regardless of the reason, Josie always looked forward to a night out with the girls. They planned to meet at The Omega Society at six-thirty to scope out the room before dinner. At least Heather and Nikki would; Alex was still scheduled to work but promised she'd meet them at the nightclub by ten. Franklin Mather had sent Josie a fee schedule for the club, and the dues were just as steep as Josie expected—it had to be pricey to keep up those buildings and activities. She responded with the names of her guests, and he sent her instructions for the evening. The room would be ready for them any time after ten, and guests staying in the rooms had their own private entrance. The girls would be in The Alpha Suite, which was on the top floor, and the parking attendant would have their key waiting.

Josie arrived downtown at six, pulled into the garage, and stopped at the office to get the key. The garage manager pointed her towards a specific area of the underground lot where four parking spaces had been assigned for the evening and handed her a key card. Josie was a little surprised; she had expected a physical key since all the rooms seemed to have their original oak doors with brass keyholes. Near the parking spaces, Josie could see a glassed-in lobby with elevators that led up to the rooms. Once in the elevator, she noticed several things. First, this elevator not only went to the upper floors, but down as well, with an indication on the buttons that the bottom level was O. Second, unlike the elevators to the main entrance, this elevator did not have an attendant. She imagined that was by design since the club hosted many high-profile guests who likely did not want to deal with more staff than was necessary. She did, however, need her key card to operate the elevator, and she pressed the button for five and began her ascent.

The Alpha Suite did not disappoint. There were two bedrooms, a lounge area, and a kitchenette complete with dishes, glasses, and high-quality flatware. A coffee maker with a built-in bean grinder sat next to a small refrigerator stocked like a minibar. The décor matched the rest of the club with beautiful dark wood and rich colors. The furniture did have a slightly more modern feel than the common areas, but it was just as expensive looking. There was something vaguely familiar about the room, but Josie couldn't quite pinpoint what it was. She almost felt like she had been there before.

A gift basket sat on the table with a bottle of Veuve Clicquot, artisanal cheeses, crackers, dried fruits, and a note from Franklin Mather.

"Ms. Ashbury—The Omega Club welcomes you and your guests. Please let us know if there's anything we can do to make your visit more pleasant. We hope you enjoy your stay."

The champagne and cheeses were cold to the touch, and Josie wondered if the parking attendant had announced her arrival so someone could run the basket in. She popped the Veuve and cheeses into the fridge and noticed the basket had been resting on a wooden tray with a cutting board and cheese knife on it. She moved the tray over to the dining table, which housed a leather-bound book containing the restaurant menu and concierge number. Josie was surprised to find that the guest rooms offered twenty-four-hour room service, though from a more limited menu than the restaurant. The list of services available through the concierge was enormous, with everything from tickets to sporting events to spa treatments available with just a phone call.

The bedrooms of the suite were connected by one large bathroom complete with two sinks, a steam shower, and a large tub. Josie thought for a fleeting moment about taking a bath, but she knew she didn't have time. She snapped a photo of the tub; it was the kind she wanted to install when she had her bathroom redone.

She heard the robotic lock disengage, and Nikki spilled into the room with her rolling suitcase.

"Holy smokes, Jose, this place…" Nikki let out a low wolf whistle.

"Right?" Josie said. "It's pretty fancy."

"I don't know if fancy even begins to describe it. It's incredible," Nikki said, running around to check out all the nooks and crannies Josie had just acquainted herself with. She quickly found the goodies in the fridge, popped the champagne, and was pouring a glass by the time Josie turned back around. She handed Josie a flute and plopped down on the couch, taking a long swig.

"You know, a gal could get used to this," she said.

"Don't," laughed Josie. "Remember, we're here to investigate, not pamper ourselves. Speaking of which, go check out the bathroom."

Nikki raced through the bedroom and shouted, "Holy crap!" and Josie could hear her turning the steam shower on and off. "Who are these people?" she said as she emerged, wide-eyed.

"The rich and famous," Josie answered, doing her best Robin Leach *Lifestyles of the Rich and Famous* impression.

"Are you sure you were an actor?" Nikki teased.

Josie tossed a pillow at her as the door to the suite engaged once more. Heather entered, looking just as bewildered as Nikki had.

"I just left a house where people were throwing Spaghetti-Os at each other," she deadpanned.

"I could throw some expensive cheese at you, if it'll make you feel more at home," Nikki said, handing her a glass of champagne.

Heather slipped out of her coat and opened the closet. "There are real hangers in here. I don't think I've seen real hangers in a hotel since…well, ever."

"Welcome to the one percent," Nikki grinned.

Josie glanced at the clock. "We've got about fifteen minutes until our dinner reservation downstairs. I'm going to change and touch up."

The girls nodded in agreement, with Nikki dragging her bag into the room with Josie and Heather into the other one. They all met in the bathroom and giggled and talked while they freshened up their lipstick and mascara.

"This place is amazing," Heather said, gesturing at the vanity with perfect lighting.

"I know. I'm taking notes for my own remodel," Josie laughed.

"When is Alex coming? Is she still working 'til ten?" Nikki piped up.

"When I talked to her earlier, she said she was going to try to get out by eight, so maybe she'll make it to dinner. If not, she'll definitely be at the club tonight," Josie answered.

"Can she get in?" Heather asked.

"They've got her name at the door," Josie said. "No passwords needed this evening."

When the ladies were satisfied with their appearances, they rode the elevator down to the restaurant level and sat at the bar. They had just put in their drink orders when a gorgeous young host came to escort them to their table.

As he walked away, Nikki mumbled, "Boy, they're really pulling out all the stops to try to get you as a member," which received a peal of laughter from Josie and Heather. Josie was having such a good time that she almost forgot why they were there. Almost.

* * *

Dinner was delicious, and they put down a bottle of cabernet between the three of them. When Josie asked for the bill, she was informed quietly by their server, "Courtesy of the club, Ms. Ashbury. Mr. Mather sends his regards."

Josie put down a large tip—she wasn't sure if she was supposed to, but she did it anyway—and they headed for the club.

Once in the elevator, Heather asked, "What was the damage?" and pulled out her wallet.

"The club covered it," Josie answered.

Nikki gasped. "Celebrities really do get all the free stuff! They must really want you as a member."

CHAPTER FORTY-ONE

"Or they'll bill me later, once I've signed the paperwork."

The women laughed their way off the elevator and walked down a long hallway leading to a lobby similar to the one upstairs. The hallway appeared to be a tunnel between the two buildings, and Josie wondered if there was maybe something to that Reddit thread about the underground network connecting the clubs. Having no coats to check with the coat girl, they descended into the anteroom and ordered drinks.

"Wow, this is complicated," Heather said.

"Right?" Nikki answered.

As they picked up their drinks, Alex entered the room looking gorgeous in a simple black dress similar to the ones the hostesses were required to wear.

"This is too complicated. Am I not in the club yet?" she demanded as she sidled up to the bar and ordered a vodka soda.

Josie laughed and hugged her. "Almost," she said.

"Do I have a lot of catching up to do?" Alex said, gesturing at them.

"Not too much. We just finished dinner and only drank one bottle of wine," Heather assured her.

"Only," Alex laughed.

They made their way into the main room of the club. To Josie's surprise, she was able to let go and have a good time. They danced, sat on the big couches and talked, and caught up on their weeks, all while diligently alternating two waters for every drink. In their text chain, they had decided they all needed to keep their wits about them (and Nikki was sort of on assignment). They had also decided it was best to assume they were always being watched and overheard.

"I wonder what you have to do to get in on one of the poker games," Alex said, craning her neck.

"I think you request it through the bartender," Josie said, stifling a yawn. "But you also have to be a member."

"Too bad," Alex said. "I could go for a game of Texas Hold 'Em. I bet I'd hand these guys their asses."

"Okay, ladies, I'm an old lady with little kids and a job that I have to be up for pretty early," Heather said after she caught Josie's yawn. "Can we call it a night?"

They agreed that it was time to go. Alex needed to use the restroom, so they waited as she wandered down the long hallway with the restrooms and poker rooms. When she returned, she had a funny look on her face.

"What?" Josie demanded.

"I think I just got invited to a poker game, but I can't be sure. Some guy just gave me this." Holding her hand low in the center of the four of them, she opened her palm to reveal a solid silver poker chip. "The thing is, when I peeked into the rooms while I was on my way to the bathroom, they all looked like they were playing with regular chips."

"I've seen one of those before," Josie said quietly, glancing over her shoulder to see if anyone was paying particular attention to them. Nobody seemed to be. She held out her hand, and Alex discreetly passed her the chip. "I found one exactly like this in Amber's jacket. Who gave this to you?"

"Ummmm," Alex said, craning her neck to look around. "He's gone. Looked like an athlete, though. Tall black guy, super jacked, very handsome. Wearing a dark suit."

"Basketball player tall or football player tall?" Nikki asked.

"Mmm, probably too short to be a basketball center, but built like a point guard or a football kicker," Alex answered. "He was probably six-three, two hundred pounds. Slim, but built."

"Ladies, are we ready?" Heather prodded, swooping her arms around them and gently guiding them towards the exit.

"We'll talk about it tomorrow after we leave," Josie murmured to Alex, who nodded. They were all looking forward to a good night of sleep in the plush comfort of their suite.

* * *

The next morning, Heather had to leave early, and she did not disturb the other girls on her way out. By seven-thirty, the other women were awake, and Nikki had made coffee. At quarter to eight, a knock came at the door, and

Josie was pleasantly surprised by a host wheeling a room service tray covered with a linen tablecloth laden with fruit, pastries, breakfast sandwiches, and orange juice.

"Compliments of the club," he announced. Josie tipped him and shooed him out the door while Nikki and Alex dove in.

"Mmmm, this is exactly what I needed," Alex said through bites of a bagel and egg sandwich.

Nikki nodded. "What do you guys have on deck today?"

"Work tonight," Alex said through another mouthful.

"Not a lot this afternoon," Josie answered. "I do have a date with Jake later."

"Ooooh," Nikki said, waggling her fingers at Josie. Josie could tell she wanted to say more, but a glance over Josie's head at the corners of the room made her stop. "Well, I've got to get to The Press," she said, going to the bedroom to pack up her stuff.

While Nikki was packing, Josie wrote Alex a note on the club stationery and passed it to her as she asked, "Are you seeing Tommy this week?"

"We're going to Masquerade," Alex said in a low voice, blushing as she casually tucked the note under her. "I think there was some talk of us getting coffee later. Speaking of which, I should probably head out, too."

"I guess I'll get going as well," Josie sighed, heaving herself out of the big, comfortable chair she had curled up in.

They rode the elevator down to the parking garage and hugged goodbye. As instructed in the note, Alex called Josie from her car as soon as they were on the road.

"Okay, what's up with the poker chip?" she demanded immediately.

"I found one in Amber's jacket," Josie answered, and proceeded to fill her in. "I gave it to Sean to check for fingerprints. I'm pretty sure she had the jacket on the night of her death."

"Pretty sure?" Alex said. "What does that mean?"

"It means, I think I remember seeing it on the water tower, but obviously the police didn't find it because it ended up in my house," Josie sighed.

"And you don't know how it got there?" Alex said slowly.

"No. I must've, I don't know, taken it or...." Josie trailed off.

"You don't remember?"

"Not exactly."

"Well, you must've taken it if it ended up in your house," Alex concluded. "Have you found any other strange things in your house that you don't remember bringing home?"

Josie thought for a second. "Not unless you count buying stuff on Amazon after a couple glasses of wine," she joked. "But seriously, not that I can recall. Stuff has been out of place, though. I've found things out on counters that I could've sworn I put away, the cats were locked in the basement the other night, and I *never* do that."

"Have you been sleepwalking?"

Josie paused. She hadn't told the girls about her conversation with Marion. If she told them, she'd have to admit that something was wrong, and she wasn't quite ready to do that.

"I don't think so," she lied.

"When is your next doctor's appointment?"

"This week. Wednesday, I believe."

"Okay, good. *Don't cancel,*" Alex said. "I mean it. With all the stress of the last couple of weeks, you need to go. When was the last time you saw her?"

"Before Amber's death," Josie admitted.

"Okay, well, yeah," Alex said. "You really need to go. Promise me."

"I promise," Josie said.

Alex seemed satisfied with her answer, so she dropped it. "Hey, I'm almost home. Talk later?"

"Sounds good."

Josie had just pulled into her driveway as well, and she quickly pulled up her texts and emails, hoping for something from Sean. No such luck. How long could a fingerprint analysis take? Unless she had totally messed it up by handling the chip. She kicked herself for being so stupid. She headed inside, looking forward to the unconditional snuggles of the cats, and wasn't surprised to find she had left the front door unlocked. She dropped her bag in the foyer and bent down to embrace Monroe and Presley, who were running towards her eagerly. As she stroked their heads and they rolled around, she decided to go for a run. Although it was cold outside, she was grateful to have the luxury of running later in the day, and she had actually slept a little last night. Hopefully, this meant a break in her seemingly endless streak of sleepless nights.

Chapter Forty-Two

Later that night, Josie and Jake were supposed to go out, but after the night out with the girls, she didn't have the energy. When she told him, he offered to come over with Chinese food and suggested they watch a movie, which sounded amazing to her.

"How did last night go?" he asked as they dug into the fried rice.

"Good," she answered through a mouthful of egg roll. "I mean, it was uneventful for the most part, but good."

"No stumbling into secret back rooms full of cloaked men?" he joked.

"Not yet," she smiled. "One weird thing did happen, though. Some guy gave Alex this silver poker chip."

She pulled it out of her purse and slid it across the table. Jake picked it up to examine it.

"Isn't this the same—"

"As the one I found in Amber's jacket, mmm-hmm," Josie cut him off.

"I guess that makes sense, if Amber was working at the club," Jake shrugged, putting the chip down on the table. Do you think it's some sort of signal?"

"No idea. I mean, it could be something as simple as an invitation to a back-room poker game, but it was awfully late in the night when the dude gave it to Alex. Plus, he didn't say anything; he just kind of slipped it to her and disappeared."

"That is odd. But you think it's somehow tied to Amber's death?"

"I don't know. And I don't have any idea how I would begin to find that out. I'm beginning to think that maybe Clinton Oldham was right; Amber's death was either an accident or a suicide, and Tony's overdose was the same.

The poker chips could just be a coincidence."

Jake wrinkled his brow. "Do you really believe that?"

"I don't know what to believe," Josie sighed. "If both of them were murdered, somebody's doing an awfully good job of making it look accidental."

"And the cops have totally abandoned their investigation into Amber's death, full stop?" Jake asked.

"They didn't have a choice. Even if they wanted to, Oldham called them off. Continuing with the investigation would be career suicide after being given a direct order from the commissioner."

"That's too bad," Jake said.

"It is, and it isn't. I may be making something out of nothing here. But even if there is some grander conspiracy going on with the club, I don't even know if there's a way to get to them. There are so many powerful people that are members—judges, prominent businessmen, celebrities, athletes—they're totally connected. If I were even to hint at an accusation, they would probably sue me, at best. Or put out a hit on me."

"Like the mafia."

"More like the Illuminati. Maybe those Redditors are right," Josie joked.

"Well, let's talk about something lighter. Are you ready for Masquerade this weekend?"

"Just about," Josie said distractedly.

"I'm stoked. I've never been to a Masquerade ball," Jake said as he grabbed their plates and the wine bottle to take with them into the living room. Josie picked up their glasses and followed him.

"There's still one thing that's bugging me," she said as they scrolled through Netflix, searching for movies.

"Oh, yeah? What's that?"

"Okay, let's say the club is responsible for Amber's death. That I understand; if they're doing something illegal and she was part of it or found out about it, they'd have motive. But why Tony? I mean, I guess they could've just assumed that she told him about what was going on at the club. But that seems like a stretch. If they assumed Tony knew, wouldn't they also

193

conclude that her other friends knew?"

"Maybe Charlotte told them that Tony knew," Jake pointed out. "She's still working there, right? Maybe she's feeding them information."

"Maybe," Josie chewed her lip. "But I don't see Charlotte doing that. Yes, she's a pain in the ass, but she would know that anyone she fingered would be in harm's way. I don't think she'd do that to Tony."

"Fair point," Jake conceded. "Maybe they really do have eyes and ears everywhere."

Josie found the thought of that deeply unsettling, but she tried to shake off her discomfort as they settled in to watch another classic '80s movie, *The Breakfast Club*. By the time the movie was finished and she was leading Jake back to her bedroom, she had all but forgotten about the club.

Chapter Forty-Three

Monday afternoon, Josie drove the short distance from her house to the Burnes residence, bracing herself for a fight. She knew she was getting closer to the truth, but she also knew Charlotte was going to be difficult. She didn't know if Charlotte would even talk to her or if she would simply slam the door in Josie's face.

The Burnes' house was very much like the Oldham estate, just without security guards and a gatehouse. Pretty and stately, the gray stone mansion sat on Lake Street about a half mile away from the Oldhams. Amber and Charlotte had played together as little kids, just as Josie and her friends had. Well, not exactly like Josie and her friends. These girls' playdates were probably facilitated by nannies while their parents were off jet-setting. Josie winced at the thought. She needed to keep in mind that no matter what Charlotte's involvement was, she had lost her best friend in all of this.

Josie rang the bell, and when no one answered, she slammed on the cast iron knocker shaped like a large lock with a thud, thud, thud. Still, no one answered, but Charlotte's car was in the driveway. Josie was leaning over the railing and peering in the large bay window when a voice behind her called, "What the hell are you doing here?"

After catching herself from falling into the rose bushes, Josie whipped around to see Charlotte stalking up the driveway. On the street, a black car that looked like it might have just backed out sped away, but Josie couldn't see the make or license plate. Though gorgeous as ever, Charlotte looked miserable. There were dark circles under her pretty eyes, and her mascara was smudged at the edges. She looked like she had been crying.

"Looking for some answers," Josie said.

Charlotte nodded, looking weary. "Come inside with me, and I'll tell you whatever you want to know." She took out her keys and fumbled until she found the right one.

Satisfied, Josie waited as Charlotte unlocked the bolts on the door. "Did someone just drop you off?"

"What? No. I mean, yeah, like, my physics study partner. We, uh, have a paper due."

What was with this girl and the lies? Josie decided to let it go for now. She needed to focus on the task at hand and not worry about who Charlotte was running around with after school.

"Come in," Charlotte said, finally swinging the door open.

Josie followed her into the house, which was every bit as lush and extravagant as the Oldham estate, but in richer colors. Instead of the subdued beiges and creams, the Burnes' house was filled with reds, golds, and greens. Charlotte led Josie into the farmhouse-style kitchen, complete with a restaurant-grade range and a faucet over the stove for pasta that was so popular in kitchen renovations these days. After handing Josie a glass of filtered water, she flopped onto a barstool at the enormous kitchen island and sighed, "What do you want to know?"

"I want to know how long you and Amber were working at the club," Josie began carefully. She knew Charlotte was volatile, but she was also obviously fragile, and Josie wanted to tread lightly.

"Around the middle of summer," Charlotte answered.

"And are you working there under your real name?"

Charlotte shifted uncomfortably. "We weren't at first, but, like, somebody must've found out who we really were at some point."

"The guy at the football game," Josie said, not really asking a question.

Charlotte nodded.

"And they let you keep working there? Even when they found out you were underage?"

"It's, like, complicated. That guy, he isn't really—he doesn't, like, *work*-work for the club. He's, like, a consultant."

"Ah. So technically, officially, the club doesn't know."

"Right."

"Why? Why not just get a job at The Oaks or someplace legal?"

"It was fun," Charlotte shrugged. "We got to hang out with all these, like, celebrities and athletes and stuff. They wanted to be around us. They thought we were, like, interesting. Not just anyone can get a job there, you know."

"It made you feel important. And you didn't mind that being groped and ogled by creepy old dudes also came with the job?"

"It's not like that. A lot of the guys there are young. And the women are cool, too. They're so smart and successful, and they have, like, connections for jobs. Plus, it's not like it's easy to get in, you know? There's *standards.*"

Digesting this, Josie studied the teenager standing across the kitchen island. Though Charlotte was tall and beautiful and could pass for twenty-five, she was still just a kid. "But Charlotte, why not just meet those people through your family? Your parents must introduce you to all kinds of amazing people," she finally asked.

"Because this way, they wanted to know *me.* I wasn't just Frank and Kelly's daughter, I was, like, an individual," Charlotte replied. "And we were bored. I know it sounds stupid or whatever, but, like, there's only so much to do in this town, no matter how much money you've got. Yeah, we could've just gotten IDs and, like, used them to buy beer or whatever, but that's so...pedestrian," Charlotte said, waving her hand. Moments like that made it easy to forget that she was, in fact, seventeen. She went on. "We wanted to do something, like, exciting with our summer, so we started doing this...this kind of game." Now Charlotte hesitated. It was the first time Josie had seen her look even slightly unsure of herself.

"What kind of a game?" Josie prompted.

"We were just...I don't know, like, seeing what we could get away with. 'Pushing our boundaries,' or whatever. It started out with dumb stuff like seeing if we could get into bars and clubs. Then we found O, and Amber and I ended up in sort of, like, a bet to see if we could get hired...and then we did. We weren't going to actually, like, work there, but then we were like, why not?"

"What about the other girls?"

"Lexi and Morgan? No way," Charlotte snorted. "They're both a little, like, conservative for that sort of thing. They wanted nothing to do with it."

"So what happened with Amber?"

"What do you mean?"

"I mean, how did your friend end up dead?" Josie said.

Charlotte looked as though Josie had slapped her. Then, she shook it off. "I don't know what happened," she said coolly. "I think she was seeing some other guy. I mean, Tony certainly didn't, you know, care. Look, I know you're going to, like, ask me a bunch more questions, but I don't know much about it, okay."

"Amber met a guy at the club?"

"Like I said, I don't know. I thought I saw her duck out with someone this one night, but I…I didn't get a good look at the guy."

"And she wouldn't tell you anything about him."

Charlotte shook her head. "She was real, like, secretive about him, you know, not like I've ever seen her. I think she met him at the beginning of summer, and they were, like, whatever until…"

"And you think this guy is the one who got her pregnant," Josie said.

"Look, I'm tired of this, okay? I just want to move on. Amber is dead. She got herself into an awful situation, and she couldn't handle it," Josie thought she saw her lip quiver, but that moment of vulnerability was gone as quickly as it came.

"And Tony?"

"Amber was Tony's best friend. He was, like, distraught, obviously. I guess he couldn't handle her death, so he started doing drugs or whatever. Or maybe they were, like, doing drugs together. You know, before."

"I see," Josie said, taking a drink. "You think their deaths were *both* accidents?"

"Does it really matter?" Charlotte heaved another in a long line of sighs. "Whether or not Amber fell or, like, jumped, we're still in the same spot, right?"

"I suppose so," Josie said, getting to her feet. "Oh, one more thing. Do you know anything about this?" she reached into her pocket and pulled out the silver poker chip, holding it out between her thumb and index finger.

Any composure Charlotte had up until that point fell away. Her face went ashen, and her eyes widened, then she dropped her gaze to the floor. Her mouth remained firmly closed, but Josie could see her jaw was clenched.

"I see," Josie said, putting the chip back in her pocket. As she turned to leave, Charlotte stopped her.

"I—I'm not doing it anymore," she said quietly. "I quit. I'm done with that place."

"Let's just hope that that place is done with you," Josie said grimly. Charlotte didn't respond, but Josie had a feeling she was thinking the same thing.

Chapter Forty-Four

While she was at the Burnes residence, Josie received a text message from Sean asking her to call him. After she was in the car with the Bluetooth connected, she ordered the phone to "Call Sean."

"Hey," he barked.

"Hey. What's up?"

"I got the fingerprint analysis back on the baggie and the poker chip."

"And?"

"And there were not two, but three sets of prints—yours, Amber's, and an unidentified set. I ran them through our system, but nothing came up."

"Damn," Josie said.

"Well, maybe," he said. "Maybe not. I put in a call to your brother to see if he'd do me a favor and run them through the FBI database and see if they got a match. They've got access to a lot more records than we do."

"Oh, good thinking. I hope he finds something."

"Me too. Keep your fingers crossed."

"I just had an interesting conversation with Charlotte Burnes," Josie said. She filled Sean in on Alex's experience at the club and Charlotte's reaction when Josie showed her the chip.

Damn," Sean said once she finished. "Please keep yourself safe. The people who belong to that club are heavy hitters. Who knows what they'd do if they knew you were snooping around."

"I will," she promised. "I'll call you later."

"Bye."

Once she got home, she spent some time with the cats and had just settled down on the couch with a book when someone knocked on her door. She tried to remember if she had made plans with anyone for tonight. She couldn't think of anything, and door-to-door soliciting was prohibited in Lakeview. When she opened her door, she was surprised to see her brother, John, standing there, his hands shoved deep in the pockets of his wool dress coat.

"Well, let me in, would you? It's freezing out here."

"Oh, sorry, I'm just surprised to see you. Did we have plans?"

"No. No, we didn't, but given the call that I got from Sean Sullivan a little while ago, I thought maybe a visit was in order," he said, stepping inside and removing his coat. John was about six foot two, and with his dark hair and green eyes, he looked like a younger version of their father.

"How are the girls?"

"Fine, fine, everybody's fine. Listen, Josie, what have you gotten yourself into here? I thought the police closed the investigation into Amber Oldham's death on the commissioner's orders. Now you're finding evidence in your house, and I've got Sean sending me unidentified fingerprint samples?"

"Oh. How much did Sean tell you?" she asked.

"Enough."

"All right. You obviously know that I don't think Amber's death was an accident. Tony Burgess' wasn't either. Amber and her girlfriend got jobs earlier in the summer at O, that new social club affiliated with The Omega Society. The club doesn't hire hostesses under twenty-one, so the girls used fake IDs. But that's the least of my worries. I'm pretty sure the club is involved in some sort of illegal activity. That poker chip? I think members give them to the hostesses to signal that they want to have sex. Plus, Amber isn't the only girl who died of a fentanyl overdose that's linked to the club. Last month, two young women were found dead of overdoses, and they both worked at the club. I think the club is engaged in prostitution and possibly drug dealing and is using O as a front."

John had been silent while Josie rambled on. One of his many gifts as an FBI agent was his stoicism. He hadn't so much as flinched as Josie laid out her theory, and now he sat quietly, absorbing the information.

"Even if what you're saying is true, do you have any proof?" he asked.

"No," she admitted. "Nothing but two silver poker chips and a teenage girl who may or may not be willing to talk."

John ran his hand through his hair. "I mean, Josie, this is quite an accusation. Let's say I could get an investigation set up to look into your claims; these things can take months, even years to play out. And that's if we even find anything. The people running The Omega Society are smart, rich, and well-connected. People like that rarely get sloppy, and when they do, they have the means to make it disappear."

"But two kids are dead, John," Josie said quietly. "And two young women. I think Amber was maybe going to go to the authorities."

"Have you found anything to indicate that she was going to blow the whistle?"

"No," Josie admitted.

"I see. And you don't have any evidence to back up your theories. Even if what you're saying is true, there's nothing to indicate that the club had any involvement in these deaths. And again, even if there was," he continued as she opened her mouth to speak. "They have enough connections to bury something like this. Or worse, you."

"You're not going to do anything?"

"I didn't say that," he said. "Unfortunately, it's just going to take some time. I'm aware of the Reddit conspiracy threads about the club, and you're not the first person that's claimed the club is engaged in illegal activity."

"Of course, if you have money in this country, you can get away with anything," she spat.

"That's more true than I'd like it to be," John said gently. "Look, Josie, please trust me. I'll keep looking into this. But do me a favor—no more recon on your own. Don't join this club just to try to dig around. I don't want to wake up one day and find that you've disappeared."

"Fine," she sighed. She knew he was right. The people that belonged to the club could likely get away with just about anything. She wondered if they had pressured Clinton Oldham to talk to the police commissioner and have the investigation dropped.

"Jose?" John said, snapping his fingers in front of her eyes.

"Sorry, thinking," she mumbled.

"I've got to run," he said, standing to put on his coat. "When was the last time you slept?"

"I sleep all the time—"

"A full night," he interrupted, looking at her pointedly.

"It's been a while."

"When was the last time you saw the doctor?"

"I have an appointment tomorrow."

"Good," he said, opening the door. "Maybe have her give you something to help you sleep, eh?"

"We'll see," she said, hugging him. "Kiss the girls for me, and tell Katie I said hello."

He gave her a salute before closing the door behind him. Josie made sure to lock it, checked the back door as well, and armed her security system. Maybe she was being paranoid, but at this point, she wasn't willing to take any chances. Plus, she was on the club's radar now, and as far-fetched as she knew it might be, that made her feel like she was being watched.

Chapter Forty-Five

On Wednesday after school, Josie drove to a building adjacent to Lakeview Hospital, where mental health services were conducted. She had a long overdue appointment with her doctor. As she entered the waiting room, which was decorated in an overly comfortable fashion with a huge bookcase of self-help books along the north wall, she pressed the doorbell to alert Dr. Gupta of her arrival. Dr. Gupta shared the office with several other doctors and counselors, but Josie never seemed to be in the waiting room with another patient, whether by design or simply coincidence.

Josie had been in regular therapy since her early twenties when she started gaining success and dealing with the pressures of Hollywood. She went at least once a month and found it incredibly helpful with managing her stress. She believed that everyone should have access to a therapist; the world would be a much friendlier place if everyone had a weekly appointment with a mental health professional. Since the incident last year, she had upped her sessions to at least weekly, with the occasional second appointment if she was feeling particularly strained. Sometimes she would do the second appointment virtually, a wonderfully convenient option in the modern world.

While she was waiting, she picked up a book, 'How to Heal Your Life.' Flipping through, she found daily affirmations, exercises, and meditations. She wondered how often saying, 'Today is going to be a really, really good day,' actually worked for people. Though she appreciated the calming effects of meditation, she had never understood affirmations. Were you just hypnotizing yourself into believing something was true? Could looking in a mirror and saying, 'Life brings me good experiences,' really alter the course of your life? She thought she was just as likely to find a body on a day when she stared at herself saying, 'I am a joyful breeze entering a room,' as not.

"Josie?" she heard a voice call. Dr. Priya Gupta stood in the doorway to her office, dressed casually in dark jeans and a sweater. At their first appointment, Josie had liked Dr. Gupta's informality; some of the other psychiatrists she had met showed up in lab coats, bringing to mind unpleasant images of hospitals and sickness. Josie appreciated that Dr. Gupta dressed like she was meeting a friend, and her sessions often felt as though she was chatting with a girlfriend.

"How are you feeling today, Josie?" Dr. Gupta said in slightly accented English.

"Kind of tired, stressed, just generally discontent."

"It's been a while since I've seen you."

"I know. It's been a hectic couple of weeks."

"Yes, I've been watching the news. These were students of yours?"

Josie nodded.

"I see. These deaths must have been especially painful for you," Dr. Gupta said.

Out of nowhere, a sob escaped Josie's lips. She felt like the dam inside of her holding back a flood of emotions had suddenly burst. Dr. Gupta passed her a box of tissues as Josie tried to compose herself, feeling a sense of relief as she was able to let out some of the grief that she had been carrying.

"Remember, it's okay to cry. It's not a weakness. Everyone cries," Dr. Gupta reminded her. "It can be cathartic."

"Everything's just been ha-, happening so fa-, fast, I haven't had time to stop and f-, feel anything," Josie hiccupped.

"I understand; take your time."

After about a minute, Josie managed to get her breath under control enough to be able to speak. She blew her nose. "Okay, I think I'm better now," she said with a weak smile.

Dr. Gupta returned the smile. "How have you been sleeping?"

"Puh," Josie made a noise. "I haven't, really. I catch one or two hours here and there, but not through the night."

"Mmm," Dr. Gupta made a note. "Have you been doing the relaxation exercises we talked about?"

"No," Josie admitted.

"Okay, Josie, you must do these. I'm still very worried about your sleeping habits. Lack of sleep can lead to a whole host of other problems, not to mention that you pose a danger to yourself even during the day. I know you don't want to take medication, and that is okay, but you must try something, or you're going to end up in the hospital one way or another."

Josie nodded. Dr. Gupta was right. She had been slacking on her meditation and relaxation exercises, and they would most certainly help her if she would just do them.

"And what about your hallucinations? Have they been aggravated by the lack of sleep?"

"Yes," Josie said reluctantly.

"See, this is what I'm talking about. You know why you're having these episodes. And they are made worse by your insomnia. We must find a way to solve both problems, or I'm going to have to recommend a hospital stay. But ultimately, the problem is internal. Until you are able to forgive yourself for the death of your parents, you're not going to be able to recover."

"I know. I just can't stop. If I hadn't flown in for Masquerade last year right after James and I broke up, and if Tommy and I hadn't drunk too much and had my parents drive us home…."

Last year on the night of Masquerade, Josie flew back to Cleveland, as she did every year, to attend the ball, and she had brought Tommy as her date. When she and Tommy arrived together in his '69 Mustang, the paparazzi had mistaken him for a new boyfriend. Neither of them gave much thought to this at the beginning of the evening. After drinking and dancing all night, they had decided to leave his car in the garage and take a car service home when her parents had offered to drive them. They had taken a car service to the ball, and neither of them were drinkers. So they all piled into the Mustang, Josie, and Tommy in the backseat and their parents up front, just

206

like when they were kids.

However, the paparazzi decided to follow them that night. The weather was terrible, an ice storm like tonight, and Josie's father was having enough trouble keeping the Mustang on the road without worrying about the car that kept flying up on their bumper. He took his eyes off the road for one second, just enough time to take a curve a little too fast, and Josie and Tommy's lives changed forever. Josie and Tommy had escaped with minor injuries, but her parents had not survived the crash. Whoever had been chasing them took off into the night, leaving Josie's life in pieces.

She recovered quickly and returned to work, but could not pull herself together. Finally, she had a very public breakdown on set during a day of filming. Production had been pissed off when she abruptly decided to leave the show, but ultimately the studio backed down after realizing that trapping a star into her contract amid a mental health crisis would not be good for their image. She promised to try to return to the show after she recovered, but a year later, she was still in Lakeview, trying to come to terms with her parents' deaths.

"Yes, Josephine, but there were other things, other contributing factors that you leave out of the story you tell yourself. Those photographers shouldn't have been chasing you. And there was a terrible ice storm. All of these things played a part. And what was the alternative? Should you or your brother have driven drunk? Do you think your parents would rather that it was you?"

"No," Josie whispered. "But if I had just stayed in LA...."

"Josephine, the story you are telling yourself is much worse than what happened. We've talked about this. You have written yourself into the role of the villain when this was an accident. Your brother understands that it was an accident, right? He doesn't blame you. And your other brothers as well. At some point, you have to stop torturing yourself."

"I know," Josie conceded. "That's one of the reasons I'm planning to go to Masquerade this year. I mean, aside from the fact that it's an important fundraiser for the Cleveland Animal Protective League. I'm hoping it will help me continue to heal. Tommy's going, too."

"Listen, I know that you do not want to check yourself into the hospital, but I think it's time to consider some options," Dr. Gupta rose and pulled out a brochure from her desk drawer. "This is a rehabilitation facility. They treat a lot of things, but many people go there who are having trouble coping, having exhaustion, et cetera. I think you should consider doing a ninety-day program."

Josie turned the brochure over in her hands. "I'll think about it. I'd have to talk to the school board and see if I can even take the time. I made a commitment."

"Please, think hard. The way things are going for you—I don't see a good ending with the path you are on. You are on a disastrous trajectory, and it's not a matter of if; it's a matter of when."

Chapter Forty-Six

The visit with Dr. Gupta left Josie feeling confused and worried, and when she awoke the next morning, she felt twice as cloudy as the previous day. She forced herself on a run and found that the cold wind helped clear the cobwebs. By the time she got to school, she almost felt like herself. She decided to check on Charlotte during one of the breaks between classes, but when she looked at the attendance record, she found that Charlotte was absent. Hopefully, she hadn't upset her too much during their conversation. Charlotte was a tough cookie, but she was still a kid who had lost her best friend, and the cracks were starting to show.

As she was leaving the English office on her way to her next class, she saw Jake pop his head out of his classroom, and her blood froze. The masquerade, It was tomorrow night. Josie had been so distracted she had forgotten to get a dress. She forced a smile and started down the hall towards him.

"Hey," he said, taking a few steps to meet her. "I've been trying to call you."

"I know. I'm so sorry. Things have been a little crazy." She made a crazy face, sticking out her tongue, then immediately regretted it. Super awkward.

Jake didn't seem to mind. "We still on for tomorrow night?"

"Absolutely."

"Great. I'm picking up my tux after work. A regular, like, Zorro mask is fine, right? I've never been to a Masquerade ball before," he said.

"I'm sure that'll be fine. It's mostly the women who wear elaborate masks; a lot of men choose to wear simple masks."

"Good, good," Jake said, glancing at the clock. "I'd better let you go. The bell is about to ring. Pick you up at seven?"

"Perfect," Josie said, looking up and down the hall to make sure they were alone before she stood up on her tiptoes to give him a quick kiss.

The bell rang, and students flooded the halls. As she walked away, she spun to look at him once and give him a little wave, then she pulled out her cell phone and began frantically texting her stylist in LA.

"SOS! 9-1-1! Need black tie gown stat. Can you help?" she typed.

Noelle, a twenty-something design phenom with blue hair, answered almost immediately. "Got you, girl. When?"

"Tomorrow night," Josie texted back with a grimacing face emoji. "I'll owe you big time."

"No worries. I'll overnight it," Noelle wrote back, with a blowing kiss emoji.

Noelle was amazing. Josie found her back when she worked on her first big movie, and Noelle had essentially built Josie's fashion image. Josie still had Noelle pick out clothes for her every season, even though she wasn't in Hollywood. Along with the clothes, Noelle sent her photos of outfits perfectly assembled right down to the accessories. She had been a godsend when Josie was being photographed regularly by the paparazzi and saved her from looking like a schlub most of the time.

Once she had finished teaching her first two classes, Josie packed up her computer bag and was about to go to the English office for a break when she was accosted in the hall by Morgan and Lexi, both looking extremely worried.

"Girls?" she said as they neared.

"Ms. Ashbury, have you seen Charlotte today?" Lexi asked anxiously.

"No, she's out today," Josie said. "I checked the attendance record this morning."

The girls exchanged a look. They both looked like they hadn't slept, and their normally perky features were drawn and hollow.

"We're worried about her," Morgan said quietly. "She hasn't texted either of us. Like, at all. And she's not answering our texts."

"Well, maybe she's sick," Josie frowned. "If she's in bed with the flu or something, maybe she doesn't have her phone nearby."

The girls stared at her as though she had just sprouted another head and begun speaking an alien language.

"Um, yeah, that's not really a thing," Morgan said finally. "She, like, *always* has her phone."

"Maybe she's sleeping. She seemed fine when I talked to her the other night," Josie said, starting down the hall with the girls trailing behind her. Lexi grabbed her arm.

"Wait, you talked to her?" she demanded.

"Yes," Josie said, turning around. "I went over to her house to talk to her about O."

It was as though the air had been sucked out of the hall. Both girls looked at Josie in horror, as if she had just told them she had held Charlotte at gunpoint and forced her to spill all their secrets.

"So she...she told you everything?" Lexi sputtered.

"Yes. She told me about how she and Amber have been working at the club since June. She also said something about the mystery guy Amber has been seeing."

Morgan and Lexi exchanged another glance.

"C'mon, ladies, enough with the guilty looks," Josie said loudly, then lowered her volume, looking around to make sure no other teachers had popped their heads out into the hallway. "Either you're going to work with me, or you're not, but enough with the weird looks and half-truths, okay? *Enough.*"

After a moment of looking down at her feet, Morgan said, "You're right," and began fishing in her pocket for her phone.

"Morgan," Lexi gasped, looking back and forth between her and Josie.

"She's right, Lex," Morgan snapped. "Don't you want, like, justice for Amber?"

Lexi looked at her worriedly for a moment, then threw her hands up and turned around. Morgan opened her phone and scrolled rapidly through it. When she turned the phone around, Josie's breath caught in her throat.

"This is a photo of Amber, and whoever that dude was she's been seeing. I know it's blurry, but it's the best I've got," Morgan said, shoving the phone into Josie's face.

Josie took the phone out of Morgan's hands and peered at the photo. She immediately recognized it as one that Charlotte had taken down from her Instagram page after the Homecoming game. As Josie stared at the photo, she realized why the guest room at The Omega Society had looked so familiar. This photo had been taken in one of those rooms.

It had been shot from a distance and looked as though it was the background of somebody else's selfie. Though blurry, the photo was definitely Amber, with her alabaster skin and pale blond hair billowing around her face. Amber's head was angled slightly towards the person she was talking to, a man, and she seemed to be about to throw her head back into a full cackle. Her left arm was wound behind the man's right arm, her hand grasping his. The two were standing close to each other, and it was clear that the man was much taller than Amber, with dark hair, but that was all Josie could make out. The man had turned his face the moment the camera took the photo, and his features blurred like a surrealist painting. His clothing was unremarkable, a green sweater and dark gray slacks, but there was something familiar about him.

Josie put her finger on the photo to see if the live photos feature would work to clear the man's face, but it didn't. "Where did you take this photo? When?" Josie demanded, shoving the phone back at the girls.

"Charlotte took it," Lexi answered. "Charlotte took a selfie and cropped the photo to put up on Insta. She took it off her account. I tried to, like, zoom in as much as I could, but I couldn't get the background any less blurry."

"When did Charlotte send this to you?"

"Monday night," Morgan said. "Around, like, seven. Probably around the time you talked to her. But, like, no text, no explanation, nothing."

Charlotte was obviously trying to expose the mystery man, even though she said she didn't know who it was. Unfortunately, this wasn't a terribly helpful way to go about it.

"And you girls have no idea who the guy is? Amber never told you?"

The girls shook their heads vigorously, their eyes as wide as saucers. They both looked petrified.

CHAPTER FORTY-SIX

"Ms. Ashbury, you have to do something," Lexi pleaded. "It's not like Charlotte to just, like, ignore her phone, even if she was, like, dying or something. Something is wrong."

"Okay," Josie said. She held out her hand. "Can I send this photo to myself, please?"

Morgan nodded and handed back her phone, and Josie quickly sent herself the photo. Then she said, "I'll check with the office to see who called Charlotte out this morning. You girls just keep your heads down and be careful, okay?"

The girls nodded in unison, and Josie handed back the phone and headed off down the hall.

"Wait," called Lexi, running after her. "Will you please text us and let us know that Charlotte's okay? Please?" Lexi's eyes were wide and shining with tears.

"Of course. I'll let you know as soon as I know anything for sure, okay?"

The girls slowly headed for the stairs to the second-floor math and science classrooms. Josie made a beeline for the main office and spoke briefly with Joan, the older, stricter administrative assistant who worked there, and learned that Charlotte had been called out by her father. When Josie pressed Joan a little, she learned that it was simply a male voice claiming to be Charlotte's father and "the school has no way of knowing whether or not it's the actual parent calling a kid out or someone impersonating a parent" and "how the hell were they expected to get that kind of information anyways?" Josie left it at that and went to finish her classes for the day.

After her next class, Josie tried calling both numbers listed for Charlotte's mother, which went straight to voicemail. She tried Charlotte's father's cell phone and finally, after calling his office, learned that he and his wife were out of the country for the next few weeks. Unless Frank Burnes called Charlotte out of school from London, someone else had called that in. This made Josie even more worried. If Charlotte was actually sick, or if she simply wanted to skip school that day, why not call herself out? She could have used some sort of voice distortion app, but those always sounded so fake the attendance secretary surely would have made a note in the system. Maybe she had gotten a relative to call her out. What else were kids supposed to do if they got sick while their parents were out of the country?

So someone, male, called the school. No need to panic, Josie thought to herself, as she felt a familiar feeling rising in her throat. Normally she could control her anxiety pretty well, but regulating her emotions was more challenging with each passing day. A friend or staff member at the Burnes residence could have called Charlotte out. A lot of these boys, especially the seniors, had deep enough voices that they could easily pass for a dad. Josie tried to push Charlotte's absence into the back of her mind as she continued teaching, but couldn't help feeling like the girls were right; something about the timing was very wrong. Just before her final class of the day, Josie texted Charlotte herself, and was disappointed to see that she received no response during the teaching hour.

On her walk home across the parking lot, she called Sean, but got his voicemail, as per usual these days. "Hey, Sean, it's Josie. Listen, I've got something important here—I'm sending over a photograph I need you to look at and see if you can enhance it or something. Amber's friends sent it to me; they say this is that guy she was dating. Please call me as soon as you can." Once her call was done, she forwarded the photo, squinting at it again as she sent it. Squinting only made the photo fuzzier. Maybe Sean would have better luck with it.

She also forwarded the photo to John. "Hey bro—you have any fancy photo enhancing software that can make out who this is?" She clicked into her phone. She knew her brothers were worried about her—she'd have to take everybody to dinner once things calmed down and show them that she was doing okay.

214

Chapter Forty-Seven

Friday there was still no sign of Charlotte. No one had called her out, and the office had flagged the absence and left messages for both of her parents for all the good that would do. Josie mentioned to Principal Crandall that she was concerned about Charlotte's absence, but as she had been called out the previous day with "the flu," he brushed it off, saying that he was certain it was just an oversight.

Lexi and Morgan, however, were in a full panic. They had gone to Charlotte's house the night before, but no one answered the door, and the house was dark. Josie tried to comfort them as best she could, with little success. Where was Charlotte?

After school, Josie went to Charlotte's house. Though Charlotte's Range Rover was in the driveway, she got no answer at the door despite her ringing the doorbell and banging and, as the neighbor who happened to be walking down the street put it, "shrieking like a banshee." Josie sent Charlotte a text and left a voicemail, begging her to check-in. She wanted to keep looking for Charlotte, but time was ticking down until Jake was picking her up for Masquerade. After trying the landline at the Burnes residence several more times, Josie decided to give it a rest for the night. She did, however, notify Sean via text that Charlotte appeared to be missing, and she was worried. He still hadn't responded to her previous text about the image.

When she arrived home, a huge brown package was on her front stoop, along with a note from Noelle that said, "The de la Renta, complete with accessories and shoes. Enjoy!"

Josie dragged the bulky package into her living room and tore it open with a box cutter while trying to keep her curious kitties from burrowing inside the box. Inside was a gorgeous off-the-shoulder red satin ball gown with a bustle and train. The front was simple but elegant, the back of the dress clearly meant to be the star. Also hanging was an intricately beaded black and red mask on a stick, a necklace made of iridescent black stones, and a small black satin clutch with a loop on the back. At the bottom of the box, Josie could see the scrawly Christian Louboutin logo peeking up at her. Inside was a pair of classic black stilettos, with soles the exact shade of her dress.

"You've really outdone yourself, my friend," Josie whispered, whisking the gown out of the box and into her closet to let it air out.

She sent Noelle a text, "YOU'RE A LIFESAVER!!! Owe you BIG TIME!!!," then went to shower and do her hair. She probably should have made an appointment to have her hair and makeup done, but with the week she'd had it completely slipped her mind. It wasn't that big of a deal; after all, she did her own hair and makeup for years before her Hollywood days. She winced at the thought of her high school dance pictures, with baby's breath in her hair and lots of sparkly eyeshadow to match. Maybe not.

While Josie was getting ready, she listened to the TV weatherman issue a warning about an impending ice storm. The night was on track to be just like last year, when there had been a thin sheet of ice covering everything by the time they left Masquerade. Josie felt a cold prickle of dread crawling up her spine, the events of last year creeping into her mind. She tried to shake it off, but the ice storm was making the evening feel too similar. Her heart ached as she remembered her parents twirling on the dance floor, her mother's head thrown back in a laugh at something her father had whispered in her ear. Then suddenly, Josie flashed forward to sitting in the backseat of the car, her father telling her that everything was fine while his white knuckles told a different story. He glanced in the rearview mirror at the headlights that were following them, and the bend in the road came too fast—

She shook herself out of the reverie. As she was spritzing on perfume, the doorbell rang.

"Shoot!" she muttered under her breath. She wasn't in her dress yet. After remotely unlocking the door, she waited a moment, then yelled, "Sorry, I'm almost ready! Come on in. There's champagne in the fridge."

She dashed out of her bathroom towards her closet and quickly, but carefully, stepped into the dress. Fortunately, the zipper didn't go too high, and years of being a single woman living alone had taught her to zip herself into a dress without assistance (sometimes with the assistance of a wire hanger as a prop). Someone really should invent a device for that. A "zipper buddy." She giggled as she imagined the infomercial for such a product, which would no doubt have a woman with both her arms behind her back, flailing and twisting around in circles like a dog chasing its tail, trying to get that pesky zipper closed. She swished her gown into place and flipped open the jewelry box that held her necklace, then slid her heels on and turned to face the mirror for a quick once over.

Satisfied that she had adequately pulled herself together and not gotten any cat fur on her dress, she shoved lipstick, blotting papers, and her phone into the clutch before hurrying into the living room. Jake stood in the center of the room, holding a flute of champagne and looking at the photos on her mantle. When he saw her emerge, he gave a low whistle, his eyes widening, then grabbed a second flute off the mantle and handed it to her.

"You look...incredible. Oscar-worthy," he said.

"Thank you. You clean up pretty good yourself," she joked, gesturing to his tuxedo.

The classic suit fit Jake's tall frame perfectly, and his hair was well-styled. His face was clean-shaven, and his eyes danced as he laughed.

"Thanks. I showered," he joked back, gesturing down at himself. "I hope you don't mind, but I got a car service for tonight. I figured that was the best way to go if we'd both be drinking."

"Oh," Josie said, surprised. "I thought we'd just take an Uber."

He laughed, then realized she wasn't kidding. "Mmmm, no. I think that dress alone is worthy of its own car."

"You're absolutely right. Hell, this dress probably deserves its own security escort," she giggled.

"Well, I hope you two will be okay with just me," he laughed.

"How about this: just promise not to let anyone spill anything on me, and we're good."

"Done. But in all seriousness, you look amazing," he said again, putting his arm around her waist and pulling her in for a kiss.

Once they broke their embrace, he grabbed the black faux fur shrug draped over the back of the couch and helped Josie into it. They were on their way out the door when she stopped.

"Oops, I almost forgot," she said, running back into her bedroom. "Can't be a masquerade without the mask, right?"

Jake grinned at her as she danced out of the bedroom with the mask held up to her face. "Wow. Mine is a lot simpler than that one."

"Yeah, like we were talking about the other day, most men's masks are pretty simple, black or white."

"Phew," Jake said with mock gravity.

Josie smiled up at him. She liked that he didn't pretend to know everything. Men in Los Angeles often behaved like they were experts on every subject, and dating there had been exhausting. It was refreshing to date someone who didn't proclaim himself to be a jack of all trades, master of everything, knower of all. The list of the many things she liked about Jake was growing longer by the day.

"Shall we?" he said, offering her his arm.

"We shall," she replied, taking his arm and holding her dress up with the other hand.

The wind howled as they stepped outside, sleet beginning to tumble from the sky. After carefully helping her down the stairs from the porch, Jake opened her door of the black sedan waiting in the driveway and made sure she was securely inside the car before joining her on the other side. The driver, an older gentleman, caught her eye in the rearview mirror.

"How are you doing tonight, miss?" he asked.

"Well, thank you. And you?"

"No complaints," he said, flashing a warm smile.

After Jake was buckled in, he said, "All right, off we go. Playhouse Square, please, Paul. And please, be careful."

As they pulled out of the driveway, Jake took her hand and squeezed it. "How are you?" he said. "Haven't seen much of you the last couple days."

"I know," she replied, looking down. "I've been slammed."

"Are you okay? I know this night must be—"

"I'm fine," she said quickly. "Ready to make some new memories."

"Well, how about this? Let's try to forget about the last few weeks—hell, the last year—and have a good time tonight. I think you've earned that."

Josie looked up at his earnest hazel eyes. "Deal," she replied with a laugh.

"Have you been sleeping any better?" Jake asked.

Josie shook her head. "Not for lack of trying. It's just a phase; it'll pass. It always does."

"How often does this happen?"

"Mmm, now and then. I haven't had a bout like this for…" she paused, thinking. "Well, maybe ever."

"Is it stress?"

"Stress isn't making anything better. But enough about me. Let's talk about you. How are your classes?"

Jake laughed. "Pretty good. No complaints. Kids are kids, you know? Doesn't matter where you put them; they still act mostly the same. Lakeview is nice, though, especially for a public school."

Josie shifted to face him. "Is it different from the school you taught at in Utah?" she asked.

"Not really." Jake shrugged. "I taught at a private school near Park City—you know, where Sundance is," he blushed a little. "Well, of course, you know. Have you been to Sundance?"

"I went one year," she answered quickly, eager to steer the conversation back to Jake. It seemed like they were always talking about her life whenever they went out, and sometimes she felt like she wasn't getting to know him, even though they had been dating for a couple of months. "The year that *The Shape of a Moment* was up for awards. We had to do a bunch of press and the festival circuit."

"Makes sense," Jake said.

"But tell me more about the school," Josie pressed.

"You know, it was a typical private school in a wealthy community. The kids were all right. Some of them were snotty, but for the most part, their attitudes came from the pressure their parents put on them to get into the best schools, get the best grades, live the best lives," Jake said, shaking his head and sighing. "The parents were the hardest thing to deal with, to be honest. It was like every time you gave a kid a B or below, you'd committed a capital crime. I'd just had enough."

"How did you land in Ohio?"

"Well, I started looking at public schools with openings," Jake said. "I knew I didn't want to live in a big city, so I looked mostly at suburbs, and Lakeview had a spot open this year after Mr. Cooper retired. It's not like I had kids I had to pull out of school or a family to uproot, so I figured, why not? It's really not all that different from what you did when you moved from Lakeview to LA, right?"

"I guess not," she said. "I wouldn't have thought of it that way, but yeah."

Josie was starting to ask him about his family when the driver announced their arrival at Playhouse Square. "Geez, that ride went fast," she remarked.

"Good company," Jake said, winking as he climbed out. As the chauffeur opened her door, Jake held out his hand to help her climb out of the sedan, saying, "Careful," and pulling up her dress so it didn't dip into the stream of dirty water running along the curb.

"Thank you," she replied as she maneuvered out and arranged her skirt.

Jake held out his arm again. "Shall we?"

Chapter Forty-Eight

The Animal Protective League's organization committee went all out for Masquerade every year. It was their biggest annual fundraising event, so they pulled out all the stops. There was a step and repeat in the theater lobby accompanied by a long red carpet.

"Looks like they knew you were coming," Jake whispered playfully, and Josie swatted his arm.

They stepped over to the backdrop to have their photo taken by one of the many hired photographers for the evening, as well as a couple of members of the press. One of them recognized her, because within a couple of seconds, they were yelling, "Josie! Over here! Over here!"

When several of the reporters started yelling, "Josie, how does it feel to be back here one year after your parents' death?" She took that as her cue to hurry inside.

"Wow, that was intense," Jake said to her. "Is that what it's like to be you?"

"It was, but not these days," she answered.

She shook off the reporters' comments as they twirled their way through the lobby. The theaters in Playhouse Square were breathtaking in and of themselves, but every year, the Masquerade decorations got better and better. This year was no exception. The lobby was festooned with shiny balloons and lush draping in black and silver, and inside the box office, volunteers handed out masks to anyone who forgot theirs. Jake held up his Zorro-esque mask and twirled it around by the elastic, and Josie responded by holding her mask up to her face and sticking her tongue out. The ball stretched across several of the theaters, with areas set up for dinner, dancing, and table games in different rooms and on the stages.

The magnificence of Playhouse Square always took Josie's breath away. The five historic theaters—the State, Palace, Ohio, Hanna, and Alan—had opened in the 1920s. Each was done in a Renaissance Revival style, opulent and decadent in its own way, with bright, sparkling chandeliers, lush murals, and beautiful arches. The Palace Theater, which is where the center of the ball was to take place, was by far the most lavish of the theaters, with a three-story lobby decked in marble, a vast backstage space that housed vaudeville performers in another life, and a Turkish smoking room. Playhouse Square was the largest performing arts center in the country outside of New York City. The neighborhood outside of the theaters had undergone its own revival recently, and there were now posh hotels flanking the district, trendy restaurants, and an enormous chandelier hanging over Euclid Avenue. The effect was nothing short of spectacular.

After checking her wrap, Jake and Josie made their way into the lobby of the Palace, and Jake let out another low whistle.

Josie laughed. "You've never been here, have you?"

He shook his head.

"We'll have to get you the full tour, then," she said, taking his hand and pulling him further into the lobby.

They got drinks at the bar, then wandered around the theaters, taking in all the beautiful architecture mingled with the fun décor. They were on the third floor of the Palace lobby, and it seemed Jake was beginning to look a little overwhelmed when Josie spotted Alex and her brother, Tommy, down on the ground floor.

"Oh, c'mon, I want you to meet Alex and my brother," she said, grabbing Jake's hand and pushing past the photographer who had been not-so-discreetly following them around.

Jake laughed gamely and allowed himself to be tugged along, looking up at the frescoed ceiling, still wide-eyed as they made their way down the marble stairs that were worn down in spots from years of patrons' footsteps. By the time they got downstairs, Alex and Tommy had made it to the bar. Fortunately, they were easy to spot, with Tommy in a very characteristic royal blue and black paisley patterned tuxedo jacket, black on black shirt and bowtie, and his hair styled into a rockabilly pompadour. He had rolled his sleeves up to show off his forearm ink, most of which he designed himself, and also wore a simple black mask like Jake's. Most of the men at the ball had opted for either the simple black mask or something akin to Phantom of the Opera. The women were stealing the show in the mask department.

Alex looked stunning in a black floor-length gown, which Josie saw was backless when Alex turned around, the material cut in a V so dangerously low that it toed the line between sexy and scandalous. They made a perfect couple, and Josie mentally gave herself a little pat on the back as she watched Tommy wrap his arm around Alex and whisper something in her ear. Alex threw her head back and laughed as Tommy gave their drink order.

"What's so funny?" Josie asked, sidling up to the bar beside them.

"Aye, sis, long time no see," Tommy said, leaning forward. "I've been trying to get a hold of you for like a week. You don't have time for your big brother anymore?"

"I just have so many of them; it's hard to find the time," Josie teased.

Tommy and Josie had always had a special bond, but their relationship had gotten stronger after their parents' deaths. "Or maybe you're too famous for me," Tommy joked.

"I'm not famous anymore."

"Tell him that," he said, gesturing over her shoulder at the photographer wildly snapping pictures.

She was about to go over and tell him to get lost when Jake strode over to him, said something in a low tone, and shook the guy's hand. The photographer casually wandered away, snapping photos of other guests as he went.

"Thank you," she said gratefully as he returned to them. "What did you say to him?"

"I told him, very politely, that though you appreciate having a personal photographer, if he didn't buzz off, his camera might end up someplace uncomfortable," Jake said.

"Oh, no," Josie laughed. "I think you've got a whole foot on him. No wonder he bounced."

They all laughed, then stood there awkwardly for a second before Josie realized she hadn't made introductions. "Oh my gosh, duh, sorry," she exclaimed. "Jake Johnson, this is my good friend, Alex Ziebranowicz, and my brother, Tommy. Tommy, Alex, this is Jake."

Jake politely put his hand out to Alex and Tommy, exchanging pleasantries with both. Then a voice came over the loudspeaker giving a five-minute warning until dinner.

"Jose, do you know which table we're at?" Alex asked.

Josie opened her purse and looked at the small card she had picked up on their way in. "Table three," she responded. "Are Nik and Heather coming? I haven't talked to either of them."

"Nikki said she might come later. She said she had some work to finish up. Heather got called in to the hospital."

"Aw, man, that sucks. I was hoping she'd be able to come this year," Josie said. Heather had missed Masquerade the last two years because of work.

While the guys chatted about sports, Alex lowered her voice and asked, "Is Sean coming?"

Josie frowned. "I haven't heard from him in days. I've sent him a bunch of texts, but he's been ignoring me. But there's nothing I can do about it tonight. I think we should just try to have some fun."

"Good call. Especially when you have such a tall drink of water to forget with," she giggled, nodding over at Jake and Tommy, who were still deep in conversation.

Josie felt herself blushing. "How's it going with you guys?" she asked, eager to steer the conversation away from her love life.

"Good," Alex said simply. Alex, a Scorpio, had always been tight-lipped about her love life.

"Great.

The announcer's voice boomed again, "Two-minute warning, folks. Please find your way to your seats. Two-minute warning 'til dinner."

The foursome wound their way through the theater to the dinner tables, set up on the stages in the different theaters. They were seated on the stage of the Palace, which was Josie's favorite. Their table was draped with a black linen tablecloth with decorations in black and silver. A towering centerpiece constructed of miniature black and silver masks swirled up to a peak, almost in the shape of a witch's hat. The plates, white with silver trim, were the only element not in black.

As soon as she sat down, Josie felt the purse in her hand vibrate. She ignored it, but it vibrated again, this time with the persistent buzz of a phone call. Pulling it out, she saw that Sean was calling her. He'd been ignoring her for days, and *now* he was blowing up her phone? Frowning, she flipped on the do not disturb as he began calling again.

"Everything okay?" Jake asked in a low voice.

"Of course," she said, smiling at him and placing her clutch on the table. "Nothing that can't wait until later."

Jake smiled and touched her hand. The wait staff, in all black with silver masks, brought their salads, and the chairman of the board began a brief speech from the middle of the theater. As she was thanking everyone for coming out in support of the APL and urging a good time, the ignored calls nagged at Josie. Looking around the table at everyone laughing, talking, and enjoying their food, she was annoyed at her unease. She stood up abruptly, realizing her faux pas as several members of other tables turned to look at her, startled.

"Sorry, sorry. Just going to go powder my nose," she whispered to Jake, brushing his arm. She could feel his muscled bicep flex under his shirt as he reached up to squeeze her arm, and her heart skipped a beat.

Josie hurried into the lobby towards the ladies' room. The bathrooms were downstairs, and despite it being dinnertime, she could see the line snaking all the way up the stairs and out the door. She did not feel like waiting in a crowd for ten minutes to use the loo. Then she remembered there were restrooms backstage in the dressing rooms. Looking around to make sure no one was watching her, she crept down the side of the theater behind the velvet curtains which led to the box seats, up the stairs to the stage door. She took the handle in her hand, said a little prayer, and was pleased to find that the knob twisted open right away.

The backstage area was simpler than the theater and lobby, more administrative looking, with several large rehearsal halls and dressing rooms. She had been in a production of "A Christmas Carol" here as a child and still remembered these rehearsal rooms like it was yesterday. There was something magical about the backstage of a theater; the excitement that lingered even when performers were absent was palpable. There were also rumors of the theaters being haunted, as most theaters were, and she wasn't too keen on having her first paranormal experience this evening. She quickly hurried into the dressing room, not wanting to get caught sneaking around backstage by security.

Even through the solid cement walls of the theater, Josie could hear the storm raging outside. She tried to ignore it as she touched up her lipstick. Getting home tonight was going to be awful. Maybe they should get a hotel room for the evening. She pulled out her phone to look for vacancies when suddenly, the lights flickered, then went out.

"Damn it," she said.

She decided to check her phone to see what Sean had wanted. Surprised, she saw that she had missed several more calls from him, as well as a call and text from her brother, John. She opened the text message from John, which simply read, "Enhanced photo attached—hope this helps."

She clicked on the photo, which had gone from the pixelated blur that she had sent John to a perfectly clear image of a man's face. Her stomach turned. No, it couldn't be. No, no, no, she thought. She was staring at the photo so intently, she didn't even hear the door to the bathroom open and close behind her.

Then everything went black.

Chapter Forty-Nine

As Josie came to, she noticed a throbbing in the back of her head. She was on her side; her dress splayed out around her. Blinking slowly, she tried to use her arms to sit up and quickly realized that they were bound behind her back with zip ties in a very uncomfortable configuration. Her mouth was gagged as well. She struggled her way to a seated position, her eyes adjusting to the dim light in what looked to be a construction warehouse. She squinted, trying to get her bearings. The last thing she remembered was being at the gala, going backstage to use the bathroom because there was a line a mile long for the lobby one, and then the lights went out. But before that...

Josie froze. The text message from her brother. She desperately looked around for her purse, her phone, something, but saw nothing but the folds of her dress, now covered in grime and dirt from the floor. Pallets of miscellaneous building materials were stacked haphazardly in rows and shelves. There were lots of buildings like this downtown. Despite the cultural renaissance that Cleveland was experiencing, there were still plenty of abandoned buildings. Beautiful structures that once housed businesses and stores sat empty or were converted into storage space. Because of the large number of these buildings, she couldn't place where she was. But she knew she was in trouble.

"Okay, Ashbury, think," she mumbled to herself through the gag, twisting her wrists as she tried to free her hands. The zip ties were so tight; she could feel the plastic cutting into her skin, breaking it, the burning sensation slowly going numb. Same thing with the gag in her mouth, which cut into the corners and burdened her breathing. She bit down on the gag in frustration, cursing her stupidity. At least she knew who had brought her here.

As she struggled, she heard muffled cries coming from around one of the stacks. She scooted herself around the pallets, trying to find the source of the noises. She rolled until she was almost all the way across the room, her dress a tangled, ruined mess. Noelle was going to be pissed. That is, if she ever saw Noelle again. Finally, she flopped herself around a corner and saw a figure propped up against a stack of plastic-wrapped plywood.

"Charlotte?" she said through the cloth. Charlotte Burnes looked like she had been through a war. Her jeans were filthy and ripped in several places, and not in the fashionably on-purpose way. Her sweater, once something cashmere and expensive, looked like a dirty burlap sack hanging from her shoulders. Her normally shiny hair hung in strings around her ashen face. When she saw Josie, her eyes widened, and she began to speak through her own gag. Bracing herself, Josie continued her clumsy roll down the aisle until she reached Charlotte's side. With some painful maneuvering, they were able to work the gags out of each other's mouths.

"What happened, Charlotte?" Josie asked quietly, her eyes darting around. She couldn't see anything because of the dim lighting and all those damn stacks of drywall.

"Ms. Ashbury, I'm sorry, I—I—" Charlotte's eyes welled with tears as she broke off into a sob.

"Shhhhh, it's okay," Josie whispered, partially to comfort Charlotte and also to quiet her down so they wouldn't be heard.

Charlotte's breathing was ragged, but returned to normal as she tried again to speak. "I wanted to tell you, that day you came to my house," she whispered frantically. "I should have. I should have!"

"It's all right, Charlotte," Josie said as soothingly as she could. She heard a metal banging noise coming from the side of the room. They were going to have to work fast if they were going to get out of here. "We can talk about it later. For now, just follow me, okay?"

"Okay," Charlotte sniffled, looking as vulnerable as Josie had ever seen her. "Your dress is really pretty."

"Was," Josie said, trying to scramble into a crouch.

Luckily their feet hadn't been zip tied, but it was still difficult to balance in heels with her hands pinned behind her back. She kicked off her Louboutins, hoping that her bare feet wouldn't freeze. There was no heat in this building, and the temperature had dropped below freezing when the storm blew in. They started to shuffle, Charlotte crouched behind Josie, towards the side of the warehouse. But the maze-like configuration of the stacks seemed to have no order to them, and every time Josie made a turn at the end of one pile, she encountered more. The wall did seem to be getting closer, though. There had to be a door there. She said a little prayer as she shuffled along the next row. As they reached the final row next to the wall, Josie felt a strong stench hit her nostrils, burning as she sucked in a breath.

Gasoline. She smelled gasoline. As she looked down at the ground, she realized her feet were wet, gasoline running in a stream towards them. She heard another bang behind them as an empty container, what she now knew was a gas can, hit the ground with a thud. A sickening feeling rose from her stomach into her throat as she realized what was happening.

He was going to burn the place down.

"Charlotte," she whispered. "My brother is an FBI agent. He enhanced that photo you sent me."

Charlotte's eyes widened. "So you know?"

"Yes. I know. I was at the Masquerade with Jake when my brother sent me the photo."

"Did he see it?" Charlotte asked.

Josie nodded. "I think so. I snuck off to the bathroom to look at it and—"

But her thought was interrupted, because Jake Johnson appeared from behind a large pile of wood, gasoline can in hand.

Chapter Fifty

His face broke into a twisted smile, one unlike Josie had ever seen before. "Well, I see you ladies have found each other. *Fantastic,*" he spat, tossing the gas can aside.

Josie stared at him, dumbfounded. With the pounding in her head, she was having a hard time focusing. It had been Jake. *Jake* was the man in the photo with Amber. Jake was Amber's secret lover, the one who had been in that photo taken in The Omega Society guest room, the one who had gotten her pregnant. The one who had murdered her. Josie shuddered. How was this man the same as the sweet, kind teacher who she had been dating for months? She barely recognized him as he gazed at them, his face an ugly mask of anger.

"Jake," she began, trying to level her voice. "Let's talk. You don't have to do this, whatever you're planning."

He laughed bitterly. "You just couldn't stop digging, could you? Everything was going fine, Jose, but you just couldn't leave well enough alone."

This couldn't be happening. How had she been so blind? She had been so focused on the club, she had missed that the murderer was right under her nose.

Jake disappeared around one of the piles of construction materials and came back with another gas can. As he poured gasoline on the stacks, Josie tried to stall him. "How did this happen?" she asked quietly.

Jake let out another laugh, and Charlotte started to cry. "Shut up. Shut. Up. I've had about enough of you," he snapped.

Josie recoiled. Moving closer to Charlotte to comfort her, she pleaded.

"Jake? Please, talk to me. If you care about me at all, please."

He looked at her for a beat. "You wouldn't understand. How could you?" he said as he resumed pouring.

"Help me try," she insisted, trying to catch his gaze.

When he made eye contact with her, he stopped and shook his head. "It wasn't supposed to be like this," he said, and for the first time, she caught a glimpse of the man she knew. "I went to *one* event at that club when I first got to town to meet people, network. It wasn't supposed to derail my entire life."

"And you met Amber at the club," Josie said, stalling. Would someone at the gala realize they were gone? What if he had told everyone that they were simply ducking out early?

Jake winced at the mention of Amber's name.

"Did you love her?" she pressed.

"It doesn't matter!" he yelled, the fury returning to his face. He drew closer to Josie, bending down to her level. "She was going to ruin my life," he said through gritted teeth. "How was I supposed to know she was seventeen? And a *student*? She told me she was twenty-one! And she was working at the club! Was I supposed to *check her ID*?"

Josie nodded, trying to keep him talking. "There's no way you could have known," she agreed.

He narrowed his eyes. "I know what you're doing. You're not on my side," he hissed.

"No, Jake," she said, "I get it, I really do. This isn't your fault."

"Yeah, unfortunately, the world wasn't going to see it that way," he said. "Teachers screwing students aren't exactly looked on kindly."

"But you broke it off with her, right? When you found out?" Josie said.

"Of course I did! When I saw her at the school, with a *backpack*, I almost had a heart attack! But she *wouldn't listen*," he said. Now he was pacing around, manic, slapping his fist into his palm as he made every point. "She just wouldn't listen. I told her it was over. At first, she acted like she was okay with it, but then she kept turning up in my classroom, at my house, pleading with me to make it work. Make it work! Like we were going to be some sort of *love story.* Then I started dating you." He continued pacing, getting angrier by the second, "And even *that* wasn't enough for her to get the message. I start dating a movie star, and what does she do? *She befriends you.* Makes you her confidante. She just wouldn't stop. She *would not stop.* And then when she found out she was pregnant—she was going to ruin me! She threatened to tell everyone. She said she wanted to get married, start a family. It was ludicrous."

"And that's crazy. There's no way that could work. It would have ruined your life. And hers," Josie agreed, glancing at Charlotte.

"Exactly. She couldn't even see that she was going to ruin her own future. But these rich girls," he said through clenched teeth, "always have to get their way. She didn't care that it was going to ruin me. Ruin my career, my life."

"She didn't leave you any choice," Josie said softly.

Jake stopped pacing abruptly, and Josie was afraid for a moment that she had overplayed her hand. "Don't mess with me, Josie," he warned, reaching behind him and pulling out the pistol that was tucked into his belt. His eyes were wild, and she was afraid.

"No, n-, no!" Charlotte cried, writhing away from him.

"Of course, she was there from the beginning. You saw her in that photo. 'I swear I won't tell anyone,'" he mimicked, gesturing at Charlotte with the pistol. Charlotte sobbed quietly.

"Jake, I understand," Josie said, trying to regain control. "I get it. Amber backed you into a corner. There weren't any options. So maybe," she paused for a moment. "Maybe," she continued, moving her face and forcing his eyes to meet hers, "this was all an accident."

Jake stared at her in shock, then started to laugh again, that same maniacal laugh she'd heard earlier. "You know," he said, sitting back in mock admiration, "I knew you were a good actress, but that—that was *Oscar-worthy* right there." He tucked the pistol into the waistband of his pants and picked up the gas can again.

"I mean it, Jake. There's still a way out of this."

He rocked back on his heels. "You know," he said finally, "I thought I was up the creek when you showed up in the field that night. Truly, when I looked down and saw you in your pajamas, staring at the tower, I thought my life was over."

At that, Josie froze, feeling the familiar prickles on the back of her neck. She *had* been there that night, just feet away from where he murdered Amber. It made her sick to think that she was helpless to do anything to stop him.

"And man, that sleepwalking, the hallucinations of your dead parents—you should really see someone about that," he said with mock seriousness. "Even when I was sleeping in your bed, you couldn't tell the difference between reality and dreams half the time. It was like I got two different women in one package."

Jake smirked at her. "I should be thanking you, really. If you hadn't been so willing to share everything that you uncovered, I might not have been able to stay on top of this. You really should have just let it go when the police dropped the case. That journal you kept really helped me out. Don't you know that you should keep all your sensitive information in your *locked computer* now? That cop friend of yours warned you to be more careful. Hell, all I had to do was say I left my wallet behind, and you gave me my own key to your house. Of course, you leave your house unlocked most of the time anyway."

"I trusted you," Josie said, but her heart sank. Her fault. This was all her fault. If she hadn't gotten involved with this creep, if she hadn't been so stupid to just leave her phone where anyone could get to it, she and Charlotte wouldn't be here with this monster.

"You broke into my house. Thanks for locking my cats in the basement," she said flatly, but he ignored her. She tried again. "How did you even manage to get Amber up on that tower in the first place?"

Jake sighed, and for a second, a shadow of regret crossed his face. "She took me there on one of our first dates. Thought I would enjoy the history. I brought her back and convinced her to go up. Said it would be 'romantic.' I think she thought I was going to propose." He laughed bitterly.

"And instead, you fed her fentanyl and pushed her off."

"I didn't have a choice."

"And you planted the drugs in the lockers. But why Tony?"

"Tony, like you, wouldn't stop snooping around. Apparently, he pressed this one a little too hard," he gestured at Charlotte with the gas can, "and she spilled her guts. He confronted me and was going to go to the police."

"And did you plant that jacket at my house?"

"What jacket?"

"Amber's jacket. The one she had on the night that…."

At this, Jake looked confused. He opened his mouth to answer her, but Charlotte's sobs grew louder as she tried to catch her breath. "It wa—wasn't my fa-, fault," she hiccupped, her breathing ragged.

"Enough! Do you ever stop yapping?" he snarled, reaching into his pocket and pulling something out. Josie's heart raced when she realized it was a syringe. "Any last words, princess?"

Charlotte began to struggle, as Jake grabbed her and sank the needle deep into her neck. Seconds later, Charlotte's movement stopped, and she slumped over.

Then he turned to Josie. "I wish it didn't have to be this way. But you left me no other choice," he stated tonelessly, striking a match and watching the flame rise, then dissipate into a small glowing torch.

The zip tie she had been struggling with finally slipped free as Josie dislocated her thumb. She yelled in pain as she lunged at him, watching him drop the match into the wood palette closest to them. Her right fist connected with his cheek as flames engulfed the pile of kindling. Then she heard the gunshot.

Chapter Fifty-One

Between the rapidly spreading fire and struggling with Jake, at first Josie couldn't figure out where the gunshot came from. She heard him cry out in pain as he fell to the ground, then scramble to try to get away from the fire he had ignited. Smoke was rising, and the fire was ripping across the gasoline that Jake had dumped everywhere, making its way towards Josie and Charlotte like a freight train. Josie coughed, the stench of gasoline and smoke filling her lungs, as she struggled to get to her feet. Charlotte was slumped on the floor, unmoving. Then Josie saw a figure rush through the haze, and found herself staring into the eyes of Sean Sullivan, who reached down and grabbed her arm.

She shook him off as she shouted, "Sean, he gave her fentanyl! Fentanyl!" and pointed at the syringe on the ground.

Sean looked back and forth between Charlotte and the syringe for a second, then leapt into action. He quickly pulled out a small bottle from his waist bag and, grabbing Charlotte's face, administered one shot of Narcan up each nostril. Josie grew dizzy from the fumes, but a wave of relief crashed over her as she saw her oldest brother, John, step through the dark plume of smoke and hoist Charlotte onto his shoulder before disappearing back into the cloud.

"C'mon," Sean yelled as he pulled her to her feet.

He pulled her onto his shoulder like John had done to Charlotte, and as she looked back towards where they had been seated she saw the pile of drywall explode into flames. Jake was still on the ground, writhing and clutching his knee, scrambling to get up as the fire edged closer to him. Josie lost sight of him as Sean carried her outside, the smoke clouding her view. Sean carried her behind John and Charlotte, moving as quickly as he could. With the amount of gasoline Jake had poured and the flammable materials, it wasn't long before the whole building caught fire. Josie could see where they had been now, in an old building across Chester Avenue near the Greyhound Station. John and Sean carried them across Chester towards the back of the theaters at Playhouse Square, traffic slowed to a halt as drivers gawked at the building dissolving into flames. Josie heard more sirens in the distance, and people spilled out the back doors of the theaters.

Sean set her down and said, "Don't move; I'll be right back."

She grabbed his arm, still coughing as she gasped, "You're not going back in there! Are you crazy?!"

But she was too weak to stop him as he shook his arm free and ran back towards the building, followed closely by John. The two men were shouting at each other as they ran back into the building. Josie was doubled over, trying to hard catch her breath. Ambulances and fire trucks were screaming onto the scene. Her breathing was slowly starting to return to normal as the EMTs spilled out of the emergency vehicles and rushed over to her and Charlotte. That's when she heard the explosion.

Chapter Fifty-Two

J osie heard herself scream "No!" as she tried to run towards the burning building, now starting to collapse on itself.

She felt an arm wrap around her waist and yank her back as she struggled against the grip, continuing to scream and cough. Feeling a soft hand on her arm, she looked over to see Nikki and Alex standing next to her, both wide-eyed and dazed and realized it was Tommy's arm around her waist. She stopped writhing and looked at all three of them, tears welling in their eyes, before crumpling into Tommy's arms. Alex and Nikki wound their arms around Tommy and a sobbing Josie as they all stood, gaping at the towering inferno that Sean and John had just thrown themselves back into.

For what seemed like hours, they waited, watching, as the building continued to crumble and burn. Another fire truck arrived, and Tommy yelled at the firefighters to alert them that three people were still in the building. Several of them immediately rushed across the street. Others attempted to hose down the building, but it was too late to save it. They did the best they could to prevent the Greyhound Station, which had been evacuated as soon as the authorities arrived, from catching fire as well.

Josie was losing hope as she sat on the back of the ambulance with Alex and Nikki flanking her, staring numbly at the fire. Tommy was pacing back and forth, swearing under his breath. After what seemed like an eternity, the firefighters came back out, empty-handed and shaking their heads at one another. Josie buried her face in her hands, feeling like her whole body was being ripped apart by sorrow.

"No, no, no, no, no," she sobbed.

"Look!" Tommy shouted, pointed towards the warehouse. A figure emerged, carrying a lifeless body on its shoulders. It was Sean, gulping for air as he collapsed onto his knees as soon as he was away from the building. Firefighters rushed to help him, and as Josie leapt from the ambulance and threw off her blanket, running towards the crowd of emergency personnel. As she got closer, she felt a wave of relief, then distress, crash over her. The body Sean had been carrying was John's.

Chapter Fifty-Three

J osie heard a knock on the door to her hospital room, but before she could say, "Come in," she saw a couple of faces peeking through the slightly opened door.

"Hey," she said weakly, greeting Nikki and Alex as they crept into her room like mice.

After the explosion, Josie had been taken to the emergency room to be examined, but after seeing her, Heather had admitted her for exhaustion. She had been in the hospital recovering for three days and had finally been able to get some good sleep.

"He-ey," the ladies sang softly in unison.

"The kitties are doing well, but they say they miss you," continued Nikki, pulling out her phone and showing Josie a photo of Monroe sitting prettily in the window and Presley mid-meow, his mouth wide open, paw outstretched.

Nikki had been taking care of the cats since Heather made the call to keep Josie in the hospital. According to her, Josie had been delirious, hallucinating, and babbling incoherently by the time she reached the ER on Halloween.

"My babies," Josie said, taking the phone from Nikki and examining it, a smile on her face.

"How are you feeling?" Alex asked, tucking a lock of hair behind her ear as she perched on Josie's bed.

"Better," Josie replied.

"And the others?" Nikki asked quietly.

Josie's eyes filled with tears, and she swallowed a lump in her throat as she tried to find the words.

"Sean's okay. Just a broken leg. Same with Charlotte. The doctors said that had Sean not given her the Narcan so quickly, and had the EMTs not given her a second dose, she probably would have died. But she's all right, still under observation. But John," she gulped hard again, unable to continue.

"John's still in a medically induced coma," she heard Heather's soft voice from the doorway. "He suffered a head trauma in the explosion that left him with swelling in his brain, so the doctors thought it best to put him under until it goes down."

The girls nodded. The kidnapping, explosion, and rescue made the national news the night of and the morning after, with the feature Nikki scrambled to put together covering the entire front page of The Cleveland Press. On Halloween night, Josie thought that her brother and Sean had made it into the building before the explosion. In reality, the men were still outside the side of the building when it blew. The blast had tossed them backwards, with Sean breaking his leg in three places. The firefighters couldn't believe he had been able to walk, let alone carry another person out of harm's way. John had hit his head on the pavement hard enough to knock him out, and when they got him to the hospital, the doctors discovered the brain swelling. They were now just waiting for the swelling to subside to bring him out of the coma, but they had given Josie no timeframe as to when that would be.

"How are the girls?" Nikki asked.

"As good as they can be," Josie answered, sniffing as she wiped her nose with a tissue. "Isabelle has talked with them before about how Daddy's job is dangerous, you know, but I'm not sure how much of that they really understand."

Nikki nodded. "And I take it you've heard about Jake?" she asked.

"Yes," Josie said. With the gunshot wound to his knee, Jake hadn't gotten out of the building fast enough. He was inside when it exploded, and his body was so badly burned that the police needed to use dental records and DNA testing to identify his remains.

"I'm sorry," Alex said. "I know he was...well, whatever he was, but he still meant something to you."

"I didn't really know him. Not the real him," Josie replied. "I don't know how I could not have seen him for what he really was."

"Don't beat yourself up," Nikki clucked. "There was obviously something really wrong with him."

"Rationally, I know it's not my fault. But I still feel guilty. If I had only seen some signs, gotten Amber to *really* confide in me, things might have been different." She rested her head back on the pillows and closed her eyes.

Seeing that Josie was fading, Heather took another step into the room. "Sorry, ladies, but she needs her rest," she said quietly.

After engulfing Josie as best they could in a four-way hug, the girls got up and gathered their things. As they headed out the door, Josie said to them, "Love you."

"Love you more," they chorused, leaving the door ajar behind them.

"Let's talk about what happens after you're discharged," Heather said, pulling out a pamphlet. It was for Hillside Treatment Center, an inpatient/outpatient facility which dealt with a variety of mental health issues. "This place is amazing. They have great treatment plans for trauma, exhaustion, all kinds of things. But they've got holistic options like meditation, yoga, and even spa treatments. I think you should do a few weeks' stay."

Josie took the pamphlet. "Dr. Gupta actually recommended this place when I saw her last."

"I think it's important that you do this," Heather said gently.

Josie nodded. Much as she didn't want to stay in a facility for an extended period, she knew she needed to find a better way to cope with her parents' deaths. The year she had spent in therapy had obviously not been enough, and the trauma of the last month was sure to have some lasting repercussions.

"I'll call them today," she promised.

"I'll check on you later," Heather whispered, starting to leave but getting stopped in the doorway. Josie heard her talking in low tones with someone in the hall, catching, "Okay, but just for a minute," as her door swung open again.

Sean clumsily wheeled his way into the room. He had been rushed into surgery when they arrived at the hospital, and when Josie had stopped by his room over the past few days, he had been either sleeping or very groggy from pain medication. This was the first time he was able to get up and about.

"Sorry," he muttered as he banged the chair into the bed.

"That's okay," she laughed. Then she burst into tears. "I'm so sorry," she sobbed.

He grabbed her hand. "Shhh, shh, shh, Jose, it's okay. We're okay," he said, gesturing down at himself. "John is going to be okay, too."

"This is all m—my fault," she gasped, trying to calm herself.

"How do you figure?" Sean asked, cocking his head to one side. But as she opened her mouth to answer, he continued. "Look, Josie, that guy was obviously unhinged. I know you want to blame yourself, but there was no way you could have known what was going on. He covered his tracks well, left no DNA or fingerprints at either of the crime scenes. Had you not sent John and me that picture, we would have walked away from this thinking that those kids both overdosed. Actually, I should be thanking you. I don't know how you got that jacket, but the print on the poker chip matched the one the school district had on file for Jake. It's the only hard evidence he left behind."

"I must have climbed the tower before I called 9-1-1 that morning. I knew I lost time, but I don't remember any of it," Josie said, swallowing hard.

Sean's brow wrinkled with concern.

"Don't worry," she said, pulling out the pamphlet. "I'm taking care of it."

Sean took the pamphlet and looked it over. "I know you probably don't want to do this, but I think it's necessary."

"I know," she said. "I'll check myself in as soon as I know that John is okay."

Sean squeezed her hand. "He's tough. He'll be awake before you know it."

She nodded.

"Oh, and if you thought the media coverage was crazy before, you should see it now. There have been news vans parked outside for days. But Josie," he said, touching her face and raising her chin to look into his eyes. "You are not responsible for this. I need you to really believe that."

"I know. I'll be okay as soon as John wakes up," she said firmly. "The thought of losing someone else—and my nieces losing their father...."

"John is going to be fine," Sean said again. "Just have a little faith."

"Faith," Josie repeated. Faith wasn't something she had much of anymore. "Promise me."

"I promise."

Chapter Fifty-Four

J osie burst into laughter as Tommy cracked one of his well-timed, clever jokes. She was sitting in John's hospital room with her three brothers, sister-in-law, and nieces, making too much of a ruckus for the hospital as they all joyfully talked over one another. The doctors had brought John out of his coma the day after Sean's visit with Josie, and he was expected to make a full recovery. He was back to his stern but happy self, looking absolutely blissful as his girls sat on his bed, Victoria resting her head on his chest and Emma, the oldest, doing her best to keep up with the adults. In moments like this, Josie swore could feel her parents looking down on them, protecting them, making sure they were happy.

"Daddy's a hero. He saved Aunt Josie. Right, Auntie?" Victoria asked, her big green eyes suddenly focused on Josie.

"That's right, baby," Josie replied, grinning. "Your papa's a hero."

"Everything's going to be okay," Emma repeated what she had probably heard a million times over the last several days, looking content with Josie's answer. She laid her head back down onto John's chest. Her brother caught her eye and winked, and despite his circumstances, Josie had never seen him more relaxed.

After Katie gathered the girls to take them home for dinner, Josie stayed behind in John's room.

"What's eating you?" he asked her. "I know that look."

"It's just, I know that Jake was solely responsible for the murders. I know that," she lowered her voice. "But The Omega Society is still partially responsible for what happened to Amber Oldham. They hired her and put

244

her in a position where she was exposed to these men. At the very least, they're running some sort of prostitution operation down there. And those other women? That can't be a coincidence."

John sighed and looked out the large window at the lake. "Even if what you're saying is true, there's no proof."

"What about Charlotte?" Josie said. She would never forget the look in Charlotte's eyes when she pulled out that silver poker chip.

"You think that the word of a teenage girl who faked an ID to get a job at the hottest new speakeasy in town is going to take them down? Josie, come on. There's no way that would be enough. And with the people who are members of that club, any sniffing around based on that would be immediately stopped. I told you I'd look into them, and I am, but there's nothing more we can do about it."

"What about the poker chip in Amber's jacket?"

"What about it? According to the club, it's an invitation to play the high stakes games in the back rooms. A chip is required to enter the game."

"And you believe that?" Josie scoffed.

"It doesn't matter what I believe. What matters is that as much as I share in your suspicions, I can't do anything about it."

John's statement hung in the air like a smoke ring. Josie knew he was right. With The Omega Society's connections, an investigation based on what little she had would be dead before it got started. With the number of political figures and prominent businesspeople who were members, there was no way they would allow even a whiff of a scandal out into the public.

"Well, then I guess I'll have to join the club," Josie said.

"Jose, haven't you been through enough lately? Now you want to put yourself in harm's way again?" John demanded. "Look, please, don't make any moves until after your stay at the recovery facility, okay? Promise me that."

"I promise," she said grudgingly, walking over to the bed and plopping down on the edge. "You don't need to worry about me. I won't do anything stupid."

"Famous last words," he mumbled.

"Get some rest, okay? They're discharging me tomorrow, but I'll come say goodbye before I leave for Hillside."

"Josie," he said, grabbing her arm as she turned to leave. "I mean it. Don't try to investigate this yourself. I'll do what I can once I'm back in the office, okay?"

She smiled. "Don't stress, bro. I won't do anything until I get back from Hillside. I love you."

"I love you, too," he said.

Chapter Fifty-Five

Although Dr. Gupta had recommended a ninety-day stay, after a month of living at Hillside, Josie was ready to go home. She had finally gotten back into a regular sleeping pattern, and her hallucinations had stopped. While she enjoyed the spa treatments and wellness exercises, there was only so much meditation and yoga one could do before going completely looney. She had been in constant contact with Dr. Gupta, who agreed that she was okay to check out and come home, if she was ready.

The intensive therapy at the center had truly helped her process the loss of her parents. Josie had opted for individual therapy sessions every other day, and the counselors were the best of the best. With the price tag this place sported, they well should be. She didn't think she was ever going to be able to completely free herself of the guilt she felt about that night, but she had at least learned how to cope with her feelings. There was no magic pill or activity that could "cure" her. The only thing that would help was time.

Time out in the country had done her a world of good, however. The center was situated several hours outside of Lakeview, in the middle of nowhere with rolling hills as far as the eye could see. There was a small lake on the grounds, and she kept up her early morning runs around the perimeter. It was cold, but she was adjusting to running in the frigid temps. The cold breeze did wonders for her in the morning. A good night of sleep helped, and fortunately, she had started falling and staying asleep easily a few days into her stay.

Principal Crandall had been very understanding when she called to inform him of her situation, and they agreed that she could come back and teach for the spring semester. She felt bad about leaving her classes in the lurch, especially when the school had already lost one teacher, but she knew she wasn't going to be any good to anyone unless she got better herself. Nikki and Alex had been rotating turns staying at her house with the cats, and she was so grateful she hadn't had to worry about hiring someone.

Her agent and manager had been trying to reach her ever since Halloween. Apparently, they had seen the story on the national news. They said they were calling to check in, but Josie had a feeling that they were eager to capitalize on her foray back into the spotlight. She filled them in about her stay at Hillside, and they all agreed to have a meeting when she was back home. They weren't going to be pleased with her decision to stay the rest of the school year in Lakeview, but she did concede that she would look at projects back in LA once the year was over. She wasn't sure if she agreed to that to placate them or because she really wanted to return to Los Angeles, but she had some time to think.

After saying goodbye to the friends she had made and promising to keep in touch, she got on the road. Though it was cold, the sun was shining, and it was a beautiful day for a drive. Once she was in the car, she dialed the number for The Omega Society and got the voicemail.

"Hello, you've reached Franklin Mather the third at The Omega Society. I'm so sorry to have missed your call…" Franklin's delicate voice sang.

"Hi, Franklin, Josephine Ashbury. I'm so sorry to have been out of touch, but I wanted to speak with you about going forward with my membership. Please give me a call back at your earliest convenience. Thank you."

With a satisfied sigh, she cranked up the car stereo and settled in for the drive. She was ready to go home.

Acknowledgements

First and foremost, a huge thank you to Curtis. Without your unwavering love and support, I would never have finished this book. I appreciate you listening to me vent when I got stuck, and helping me to find solutions for problems that I thought were unsolveable. You are the best partner I could ask for.

Thank you to Cindy Bullard, my agent, for taking a chance on my debut novel and championing my work. I am so grateful for your advice, optimism, and support.

Thank you to my editor, Shawn Reilly Simmons, for your keen editorial eye and publishing prowess. My work is better because of you.

Thank you to Lisa Daily, my publicist, for working so hard to make this book a success. You are an amazing force of positive energy, a phenomenal writer, and I cannot wait to work on more projects with you.

A huge thank you to my parents, for encouraging my creativity as a kid, buying me a seemingly endless number of books, and providing a first-rate education that prepared me for the career of my dreams. Thank you to Amanda for always lending an ear when I needed to talk, and to Jesse and Jagger for providing some much needed entertainment when I needed a break. And thank you to Gio, for sharing your creativity with me—your story ideas are incredible.

Thank you to Amy Bistok, for always being in my corner; to Amiee Collier for being available to chat day or night; to Stephanie Janesh for your positivity and encouragement; and to all my other friends who were there in more ways than I could possibly list.

Thank you to Oreo, for offering me snuggles while I was writing and walking breaks when I needed them. And thank you to Lap of Love's Pet

Loss Support group for helping me through her loss. And to my other fur babies, though I'm not sure walking across my keyboard and laying on my laptop were particularly helpful.

And finally to Kevin, who I will miss for the rest of my life, you meant more to me than I could ever articulate. You brought joy and light to everyone around you, and the world is better for having had you in it.

About the Author

Amy Young is an author, comedian, and actor based in Cleveland. After spending a decade in Los Angeles working in the entertainment industry and writing her debut novel, The Water Tower, she returned to Ohio to be closer to family. Amy is working on her second book, a thriller, and in her free time she enjoys going to the theatre, bingeing reality TV, and spending time with her husband and many, many cats. She has a B.A. in English from Kenyon College.

SOCIAL MEDIA HANDLES:
  Twitter: amypcomedy
  Facebook: amy.pawlukiewicz
  Instagram: amypcomedy
  LinkedIn: amy-pawlukiewicz
  Tiktok: @amypyoung1

AUTHOR WEBSITE:
https://authoramyyoung.com/

CPSIA information can be obtained
at www.ICGtesting.com
Printed in the USA
JSHW022332050723
44275JS00001B/58